Faux Beau

ALSO BY MARINA ADAIR

Sierra Vista series
Faux Beau
Second First Kiss

The Eastons
Chasing I Do
Definitely, Maybe Dating
Summer Affair
Single Girl in the City
Four Dates and a Forever

Romcom Novels
Situationship
RomeAntically Challenged
Hopeless Romantic
Romance on Tap (novella)

Sweet Plains, Texas series
Tucker's Crossing
Blame it on the Mistletoe (novella)

Nashville Heights series
Promise Me You

Sequoia Lake series
It Started with A Kiss
Every Little Kiss

Destiny Bay series
Last Kiss of Summer
Like the First Time

Faux Beau

MARINA ADAIR

To
Kerri Gambino, the original
PurpleSneakers.

Table of Contents

Chapter One

Take Life by the Balls
Try on something new.

When Milly Smartt decided to walk a mile in her sister's shoes, she had no idea just how badly her feet would ache. She considered it a win that she'd been able to make it up the tiny slope and snap on her skis without breaking her neck. Or falling on her face. Or the other million ways a person might die when they decide to go skiing for the first time in twenty years. So she wasn't surprised when, standing on the iced-over powder, staring down the ten-foot slope, her legs began to wobble.

To clarify, she hadn't actually made it to one of the big-people slopes—that would require a ski lift, and the only way Milly's feet would ever leave the ground would be for a pedicure.

No, she'd opted for the bunny slopes.

"Shins out, hands forward, shoulders in front of your hips," the instructor, Kelly, called out.

Kelly had blue-streaked hair, enough body ink to fill a dictionary, and the patience of a kindergarten teacher on a field trip. Which was fitting since Milly was the only student over three feet tall. Yup, she was standing in the middle of a group of elementary schoolers, struggling to keep up.

Milly looked around at the snow-blanketed Sierras, the forest of deadly icicles hanging from the sequoias, and was surprised by how everyone hadn't keeled over and died of hypothermia. The big flakes that were coming down were hindering visibility, and the winds coming off the white-capped mountains had turned her nose Rudolph-red. In fact, she would sell her soul for a hot cup of cocoa—spiked of course.

Except Milly wasn't a quitter. Something she'd learned growing up with an independent, impulsive, don't-take-crap-from-anyone older sister, who never walked away from an adventure and never gave up when things seemed impossible. Zoe was the outdoorsy and outspoken sister with this bold look on life, which was how she'd lived—spontaneous. On the other hand, Milly was more introverted and bookish, and god, did she love a good plan—color-coded with itemized checklists.

But today wasn't about Milly's lists, it was about reconnecting with her sister's memory in the only way she was ready for. And that meant spending an afternoon in her sister's skis. No matter how ridiculous she looked in Zoe's Barbie-pink snowsuit and white snow cap.

She only had another couple of weeks to pack up her sister's belongings before her parents showed up on the doorstep and insisted on helping. Sorting through her sister's personal items was like sorting through her sister's life—which always brought on an acute sense of loss. But it was time to stop grieving and move on with her own life. It had been nearly nine months since Milly had walked away from her dream life in New York and returned to Sierra Vista to become Zoe's caretaker. Four months since cancer took her sister. And four months since Milly promised her sister that she'd live a full life—a life big enough for the both of them.

Then last week her dad had a heart attack and had to be airlifted to a bigger hospital in Reno. After spending three nights by his side, Milly was sent home at her parents' insistence. Milly would have argued but she'd landed a contract job to help plan an event in town. Still, after only a few days home, she needed a distraction from the stress of everything.

"Chase happy," Zoe had always said, and Milly was ready for some happy in her life.

"Using your poles, push yourself forward to get a little momentum going. As you pick up some speed, remember to use wedge turns for better control as you glide over the snow," Kelly instructed.

Nerves rioting in her stomach, Milly did as instructed. She gave a little push, a snail-pace push, and slowed to a stop less than three feet from where she'd begun, while the rest of the class zigged and zagged down the hill that, from Milly's angle, suddenly appeared to be a hundred-foot drop.

"Give it a little more elbow grease," Kelly said. "The goal is to make it to the bottom."

Milly glanced around and realized she was the only student still standing at the start of the run. Zoe would have laughed her ass off if she could see Milly now, scared shitless of a little adventure. Then she would've shoved Milly down the mountain, screaming for her to take life by the balls.

A twisting heartache knotted in her belly at the reminder of her sister. God, she missed her wit and brazen take on life. She also missed her over-the-top encouragement—which Milly could use a dose of right then.

Channeling her inner ballbuster, Milly took a deep breath, leaned her shoulders over her hips, and pushed forward with her poles. No longer at a snail's pace—she'd managed to upgrade to sloth mode—Milly watched as three fellow classmates passed her while taking their second run down the mountain.

"Remember to make a triangle with your feet, turning your toes in. The wider your stance, the slower you'll go," Kelly instructed from beside her.

Milly made a tight triangle—Pythagorean theorem tight—then dug her poles twelve inches into the powder, scooching herself forward ten feet and stopping with the front of her skis sticking out over the ledge of the hill.

She closed her eyes and blew out a nervous breath. "Baby steps," she whispered.

"Baby steps are for babies," the little girl next to her sang as she walked back up the hill. She was barely taller than Milly's ski poles but had the 'tude of a teenager.

"I am not a baby but a beginner, like you," Milly said primly.

"Then how come you haven't moved?"

"I've moved." Nowhere near as much at the others, but she'd moved just enough to remain upright.

"Not enough to zig or zag like Miss Kelly told us to," her powderpuff of a bully said.

Milly gave a little hop and landed with her skis slightly to the right. "Zig." She hopped angling them to the left. "Zag. Happy?"

Powderpuff rolled her eyes and said, "Baby," then took off down the slope, zigging and zagging like she was an Olympian.

Frustrated with herself, and feeling as if she were letting Zoe down, Milly bent at the waist to tighten her bindings, only she leaned too far forward. The slight shift in position caused the front of the skis to slide until Milly was teetering on the edge of the world.

"No, no no!"

"*Yes, yes, yes,*" the Universe said and suddenly she wasn't teetering, she was moving. Slow at first, then picking up speed. As the trees raced by, Milly tried to remind herself the rules of skiing.

"Zig and zag, Milly. Zig and zag." Forcing her feet to turn, Milly zigged to the left, but that put her on a direct route for the parking lot, so she zagged to the right. Only she zagged too hard, overcompensating and picking up speed. She tried to turn but her legs weren't listening. Maybe because they had morphed into two big trembling wet noodles.

"On your left," she hollered as she zipped past two of her classmates, nearly taking them out at the knees.

"Kelly," she hollered over her shoulder, one octave away from manic. "What do I do?"

"Turn your feet in to make a triangle. Like a slice of pizza," Kelly hollered back. But Milly's legs stayed knees forward, pointed straight ahead.

Milly looked down at her feet, willing them into a pigeon-toe, but nothing happened. It was like her body wasn't getting the memo that if they didn't point in, they were going to die. And how embarrassing would it be to die on the bunny slope.

"Fore!" she called out to everyone around her, her gut telling her she was using the wrong sports metaphor. "Avalanche on the move!"

People scattered out of her way as Milly's arms, neon-pink poles in hand, flailed in the air, grasping for balance as she barreled forward like Lindsey Vonn in the 2010 Vancouver Games. She nearly buzzed a massive sequoia, veering at the last minute, setting her on a direct course with—

"Oh shit."

—the stone wall of Sierra Vista Lodge, a luxury ski resort based at the foot of the most treacherous runs in all the Sierra Nevada mountains.

The faster she went, the more imposing the wall became, until she was certain she was going to die. And wouldn't that piss Zoe off. For Milly to die before at least trying to live balls-to-the-wall. Zoe would accuse her of purposefully dying rather than facing a few of her fears—like ski lifts.

Milly prepared herself for impact, raising her arms in front of her face and closing her eyes. Except when she plummeted into the wall with an *oof*, she fell forward, rather than bouncing back, in a landing that was softer than expected.

"Ow," she moaned, putting her hands in front of her to push herself up. Instead of snow, her hands came into contact with hard ridges and valleys. Warm, hard ridges and valleys. Raising her head, she blinked up into the most mesmerizing green eyes she'd ever seen. Eyes that were swimming with concern and a tiny bit of recognition.

"Milly?" her unexpected savior said.

"Am I in heaven?" she asked, and that concern flipped to amusement, but the recognition remained.

"Why? You hoping to see me in heaven?" His voice was rough and low, like tossed gravel on steel, and so familiar she'd recognize it anywhere. It was her first crush.

Lucas Macintyre. Who also happened to be her newest, and only, client—at the moment.

When Zoe discovered she had just a few months to live, Milly relocated to Sierra Vista to live in the family's weekend home. Not wanting to miss even a moment, Milly took personal leave from her job as a logistics coordinator for a publishing house in New York. She liked problem-solving and spreadsheets and anything color-coded. The way she viewed the world, like it was a big Tetris puzzle waiting to be solved, made her good at what she did. And even with the stress associated with her job, she loved what she did.

Her boss allowed her to telecommute for a time, but when it became too difficult Milly had to choose. She chose Zoe, and she'd choose her again, but there were times that Milly wondered what her life would have been like had she stayed in New York.

Would Dillon have followed through on the engagement? Would she have landed the promotion she'd been working toward? Mainly, would she be happy?

Everything had moved so quickly. One second, she was on her way to ticking off life's boxes—dream job, dream husband, dream house—the next she was a caretaker to her sister. A job which had consumed the past nine months of her life.

After a while, her work friends had stopped calling, as if unsure what to say as the grief extended from weeks to months or somehow afraid that they'd remind her of her sister's death. Not that it would have mattered. She remembered every waking moment of every day. Some of the sleeping ones too.

Her life was stuck on pause while the rest of the world moved forward without her.

"I'd be lucky if I saw tomorrow at this point," she said to him.

His eyes lowered and she followed his gaze, realizing that she was cupping his pecs, one massive muscle in each hand, like she was copping a feel.

"Oh my god. I am so incredibly sorry. This is so unprofessional." She tried to jerk her hands back, but his arms wrapped around her, holding her firmly against him.

"I'm the one who caught you."

"You caught me?"

"I couldn't let you crash into the wall, now, could I?" he said in a warm tone that had the power to turn Siberia into one big puddle. "That was a pretty epic run."

"Followed by an epic fall."

"Which is why you should take a minute to make sure you're okay."

"I should be asking you that."

His eyes twinkled with mischief. "Never been better. Hey, Milly."

At the sound of her name rolling off his lips, all kinds of warm fuzzies ignited—in her southern region. Parts of her that she thought had gone on a permanent vacation were stamping their passport and arriving home.

"Hey," she breathed, feeling like a teen all over again.

Having a crush on one of her clients—especially when he hadn't so much as given her a hint of reciprocated feelings—was a bad idea, which was why she'd never acted on it. That didn't mean she didn't take a moment to appreciate how good he looked in a pair of jeans and black snow jacket. It was strange seeing him out of his usual suit and tie uniform.

She wasn't sure if it was seeing him outside of the office in such a casual setting, or that she'd lost her glasses in the snow, but he looked bigger, broader. Then there were the slight crinkles around his eyes as if smiling was his day job. And he was smiling now.

She slowly became aware of their position. She was on top of him, her thighs resting between his spread hips, all their good parts lined up. Clearly, she'd hit him head-on. "I should, um…" Using his yummy chest for leverage, she rolled off him, landing with a thud into a snow angel position. Her skis were standing up like roadkill, her poles scattered around her, and her snow cap lying limply a good foot from them.

He gracefully got to his feet and lent her a hand, pulling her up. Even through the double layers of gloves, a spark ignited. If he noticed, he didn't let on.

"Thank you," she said, dusting the snow off her butt.

"You need any help with that?"

Milly froze and met his gaze, pleasure and uncertainty playing a game of tug-of-war in her belly. Was he flirting with her? Was Lucas Macintyre really flirting with Milly Smartt? She wasn't sure. It had been so long since she'd flirted with a man, she didn't even remember what it felt like. The last man she'd flirted with was Dillon, who had bailed when life got hard.

Play it cool, she told herself. But her mouth didn't get the message and before she could stop herself, she asked, "Are you flirting with me?"

Gah! As a logistics specialist she had excellent communication skills. Normally. Around him she became a blundering geek. Heck, she was surprised that he'd contracted her at all. She'd stumbled through her presentation, but her strategic approach to their upcoming Sierra Vista Cup—a snowboarding and ski competition—won her the job.

He looked down on her. Those crinkles deepened. "Do you want me to be flirting?"

She stood there, mouth gaping like a fish, because did she want him to be flirting with her? She needed this contract and she didn't want to make things awkward—hard task since she was the queen of awkward. A title she'd worked hard to change. Sometimes she was successful. Around sexy, flirty guys? Not so much. So she went for honest. "I'm not sure how to answer that."

He laughed, a low rumble of a laugh. "Let me know when you decide."

He was even more funny and charming than she'd realized. Out of his suit he seemed taller and more filled out. Damn, the man was gorgeous. The last time they'd spoken about something other than ski wax and porta-potty deliveries, they'd both been teenagers, not even legally old enough to drink. That didn't stop them though. Her sister, Zoe, and his wilder identical twin, Jaxon, always made sure that the kegs were flowing.

Not sure how react to that kind of laugh, she blurted out, "How's work going?"

His smile dwindled. "Busy."

"Are you excited about the Sierra Vista Cup?" she asked. "I can't believe it's almost here."

It was just four weeks away and Milly was starting to sweat. Oh, she was on top of everything, but overseeing all the moving parts of an event that size was intimidating—and all encompassing. So that fun Milly was supposed to be chasing had taken a back seat.

"I'm guessing you're not entering," he teased, and she laughed.

He picked up her snow cap from the ground and settled it on her head, tugging at the dangling ties. "I like your hat."

"It's Zoe's." Millie looked down at her snowsuit and swallowed hard as a memory of her sister flittered through her mind. Memories of her sister that were slowly fading away. Milly didn't want to remember those final images, but she didn't regret spending every last minute caring for Zoe. Even when Milly's fiancé walked away because her life was too much for him.

"I found it cleaning out her things." Her eyes welled up and she knew she was about to lose it. She'd gotten better with talking about her sister, she really had. But after today, after attempting, once again, to live life full-out, it was all too much.

"I'm sorry about your sister," he said quietly.

"I don't want to talk about it. Today is about having a good time." Her breath caught. "I just wanted to clear my mind before I clear out the rest of Zoe's room…" She waved her hand in front of her face. "I don't even want to think about it, which is why I came here, hoping a lesson would take my mind off everything." She felt her throat closing in, a panic attack barreling down on her like a freight train.

Then he rested a hand on her shoulder and said, "Do you smell that?"

She took a deep inhale. "What?"

"Can you smell it?"

She took another breath. "I can't smell anything."

"It's the scent of a fun, carefree day."

Realizing what he'd just done for her, she swallowed hard. He'd distracted her. She was breathing regularly, and the panic was gone. "Oh, you're good."

Where her ex had chosen to walk out the door when she had a panic attack, this guy soothed her anxiety with his calm and reassuring patience. In that moment she didn't feel that her life was too much.

"That's the Macintyre way." The adult male confidence was sexy as hell. He bent over and plucked her glasses from the ground, shook them off and snugged it on over her nose—which brought him into twenty-twenty view—and into breathing distance. He smelled like pine and fresh snowfall. "How about that ski lesson?"

"Oh no." She shook her head. "I've had enough snow for one day."

"You didn't even make it to the slopes."

She looked back at the imposing mountain and shook her head. "Close enough for me."

"Well, then can I buy you a hot cocoa?" His gaze dropped to her mouth and a vaguely sensuous lightness passed between them. "Actually, I'd like to do something else." He stepped closer.

"Like what?" She was strangely flattered by his interest.

"You know what or you wouldn't have been sneaking peeks at my lips for the past five minutes."

"I didn't have my glasses on, who knew where I was looking." Even saying the words, she felt a hive break out on her forearm.

"Now, that's a lie."

"Maybe I have been sneaking peeks, but I'm a little out of practice. I haven't been with someone in a very, very, very long time."

This time his eyes definitely dropped to her lips, then back to meet her gaze. "How about we go to Bigfoot's Brews and grab a hot cocoa."

She blinked—three times. "Are you asking me out?"

He moved even closer, resting a big, manly hand on her hip. "Is that a yes, Mills?"

Before she could answer, his phone blew up with texts. One after another in rapid succession. He took a deep breath and sighed. "Dammit, I have to go. That's my sister bugging me about tonight's dinner."

"Is that like telling me you have to wash your hair?"

"No. This convo is to be continued at a time when my family isn't hounding me."

"I get it." Oh, she really got it. She too was the good kid and knew what it was like to give up what one wanted in order to be what others needed. Lucas's brother was a lot like Milly's sister, a free spirit. Just like his troublemaking playboy of a twin, her sister used to find trouble like nobody's business. Which was why she'd always felt a connection with Lucas. "Family always comes first."

His expression changed into something more serious. "It's not always that easy."

Wow. It was as if they were speaking the same language. She really got what he was saying. And that made him all the more attractive. She'd never been attracted to just the physicality; it'd always been the thing between the ears. And she was definitely attracted to that right now. Still, when he bent to pick up her poles, she couldn't help but admire his ass. And maybe it was a combo of brains and brawn.

Chapter Two

Take Life by the Balls
Bucket list: Fill it with beer. Drink it.

Growing up, Sierra Vista Lodge had been his siblings' own personal playground. The historic and remote adventure resort was perched atop the Sierra Nevada mountains and a destination for weekend warriors and families alike. He and his siblings had claimed, climbed, and ran across every inch of the mountain, a pack of hellions on skis. But Jax been gone a long time.

As a professional boardercross snowboarder, Jaxon Macintyre spent his time dominating slopes from Tahoe to Switzerland, but he hadn't tackled Sierra Vista in over a year—ever since the day he and his identical twin, Lucas, had a major blowup.

Words were exchanged—along with a few swings—and Jax did what he always did, he went fugitive, running off to play the circuit and leave the anger behind. He still hadn't forgiven his brother, something Jax was hoping to change.

But that wasn't what he was thinking about as he walked to his cabin to change for his first family dinner since he'd taken off. That trophy went to Milly, in her pink ski suit, white hat, and adorable glasses. She was like Barbie and a librarian had a love child. Only she wasn't a kid anymore. Oh no, Milly Smartt was all woman and curves.

Jax drove along the road, which circled Sierra Vista, and when the lodge came into view an overwhelming feeling of comfort and contentment filled his chest. God, he'd missed this place.

In addition to the hundred luxury rooms, the lodge housed a gift shop, equipment rentals, a bar and grill, and an outdoor café that had firepits and a s'more station. Neighboring the building that housed ski patrol, search and rescue, and some of the seasonal instructors was a small amphitheater used for hosting weddings and events.

But it was the location of the lodge that drew people there. Bordering the Tahoe National Forest, Sierra Vista was surrounded by dense sequoias, sugar pines, and Douglas firs, giving the feeling that one was in the middle of a forest rather than a five-minute drive from the quaint downtown. With gas lamp–lined streets, shiplap-fronted shops, and a million strung twinkle lights crisscrossing overhead, Sierra Vista was the gem of Lake Tahoe. And with views overlooking the crystal-blue lake and backdrop of mountains, it was a prime destination for tourists and locals alike.

Even though the temperature was falling below thirty, Jax rolled down his window, enjoying the sharp punch of frost and the fresh scent of recently fallen snow. His breath froze on contact with the air. He might have had his reasons for staying away, but as he pulled up to the lodge and noticed a familiar person standing in Jax's designated parking spot, those reasons didn't hold the same weight they had just a few days ago.

It was his older brother, Nolan. Well, not a blood brother, but a brother in every sense of the word.

Dressed in his federally issued uniform and strapped to the teeth, US Forest Service Special Agent Nolan Carmichael leaned against the newly installed sign pole, which read THE LAST CAR THAT PARKED HERE IS STILL MISSING.

Jax threw his truck in Park and slid out of the vehicle. He'd barely slammed the door when Nolan, who was a beast of a man, wrapped Jax up in a bro hug, curling his burly arms around him and nearly shaking the common sense out of Jax. Getting his teeth rattled by the massive Nolan was always an experience. But the welcome warmed a part of his heart that he hadn't known was frostbitten.

"Damn. It's good to see your ugly face," Nolan said when they both pulled back.

"Right back at ya." Nostalgia and love swelled at the sight of his best friend. "How's things? How's Nina," he asked, referring to Nolan's longtime girlfriend.

"Hanging in there, and she moved out a few months ago. Took her kids to Montana to be closer to her parents."

Jesus. How out of touch had Jax really been? To not know that his in-love brother was now single? "I'm sorry, man."

"Me too." Nolan said lowly. "Now, you want to tell me why Lucas found out that you're back through Mom's hairdresser's sister?"

When Nolan said *mom*, he was referring to Peggy Carmichael, a saint who'd taken two misplaced brothers into her family. After the death of his dad, his mom disappeared into a bottle, leaving a very young Jax and Lucas to fend for themselves. By the time they'd reached first grade, they were basically on their own.

Then they were saved by the Carmichaels, who taught Jax about friendship, family, and unconditional love—which was why he was so disappointed in himself for being absent lately. Okay, that was BS. He'd been gone because of his job, yes, but mostly because of the fight with Lucas.

"I called Lucas and he never called back."

"That was a year ago, bro. When are you two going to fix this? The rest of us are over here tiptoeing around this war zone. It's not fair to Mom and Dad."

As the middle child, Nolan was the self-appointed arbitrator of the family. It was what made him such an effective officer of the peace. There wasn't an escalation he couldn't handle, a problem he couldn't solve, or a situation he couldn't masterfully navigate through. And Jax knew that Nolan was irritated by the fact that he hadn't been able to fix the whole feud between Lucas and Jax.

Jax ran a hand down his face. "I know. It's on the list."

"Well, move it to the top. Mom is expecting you at dinner tonight. And Lucas will be there."

How could he forget. "Brynn sent me a zillion texts reminding me." Somehow his pseudo-sister had learned about his stealth arrival into town. He shouldn't be surprised. With an off-season population of only five thousand, gossip in Sierra Vista was a commodity.

"I'm glad you're here, but I thought you couldn't make it?"

Up until yesterday, Jax wasn't going to come. Nope, he was going to use the competition season as an excuse and send Peggy's present by mail. But then a buddy of his just buried his mom and Jax got to thinking about how long it had been since he hugged Peggy and Kent. What would he have done if it had been Peggy who'd died? It could have easily been her. While he called her once a month, he hadn't seen her since last fall when they came out to visit him in the Italian Alps while taking their thirtieth wedding anniversary trip to Europe.

"It was going to be a surprise," he said.

"Keep lying to me, man."

"Really, I have a present and everything."

"I think you're full of shit."

Jax raised an inquiring brow. "Do we need an interrogation room?"

Nolan went in for another grizzly bear hug. "Nah, I'm just glad you're home."

Jax didn't want to admit it, but he was too.

Jax was still thinking about his run-in with the sexy bookworm when he parked in front of the Carmichael's cedar log-style cabin with a bright red tin roof, which held all his favorite childhood memories. His mind flashed back to that first day when he and Lucas had followed Nolan home on their bikes. They'd played Navy SEALs in the river and when the sun was setting and his mom still wasn't there, Peggy had invited them in for dinner—into their home and into their hearts. The same hearts Jax broke when he had turned tail a year ago and never looked back. He'd called and sent updates on the family text thread, but he hadn't had the balls to come home and face his brother.

Jax sat in his truck, stomach bottomed out, staring out the front window. The surrounding pines were heavy with snow and the sinking sun cast a warm glow off the icicles hanging from the eaves. The driveway was full, calling out that everyone was there except Lucas, who was probably still chained to his desk at work.

With a sigh that was part relief and part disappointment, he hopped out, his legs still cramped from making the long trip from Vail earlier that day. He'd make the trek in one shot, afraid if he stopped, he'd turn back around and head to the next competition, which was tomorrow. He had been cut from the roster, which worried his manager. Jax was staring down twenty-seven and with the average age of a pro-snowboarder being twenty-two, he was the old guy in a young man's sport. His seasons were numbered. So competing whenever possible and maintaining his conditioning routine was imperative, which was why he'd gone to the lodge earlier—to get in a few runs. Only he'd run into his old crush in those ass-hugging ski pants and couldn't think past sharing a cup of cocoa with her and catching up. Then Brynn blew the moment, hounding him about the family dinner.

So there he was, purposely a half hour early, hoping to have a moment with Peggy and Kent, his chosen parents. The phone call from Peggy asking him to come to her birthday party, he had to admit, hurt his heart a little. That she'd assumed he wouldn't be coming to her birthday party, especially her sixtieth, made him realize just how out of touch he'd been with the people he'd loved most.

Nolan was right. The beef between him and Lucas was affecting the entire family.

Tucking the birthday card into his shirt pocket, he reached the front door and hesitated. After his recent behavior, was he supposed to knock or let himself in? He still remembered the first time he'd been invited into the Carmichael house; he and Lucas had nervously stood outside in the snow, looking through the front door at the loving chaos that erupted when Brynn, Nolan, and Harris had arrived home. Peggy had gone ballistic with hugs and cheek kisses and chatter about their day. Unsure what to do, and unaccustomed to that kind of greeting after just a few hours being at school, Jax had toed the front doormat.

It hadn't taken but a moment for Peggy to walk over and give him and Lucas a hug, before ushering them inside and feeding them peanut butter cookies and milk. That snack turned into dinner around their table. And when night fell and Jax's mom, Cindy, still hadn't shown, Peggy called to see if the boys could spend the night, but the boys ended up staying the whole weekend.

"If you ever need a hug or a family dinner, our table is always open. No knock needed, just come in," Peggy had said when she'd dropped them off at their home Sunday night. With a hug she handed them a bag of fresh-baked cookies. "Because every kid should have cookies in their Monday lunch bag."

It wasn't the first time Cindy had been too caught up in her addiction to play doting parent, but it was the first time Jax was given a safety net. And that's what the Carmichael family represented to him, a safe place to land—no matter how bad the storm—even if the blizzard was a result of Jax's rebellious side. Peggy and Kent had taken a chance on two kids who would have otherwise fallen through the cracks, and given them a home and more love than Jax felt he deserved.

Whenever he and his brother needed a place to stay, a meal that didn't come from the freezer, or even just reassuring words, the Carmichaels were it. Kent and Peggy didn't just pull them into the fold, they treated the Macintyre brothers like they were their own kids, even paying for Jax's snowboarding passion and Lucas's college.

Jax was always trying to pay them back, but Kent refused to cash the checks, saying, "I'll take your money when my other kids pay me back."

His *other kids,* as in Jax had finally been claimed. He was no longer the kid without a family, even though most of the time he felt like an interloper. So every year, to repay them for their generosity, he sent them on all-expenses-paid vacations to their dream destinations. Which made Jax a grade-A asshole for staying away this past year.

He stood on the front porch watching his breath come out in frozen puffs. Deciding not to knock, because Peggy would have his ass, Jax let himself inside, dumping his snow boots and winter coat in the mud room. He was touched to find his hook still empty, hanging below a small wood carving that said JAX'S PLACE. He opened the interior door and was greeted with the warm scent of a wood-burning fire, Peggy's infamous double chocolate brownies, and the sounds of laughter, which ignited a hot pang of longing in his chest.

How many nights like this had he missed out on over the past year? How many family dinners and Sunday afternoons, where the crew took to the slopes, had he opted out of? Too many. And he was starting to realize he was the driver of his own car and it was his choice to miss out on all these things.

He walked into the dining room and discovered that they were halfway through dinner. People were passing plates, sipping beer, and stuffing their face with Kent's famous lasagna. Shit, he was late. He looked at his watch and his brow furrowed; the party was at six sharp, it was only five thirty.

He knew the moment Peggy sensed that one of her cubs had come home. She went still and turned her head, her gaze locking right on Jax. He shuffled in his socks for a moment, unsure what the reaction to his presence would be after a year away. But he needn't have worried. Peggy's eyes filled with sheer joy and her hands flew to her mouth.

"My Jax is home," she breathed.

"Uncle Jax!" his three-year-old niece, Emma, said, sprinting toward him like a colt. Jax picked her up right as she launched herself into his arms. He held her close, noticing that she didn't quite fit the way she used to. She was longer and dressed like a kitten, but, god, she smelled the same. Like crayons, chocolate brownies, and all things little girls.

"Hey, Bug."

Before Jax could say another word, everyone was on their feet. In the blink of an eye, the entire family descended upon him, but Peggy pushed through the pack.

"Get out of my way, I can't even see him." She pulled on Brynn's hoodie, tugging her back. "Don't you dare hug my favorite son before me."

Faster than a NASCAR speedster at the Indy 500, Peggy was across the room to throw her arms around him. Being the shortest of the family, she didn't even reach his chin but, man, did she hug like she was ten feet tall. Or maybe that was how her hugs made him feel, like he actually belonged. And, because Peggy was the heart of the family, she started a good old hug fest.

She rested a hand on his chest and when she met his eyes hers were filled with tears. "Oh, my favorite boy."

"You say that to all the guys," he said gruffly, holding on to her tightly.

"But I mean it when I say it to you." She patted his cheek. "You've been away too long."

"I thought I was your favorite," Nolan said.

"She only says that because you bribe her with trips to Cancun and Italy," said Harris, the oldest brother and single dad to Emma, coming around to hug Jax from behind. Before he knew it, Kent had joined the group and was rubbing the top of Jax's head. Then Brynn, the baby of the family who wasn't much taller than Peggy, squeezed in, shoving everyone aside so she could wrap her arms around Jax's middle, and they all made room.

They might treat her like the annoying baby sister, but the entire family was protective of her. Not only did she suffer from heart problems as a kid, she was also too sweet for her own good, which led to other kinds of heart problems.

"I missed you," Brynn said. Her fingers were too short to make it fully around his waist but her grip was like a vise.

The family huddled around him and there they all stood like the San Francisco Forty-Niners after winning the Super Bowl.

He soaked up the love like a starving man. The love that was given so easily made him wonder how he'd stayed away so long. Then he met his twin's gaze over the top of everyone's heads and it all came rushing back. The hurt. The betrayal of finding his brother meeting with their mom behind his back. Laughing and hugging, all the while keeping Jax in the dark. He remembered the argument that followed, the surging anger, the words and the feel of his fists splintering Lucas's nose.

They continued to stare, Jax's heart in his throat. Lucas's face blank, an impenetrable shield of *I don't give a shit*. For the first time in Jax's life he couldn't read his brother.

As twins they used to be able to read each other's thoughts. Finish each other's sentences. Not tonight. Not since the night their brotherhood was broken.

One time Jax had been surrounded by a group of bullies who were saying shit about Cindy being a junkie. He knew his defense of his mom was going to get him pummeled, but at the last minute Lucas had shown up saying he felt Jax's fear and just knew where to go.

No matter that they were younger, Jax and his brother had bashed those kids. Because of the neglect and indifference they'd experienced in their childhood, he and his brother had to become scrappy, resourceful, and independent at an early age. And because of their mom's drinking habit and reputation, they'd had to become tough as hell.

Lucas had long ago given up on trying to defend the woman who chose her addiction over her sons, but Jax still held out this ridiculous hope that she'd show up one day, be the mom they knew before their dad killed himself. Twenty years later, and it still hadn't happened. He wasn't sure how to fix it, just like he didn't know how to fix things with Lucas.

"Hey," Jax said with a nod to Lucas.

"What are you doing here?" Lucas asked. No "nice to see you." No "Have you missed me as much as I've missed you?"

"I wouldn't miss Peggy's birthday," he said. His siblings' eyes were wide with disappointment, bouncing back and forth like it was a Wimbledon match.

Lucas gave a judgy shake of the head. "You're a little early."

Jax looked at the table and confusion lit his eyes. "What?"

Peggy shook her head. "I made you boys' favorite, double chocolate brownies. And if the two of you fight in my home, you're both on dishes duty, and your dad cooked so you know that the kitchen is a disaster."

"No need to fight, Mom. We're fine. Aren't we fine, Jax?" his brother said as if Jax were the one to start it.

"Yup, we're fine," Jax said when all he wanted to do was punch him in the face for lying. And he didn't even have to look at his twin's scowl to know Lucas felt the same.

Brynn looked at the birthday card in his pocket, which Jax had stuffed with two first-class tickets to Puerto Rico, and her smile faded. "What's that?"

"Mom's present."

All of his siblings shared a look and Brynn said, "The birthday party isn't for another two weeks. We had to move it because Grandma couldn't make it."

Jax's face heated with embarrassment and a little anger. "Why didn't anyone tell me?"

"I thought I put it in the text," Nolan explained, sounding genuinely confused.

"I didn't get it."

Peggy smacked Nolan in the stomach with a whack. "I told you guys you shouldn't have started that new text thread without him."

"He's not a part of the lodge so why would he be a part of the thread?" Lucas said.

Jax shouldn't be surprised that Lucas left him out of the loop, but the fact that the others didn't fight for him left him feeling like he was once again the outcast. Why did he feel as if he was always the last to know shit? And not just since last year; it had been that way since he left for his first circuit tour.

"I'm part of the lodge. I'm on the board for Christ's sake."

"Emma, honey, why don't you go in the kitchen and sneak one of Grandma's brownies," Harris said, shooting daggers at Jax for his language.

Emma's eyes went as big as Frisbees, but she didn't give anyone time to renege on the offer of dessert without finishing up her salad.

"You haven't made a single meeting in three years," Lucas said when his niece was out of earshot.

"My season is five months, and the other seven I'm training." When were people going to get this? Competing at the highest level meant he trained as hard as any other pro athlete. Just because the snow season in Sierra Vista only lasted November through April, the glaciers in New Zealand were ski-ready year-round.

Lucas crossed his arms. "Well don't be on the board then."

Mom whistled like she was an NFL-certified referee. "Enough. Both of you!" Her tone was sharp enough to remind everyone that no one messes with her kids—even one of her kids.

"I swear if Emma comes back out and sees you two about ready to jump into an MMF cage, I'm going to kick both of your asses," Harris said. "It's stupid enough that you guys are bickering like a couple of grannies at bingo, but the rest of us don't want to hear it anymore."

Lucas ran a hand down his face. "You're right. Sorry, Mom."

Where Lucas took to calling Peggy Mom from the start, it had never felt right to Jax. Even though Cindy was the furthest thing from a present parent, she was still his mom, and calling someone else that felt like a betrayal. But he didn't want to hurt Peggy's feelings either, which left him somewhere in the middle.

Always in the middle.

"It won't happen again." Not the fighting, but it wouldn't impact the Carmichael family again. He'd make sure of it.

"Good." Peggy patted his cheek. "Family is thicker than ego."

Jax read the temperature of the room, the expressions on everyone's faces, and felt his turn hot. Was that what they thought? That this was about ego? Because it wasn't. It was about trust and brotherhood. Two things Lucas broke.

"Under the bridge," Lucas said, approaching and offering his hand. He wasn't offering an apology, Jax noticed. But that was a talk for another day.

"Under the bridge." Jax took his hand, and they shook. Hard.

"Now isn't that nice. My two boys together again." Peggy took them both by the hand and pulled them into her, her arms going around each twin's waist. "Let's hug it out, shall we?"

"Nothing says I love you like a healing hug," Kent said, coming in on the other side. It was the most hugs Jax had gotten in a year. He cleared his throat and it felt surprisingly thick with emotion.

Jax met Lucas's eyes over Peggy's head and something charged passed between the brothers, but it didn't feel hostile. More like exhaustion.

With a firm clap to their backs, Kent wiped his eyes a little. Unlike Jax, Kent wasn't afraid of hugs, cheek kisses, anything that showed his overflowing love. In fact, he was more outwardly affectionate than Peggy, and that was saying a lot.

After a Guinness Book of World Records hug, everyone stepped back and Jax could finally breathe. Lucas stayed where he was, keeping an arm around Peggy and Kent. He gave a tight squeeze.

"You're not heading out, then coming back for the party, are you?" Brynn asked Jax, so much hope in her eyes he didn't want to tell her that he couldn't stay. He had exactly one week off before his next competition. Brynn might be a decorated soldier in the National Guard, but beneath the camo and ranking she was a sensitive soul.

Before he could deliver the news, Kent spoke. "Of course not, he's staying right here with us."

"I can make up your bed with fresh sheets," Peggy said and went to move to do just that when Jax tucked her under his shoulder.

Jax opened his mouth to tell them the truth, but instead he said, "No need to make up the bed, I've already got a room at the lodge."

Lucas stilled. "You're staying at the lodge?"

Jax knew what his brother was really asking. Why, when Lucas worked, lived, and breathed the lodge, did he not know his brother was there?

"Why didn't you tell me?" Peggy batted his chest. "I would have stocked the fridge and made you a container of your favorite cookies."

"I wanted to surprise you. But I'll take some of those brownies to go."

"You better not be paying for the room, son," Kent said.

"It's fine."

Jax hadn't used the free family rate, he'd paid for his room with his own damn money. The Carmichaels had given him so much, he didn't want to take any more.

"No, it's not," Kent objected. "Lucas, make sure he gets a full refund. And Jax, you can stay as long as you want."

Lucas cleared his throat, then shared a look with Peggy that Jax couldn't decipher.

"Now?" Peggy whispered.

Nolan looked around the room, trying to use his secret agent vibes to sniff out the truth. "Time for what? What's going on? And don't you dare tell me nothing because I can smell the BS in the room."

"He's right, love," Kent said, but Jax could tell by his expression that he wasn't prepared for it to be time. In fact, he looked as if he never wanted it to be time. What the hell was going on?

"Your dad and I wanted to wait until after my birthday party." Peggy glared at Lucas. "But clearly someone doesn't know how to keep a secret." Kent took Peggy's hand as her eyes filled with tears. "Your father and I have some news."

Brynn looked at Kent, her expression dialed to *scared shitless*. "Oh my god, is Nana okay? Is that why she canceled on the party? Is it her diabetes?"

"No, sweetie," Peggy said. "She's managing her blood sugar like a champ." Kent put his arm around Peggy and they both held tremulous smiles. Jax's gut hollowed out. "In fact, we're both feeling better than ever. And a big part of that has to do with our decision." She looked up at her husband with pleading eyes. "I can't say it."

Kent squeezed Peggy closer. "After weighing the pros and cons—"

"And trust me, I made a list," Peggy added.

"—we're selling the lodge."

There was a beat of silence where nobody even breathed. Except Lucas who was clearly in on the "secret" news. As if he'd been expecting the bomb to drop and had once again left Jax out of the loop.

"You knew!" Jax accused, unable to hide his disdain.

"Of course, I knew. Unlike you, I'm at that place twenty-four seven. So while it's your job to play in the snow, it's Mom and Dad's job to run the place."

"Don't let him fool you," Peggy said. "Lucas has been running the place for the past few years. Dad and I try our best, but it's a big job. Bigger than the three of us."

"This is a joke, right?" Harris asked, his face slack with shock. "Emma thinks of that place like her second home. We all do."

"We are as serious as a blizzard," Dad said. "Between social media, marketing, hosting events, needing to really be a brand to make the cut, well, being in the hospitality business has changed so much from our days. It's just more than we can handle anymore. The lodge needs an executive team, one that has a clear and fresh direction. One that can dedicate the time to really make the place shine. That isn't us."

"So we hire a team," Harris said, and all the siblings nodded in agreement. All except Lucas.

"Hiring leads to managing, and your mom and I are just tuckered out. We want to enjoy our retirement, not work through it."

"We got an offer we couldn't refuse," Lucas interrupted sharply, as if he were the only sibling who was a part of the "we." "Matrix Resorts approached us a few months back about a buy out."

"And you're just telling us now?" Harris said with heat.

"Matrix? This is a family resort. Not fancy, or bougie, but family focused." Jax looked at Peggy. "It's been in your family for over sixty years. Why would you want to sell?" he asked, because Peggy and Kent were fixtures in Sierra Vista, and he knew that Sierra Vista was a fixture in the Carmichaels' genetic makeup. He could tell that the idea of some fancy company turning their mountain lodge into something unrelatable was eating Peggy up inside.

"This offer would set Mom and Dad up for life," Lucas said. "And that was just the starting offer."

"What about Brynn?" Harris asked, looking at his little sister who was holding back tears. "She lives on the grounds." Harris glanced at Lucas and shrugged. "Where will you live, bro?"

Peggy put a supportive arm around Lucas, as if he were suddenly the one who needed protecting from this gut-wrenching news. "I think Lucas needs to run away from home. Go out on his own, instead of being trapped here."

"I've never felt trapped, Mom," Lucas said, giving Peggy a loving squeeze. "I just know how tired you and Dad are, and you deserve to spend your retirement being retired, in a house on the beach like you always wanted."

"But you guys love this place!" Brynn exclaimed. "I love this place! We all do."

"And you still can, just under someone else's ownership," Kent said.

"It won't be the same," Brynn said. "Not having you here won't be the same."

"That doesn't mean that we'll be moving permanently," Peggy said hurriedly, almost pleadingly. "We'll visit in the off season and holidays."

"Visit?" Harris looked panicked. "Emma will go from seeing her grandparents every day to drive-by visits?"

"Santa Barbara is but a few hours by plane and just around the corner from Disneyland," Peggy said. "Plus, there's the beach and the zoo. And we'll be coming home often enough that she won't even miss us."

"We'll all miss you," Harris said, and Jax knew the man had to be panicking. The lodge was Emma's home away from home. As a single parent and general contractor, Harris sometimes worked long hours and relied heavily on his parents to watch Emma.

"Enough," Kent said in a tone that left no room for arguing. "This is hard enough on your mother."

"Then why are you selling?" Brynn whispered.

"Because it's time."

"Nana and Grandpa ran the lodge until they were in their eighties," Nolan pointed out.

"Because your dad and I did the heavy lifting. And I don't want to look back and realize all I did was work."

"But—" they all said in unison until Peggy put out her hand.

"You're not going to change our minds. I want to retire on the beach, travel the world, see other places. End of story."

Jax was as stunned as his other three siblings. It may have been his adopted home, but it was the only home he had growing up. And he hated the thought of losing it.

Chapter Three

Take Life by the Balls
Keep moving forward.

Milly had dragged every box out of her sister's room and now the family room looked like a moving truck exploded, yet she hadn't opened a single box. The hospital bed and medical equipment had been dispensed of days after Zoe had passed, so all that was left was Zoe's personal effects.

The hard stuff.

The stuff that held memories and longing.

Milly sat there eyeing the boxes when her best friends, Gemma and Kat, walked in, their arms full of boxes.

"I think that's the last of it," Gemma Ward said.

Gemma was an award-winning mural artist. She was also one of Milly's ride or dies. The two had met one summer when they were eight and Milly's parents bought the weekend home next door to the Ward's; the connection was instant. But it wasn't until Milly's sister was diagnosed with cancer that Milly and Gemma went from besties to sisters, supporting each other through the trials and heartache that came with losing a loved one. Milly had lost Zoe and Gemma had lost her baby, then her husband. The grief was still raw for the both of them.

"No, there's still a few boxes in the garage that need to be gone through," Kat said.

Kat Rhodes was the local cyber expert and ball-buster, not to mention the third musketeer in their posse. Originally Zoe's best friend, she and Milly alternated taking care of her sister in the last few months of her life. Dressed in a vintage Metallica tee, camo pants, and black Doc Martens, she looked like she was the guitarist in a rock band.

While Milly and Gemma spent their time playing fairies and making snow animals growing up, Kat and Zoe were out climbing rocks and causing trouble. But when the sun set and sleepovers were to be had, the four would pile under a blanket fort and tell ghost stories.

"I already went through the ones in the garage," Milly said. "I had to make some progress, or my parents threatened to stage a surprise visit."

"Would that be so bad?" Gemma asked compassionately.

It would be a disaster. The last thing Milly wanted was for her parents to be reminded that their daughter was gone. They'd had a hard enough time accepting just how quickly Zoe had passed, Milly didn't want to add to their pain. Plus, after her dad's heart attack last week, Milly was even more concerned about adding additional stress to her parents' lives. The doctors said it was mild, but a heart attack all the same. Her mom blamed it on his diet and high blood pressure, but Milly knew better. It had been the grief that took her dad under.

So she wanted her parents right where they were, healing at home recharging and reclaiming their lives. Milly knew how soul-deep exhausting being a caretaker could be and the sacrifices it took. It cost her a relationship she'd thought would go the distance and a promotion at work. It had also cost her a chunk of her heart.

Not that she regretted even a moment of her time with Zoe. She'd treasure each and every one of them. Sleeping in the same bed as if they were kids again, marathoning all fifteen seasons of *Supernatural*—twice—and hiding in bushes waiting for the exact moment a bald eagle soared overhead so Zoe could snap the picture.

Zoe had moved into the cabin after getting her degree in photography and deciding to focus on photographing nature. Milly wondered how her sister had accumulated so much stuff when she was supposed to have been outdoors taking pictures all the time.

Some of her sister's best photography came from their time together. As were some of Milly's best memories. But she'd been cleaning out the last of her things from her New York apartment when Zoe passed. The rapid decline happened overnight and Milly didn't get home in time, leaving her parents to carry the massive load alone.

"They're really worried about me, I think," Milly continued. "I couldn't stand the looks on their faces, so I blurted out that I was seeing someone. My mom looked so happy."

"You did go on that one date with what's his face," Gemma added.

"Right, and I just didn't correct my mom when she assumed 'seeing someone' was more than that one date. I should probably be insulted that they think a man will magically fix my problems, but I know they just want me to be happy." Milly looked around at all the boxes. "Mom and Dad did some of the heavy lifting when Zoe was alive, the least I can do is the heavy lifting now."

"Well, this shit really is heavy," Kat said, plopping a box on the floor. "There must be a bowling ball in here."

Milly looked at the writing on the box and laughed. "It's Zoe's boot collection. I bet every one of them have steel toes."

"Seriously?" Kat opened the box, pulled out a pair of purple Doc Martens boots, and swooned. "Damn, she had impeccable taste."

"Do you want them?" Milly asked.

Kat stopped, her expression somber. "Are you sure? You don't want them?"

Milly waved a hand in front of her face. "You two are the same size and let's be real, Doc Martens don't match pencil skirts and glasses."

"Docs match everything," Kat said, dumping the entire collection onto the only spare patch of floor. She picked up a pair of thigh-high boots. "Even these?" Milly didn't bother to answer since Kat was already distracted with trying them on.

"This one is pretty heavy too," Gemma said, setting it down in front of Milly. "It's full of party supplies." There was a weighted pause that had Kat and Milly look up. "There's a note with our names on it."

"Our names?" Milly asked.

"All three of us."

Milly took the box from her friend and placed it in front of her. One glance at the handwriting on the note and Milly covered her mouth with trembling fingers. It was Zoe's handwriting. "What do you think it is?"

Gemma sat next to her, then Kat, all of them now cross-legged on the floor in a circle, creating so much support and love around her that Milly's heart pinched.

"We'll only find out if you open it," Kat said.

"Me?"

"Your name was first. Therefore, you get to open it."

Milly's head nodded of its own accord and slowly her hands creeped toward the note. With a shuddered breath she picked it up and pulled it out of the envelope. The card was a dark blue with metallic silver writing that read SPEND YOUR LIFE DOING STRANGE THINGS WITH WEIRD PEOPLE. There was a heaviness to the note that carried a significant weight.

Milly held the card to her chest and took in a deep breath, almost as if she could smell her sister's earthy perfume. Opening her eyes, she found both of her friends watching her seriously.

"Do you want to be alone?" Kat asked.

Milly shook her head. "She'd want us all to be together."

Milly opened the card and three mini notes fell out. Each one with the respective woman's name on it. They shared a curious glance, then Milly read the main letter aloud.

Weirdos,

You're probably thinking this is my final, sad, sappy goodbye. Pa-lese. There is no sad or sappy to be had because tonight is my Ghost-lorette Party—it's kind of like a bachelorette party but with more dares and a lot more stares, because we're all going out.

Yup, you're bringing me and my ashes along.

I want my urn to have a tiara and sash, enough glitter to rival a disco ball, and my three best friends by my side. We're talking cosmos, snarky convos, and a couple of hot fellas. Then comes the dares. I have made one out for each of you.

Now, if any of you choose to skip your dare, I will haunt you until the day you die. And I'm talking hanging your granny panties like a flag from your roof, hiding your favorite heels, cursing you with seven years' bad sex. You get the point.

Now, turn off the television and get dressed for a night out. Supernatural reruns can wait, because tonight is going to be one hell of a wild ride.

Forever your weirdo,

Zoe

PS. I've never quite figured out if people who wear pajamas in public have given up or if they're living their best life. Just to be sure, wear lace.

PPS. Enclosed in the box is a surprise from me. Wear them loud and proud, ladies.

PPPS. Mi closet es su closet.

PPPPS. Don't open the dares until you're at the bar with cock or tails in hand. (Assume your own meaning.)

By the end of the letter all three women had tears streaming down their faces. Not from crying, but from laughing so hard. Because they were all in pajamas and in the background Dean and Sam were exorcising a demon.

"God, I miss Zoe," Milly said, but for the first time since her sister's passing, she didn't feel the hollowing of her gut when saying her name. The pressure had subsided a fraction.

"Me too," Gemma said.

"I'm withholding my opinion until I see my dare." Kat held up a pink Mr. Darcy–themed thong and bralette, which had TURN MY PAGES in typewriter font on the back side. In her other hand was a paint-splattered set that read CAUTION. SLIPPERY WHEN WET. Gemma groaned.

"What does yours say?" Milly asked.

Kat pulled out a black set and grinned. "*Badass and brilliant.* She nailed it on the head. Huh, I guess that's what these are for. Nailing."

"I'm not getting nailed with *Mr. Darcy* on my hoo-ha," Milly said.

"Why not?" Kat asked. "I'd do a menaj with Mr. Darcy and Dean."

Milly took the mini note with her name on it and flipped it over in her hand. "What do you think it says?"

Gemma snatched it out of her hot little hands. "We can't open it until we get to the bar. That's the rules!"

"Yes, Mom," Kat and Milly said in unison.

Kat snatched the note and held it to her head. "I'm getting a sexy vibe. As in Milly really needs to get laid."

Gemma clapped her hands with excitement. "There's this guy I met—"

"No!" Milly said quickly. "The last time you set me up with a guy and he heard I worked for a publishing company, he assumed I had pull. He brought a manuscript for me to read because you know everyone in New York has a story to tell."

Milly was used to people pitching her their ideas in the most random places, like on the subway, in line at the grocery store, even once in a public bathroom. As soon as someone asked what she did for a living all bets were off. But that was the first time it had happened on a date while she was sucking down a bowl of tom ga soup.

"Well, at least he got you out of the house for a few hours."

Milly laughed. "A few? Try six! Six hours of having the hero's journey mansplained to me. He started in on symbolism as he was kissing my neck. Plus, who says I haven't gotten out? I went skiing the other day."

Both friends blinked.

"But you're allergic to snow, altitude, and fun," Kat said.

"Hardy-har-har. Do you do stand-up?"

"No, but I do sex. On the regular. How about you?"

Milly stayed mum on the topic. The last time she'd had a manmade orgasm was with Dillon, who left for cancer-free pastures. Okay, so manmade might be a stretch. She'd had an orgasm with a man in the room and her vibrator working overtime.

"Actually I crashed into Lucas Macintyre on the slopes. Like out-of-control crash, knocking us both on our asses. Well, he landed on his ass and I landed on him, all sprawled out with my hands groping his pecs like some kind of pervert."

Gemma covered her mouth. "You did not!"

"I so did. It was completely humiliating. But he actually flirted with me."

Sixteen-year-old Milly would have died and gone to heaven. Back then, he hadn't even known she existed. In fact, it took him a moment to place Milly during her presentation. Which was super embarrassing. But they had run in different groups. While Zoe was the outgoing, social one, Milly tended to watch from afar or disappear into a book. She had her two friends and that was all she needed. Zoe's life was about quantity and Milly's was all about quality.

"Lucas? Mr. Serious-and-Uptight flirted?" Kat snorted. "I didn't know that the guy could even speak in sentences that didn't include spreadsheets and business plans."

"Spreadsheets are sexy." Milly thought back to how he'd openly checked out her butt, and her face heated. "He even invited me to a cocoa date."

"Wait, you went on a date and you're just now telling us?" Kat threw her thong at Milly, pegging her in the head.

"Well, he got a call and had to take a rain check."

Kat snorted. "*That* sounds like Lucas. Business first, fun coming in last place. I never knew what you saw in him."

"What do you mean? He's responsible, mature, giving. And he is so devoted to helping his family. It's sexy."

"Sexy is his brother," Kat said. "Jax is fun, outgoing, and with a touch of bad boy."

"He once snowboarded in nothing but his underwear," Milly pointed out.

"Like I said, fun and outgoing."

"I dated fun and outgoing once and he bailed when life got complicated. As for bad boys, they aren't my type."

Gemma's smile faded a little bit when she looked at Milly. "Dillon was an dick. You deserve better, and he was an ass for making you feel like you didn't."

"Then there's a lot of asses in my past." And a lot of heartbreak. Well, she'd thought so until she lost Zoe and then she learned what heartache really felt like.

"It's because you date the same guy in a different suit. In Manhattan, women outnumber the men. It's a neanderthal market, and they can date and date and date without commitment. Who can blame them? It's a smorgasbord of women."

"I can," Kat said. "I've had my fair share of assholes."

"That's because you date Mr. Wrongs," Gemma said.

"Is it too much to ask for a bad boy who is hot, dangerous, *and* loyal?"

Gemma leveled Kat with a *seriously?* look. "Men are a complex combo of ego and testosterone, which renders them stupid. Especially suits who live in New York."

"And how is it different here with all of the ski bums?" Milly asked.

"Because ski bums are fun, and you need a little fun in your life. Sooo, let's swipe right on that." Kat held up her lingerie set. "Here's to the best Ghost-lorette Party in the history of Ghost-lorette Parties."

Chapter Four

Take Life by the Balls
Always opt for lace over cotton.

Milly was out.

She took one look at the overflowing crowd in Bigfoot's Brews, the rustic bar situated at the base of Sierra Vista Lodge, and nearly turned face to head home. This was not her scene. But it was Zoe's.

She looked down at the blinged-out urn and sighed. "Pull on your big girl panties and go have some fun."

"You mean your Mr. Darcy panties," Kat reminded her. She shoved Milly into the closest available bar stool and scooted in beside her, with Gemma holding down the opposite side. "Just in case you decide to bolt."

Milly sat the urn on the polished timber bar top. The urn was black marble decorated with a crystal tiara and a custom-made, urn-sized sash that read GODDESS. They'd also discovered three other sashes in the box, each with a bedazzled saying: ANGEL, DEVIL, FAIRY GODMOTHER. It wasn't hard to decipher which belonged to whom.

Kat ordered a round of cosmos and the second the server was gone the women fell quiet. On the bar sat three envelopes, waiting to be opened.

"Who should go first?" Gemma asked.

"Whoever smelt it dealt it," Kat said. "You brought it up, you go. And before you claim we should go in alphabetical order, remember your name comes first."

"I was going to say youngest to oldest."

Which would mean Milly would go first. "I'm with Kat. You're up."

Both Kat and Milly looked expectantly at Gemma. "Fine. I'll go, but if it says I have to run naked through the bar, it's a hard no. No one wants to see my stretch marks."

Neither Milly nor Kat said a word. Gemma never spoke of her pregnancy. Never. She'd once done the whole love, marriage, and baby carriage thing, but her little girl was born with a rare neurological defect and died heartbeats after delivery. Gemma was still under anesthesia due to the emergency cesarian and never even saw her baby. Even worse, the odds of her next child suffering the same fate was more likely than not, leaving a natural born nurturer without the hope of ever getting pregnant again.

Gemma took a deep breath, opened the envelope, and pulled out the letter. Her eyes went wide, and she shook her head. "I don't think I can do this." She dropped the card.

Kat picked it up and burst out laughing. "The game is, *Sign Me Up. Have a cute man autograph a part of your body that is usually covered by clothes.*"

Milly snorted.

"This isn't funny. I'm wearing a dress and Slippery When Wet panties."

"If you're calling them panties, then you need to do more than have some sexy guy sign your butt," Kat said. "Wait, it says to turn it over." Kat did and silently handed it over to Gemma. "You need to read this one yourself."

"*Gemma,*" she read aloud. "*I dare you to dream big and follow your passion. To get you started on your way, I left you ten thousand dollars. Go big!"* Gemma clutched her heart, her eyes swimming with tears. "Did you know about this?"

Milly nodded. "In her will she specified that you get the money on your next birthday. I was sworn to secrecy. So the question is, are you going to go big?"

Gemma nodded. "I'm going to use the money toward opening my art studio."

Kat placed a supportive hand over Gemma's. "We're really proud of you. I know how much you've wanted to do this."

"Since I can't paint murals anymore, I'm looking forward to teaching newbies the beauty of art."

Gemma had been talking about opening Sip and Splatter, an art and wine bar, where people can paint a picture while enjoying good friends and a glass of wine. The idea started after she lost her baby. Her specialty had been nursery murals, which served as a painful reminder of what she'd lost.

"However we can help," Kat said. "Now, since you're brave enough to chase your dream, you're brave enough to show some flesh." Kat held up her hand and flagged down the server. He was tall, ripped, and looked like a sexy lumberjack with his full beard and red flannel shirt. "Do you have a pen on you?"

He pulled one from his back pocket and held it out to Kat. "Oh, no," she said, declining the pen. "I meant for you to use it. On my friend's ass."

"Kat! That is sexual harassment!" Gemma said.

"Not if he agrees. Plus, I'm off the clock." Kat looked at Paul Bunyan. "Am I harassing you, Tim?" Kat said with a flirtatious that expressed a familiarity. Not surprising since Kat knew everyone in town. Plus, she worked a few nights a week at the bar to bring in extra cash.

Tim looked Gemma up and down, then smiled slowly. "Not at all. Signing your ass would make my night."

"It *would* make his night," Kat said with a laugh. Gemma was not laughing; she looked horrified.

"Buns out," Milly said. "Just a quick peek-a-boo. Easy peasy."

Gemma glanced around the bar, which was packed with ski bums, weekend warriors, and a smattering of locals. "This is going to be so embarrassing." She glanced up at the waiter. "You have to promise not to laugh at my panties. My dead friend picked them out."

Tim grinned. "Is that like picking out shoes?"

"Worse." Gemma stood and with a big breath she slid her dress up just enough to show one cheek.

Tim chuckled. "Slippery when wet?"

"You promised not to laugh."

"And you said these were panties. Honey, these are not panties."

"Told you," Kat said.

"Can you just sign?" Gemma said, and Tim did, slowly, making sure to dot the I and cross the T. Then he continued writing. "That seems a bit long for *Tim*."

"First, middle, and last name. Plus, my number. Just in case." With a parting wink, Tim went back to tending to his patrons.

"Before you ask if I'm going to call him, the answer is no. Now, Kat you're up."

Kat excitedly rubbed her hands together, then picked up her note. Unlike Gemma, she tore through the envelope. Closing her eyes, she flipped it over a few times, like she was playing heads or tails. "This side. *Get Buckled*," she read. "*Walk up to the next man who walks through the door and remove his belt ... with your teeth.*" Kat picked up the urn and gave it a big kiss. "Bring it on, Zoe!"

All three ladies looked at the door expectantly, and Gemma and Milly laughed when their sexy neighborhood law enforcer entered the bar. He was a mountain of a man, strapped to the teeth, and looking fine in his government-issued uniform.

"No way." Kat shook her head. "Anyone but him."

Nolan Carmichael not only enforced the law on federal forest land, he was also Kat's disgruntled neighbor. The two of them had a war going ever since Kat adopted a miniature horse who not only neighed at the top of every hour like a rooster, but he tended to faint when startled. He also thought Nolan's driveway was his own personal pooping grounds.

"That's not how this is played," Gemma pointed out primly. "'Bring it on' I believe were your exact words."

"Fine." Kat stood, threw her shoulders back and, chin up, hollered across the bar. "Hey, Ranger Tight-ass, it's your lucky night."

Nolan looked over the heads of the crowd, easy to do since he was six foot a-million. But it wasn't Nolan who caught Milly's eye. It was the sexy man following close behind.

Lucas.

He was dressed professionally in a buttoned-up blue shirt, rolled at the sleeves, showing off a powerful set of forearms that were lickable. Then there were his slacks, dark and pressed to perfection. Dress shoes. His hair was windblown and his lips...

Milly let her gaze linger for a moment, just taking in the breadth of him. But when she reached his face, he was staring right at her. He winked.

Milly spun around in her seat, her cheeks aflame. Oh my god, he caught her checking him out! She could almost hear his chuckle over the crush of the crowd. She buried her face in her hands. "That did not just happen."

Thankfully, her embarrassment was cut short when Nolan approached the table. Only he wasn't alone. He'd brought Lucas along. His gaze swept languidly down her body and back, a look of male appreciation flaming in his gaze. She sat up a bit straighter and arched her back slightly to put her girls on display like, *Take that, you flirt.*

He laughed.

"Did you finally shoot your horse?" Nolan asked, and Kat's eyes narrowed.

"Tiny Dancer is going to shit on your front porch for that," Kat said.

"He already shit on my porch. Then nibbled all my tomatoes. He's a menace."

"Oooh, big bad lawman," Kat feigned a scared look. "Are you going to arrest him?"

"I should arrest you."

"Will you bring out the cuffs?" Kat said.

Milly was so busy watching the fireworks, she didn't notice that Lucas had moved behind her until she felt his breath on her neck. "No pink tonight?"

She turned her head to look him in the eye when she remembered that she had on pink undies.

"I see," he said, all knowing.

"That's just a lucky guess."

"No luck about it. Sheer talent." With their faces this close she could see the little specks of gold in his warm green eyes. The ocean, she decided. His eyes reminded her of a tropical ocean, with the waves breaking at sunset.

"You look beautiful," he said softly, and it was like the noise of the bar faded away until all she could hear was her breathing—and his.

"Thank you." She nervously smoothed her hands down her dress and when her fingers hit skin, she remembered just how short her sister's dress was. "And you look dashing." God, did she just say that? *Dashing?* Who uses that word? A book nerd who spends her time with her face between the pages, that's who. "I mean charming." Was charming any better? "I mean, good.

You look good." She groaned, but to her surprise he didn't even blink, the beginnings of a genuine smile tipped the corners of his mouth.

"I liked dashing better. You seem like the kind of woman who deserves dashing in her world."

Lucas wasn't just dashing, he was charming, and he was charming her right into a serious crush. She wondered if he could tell by her big, goofy grin. He winked again and, *lord help her*, she was going to have to practice her poker face since she was going to be spending more time around him as the event got closer.

"Are you offering to be my dashing for the night?" she asked.

"Does that mean you're accepting applications?" His smile was half-cocked and fully loaded with swagger. Her heart jump-started like it had connected with the end of a live wire.

Was she accepting applications? And if the answer to that pressing question was yes, then what kind of timeline was she looking at? Not long. She didn't have room for long. If all went well, she'd be headed back to New York soon, to the publishing world, where she would, hopefully, work daily with the kind of authors who shaped her ideas of what romance looked like.

Milly lived with her nose between the pages of a book or a spreadsheet, rarely looking up long enough to take chances. Then again, the last chance she'd taken on love left her with a broken heart. At a time when she'd needed support and companionship, she'd been hung out to dry.

"And what makes you a good candidate?" she asked.

He cleared his throat and leaned in; his mouth was so close she could feel his breath skate down her neck. "I guess you'll have to interview me. But I must warn you, I excel in practical application."

Seconds ticked away as he waited for her to respond and, well, she had nothing to explain away what was transpiring between them. It was electric and heady, and nothing like she'd ever felt before. Maybe it was because he was showing interest or maybe it was timing—but this moment felt different than the other times they'd spent together over the past couple of months. Not that they'd spent more than a few minutes in the same room, or even alone. While she worked for the lodge, she was a consultant who worked most of the time from home, not an employee with an office, so she rarely saw him. But he'd never looked at her the way he was right then.

"Are you watching this?" Kat asked, smacking Milly's arm. That's when Milly realized she'd been staring at Lucas's mouth.

He grinned. "Like I said, practical application."

"Hello? Earth to Milly!" Kat said. "Pay attention or you'll miss it."

Milly dragged her gaze to Kat. "You're really going to do it?"

"A dare is a dare, even if it is with Big Bad Lawman." Then her friend locked her hands behind her back and dropped to her knees in front of Nolan.

Nolan didn't even budge, except to put his hands on his hips, but Milly noticed that the "Big Bad Lawman" was actually blushing. "Is this some kind of joke?"

"No joke. A dare," Kat said. "I have to take your belt off. With my teeth. You game?"

"Should we time it?" His left eyebrow rose a fraction. "Say, sixty seconds?"

"Thirty and the next round is on you."

"Deal."

Gemma took out her phone and pulled up the timer app. "Thirty seconds...and...go!" Her finger crashed down on the Start button.

Kat went to work, expertly unfastening the buckle and then yanking hard with her teeth. The bar went silent as everyone watched with rapt attention. Kat took her dares seriously, so it wasn't a surprise that when she was finished, she triumphantly lifted her hands in the air like a goal post, belt still hanging from her lips. "Well?" She looked at Gemma expectantly.

"Eighteen seconds," Gemma said.

"Take that." She threw down the belt like a football in the end zone, then stood and puffed her chest out. Nolan laughed, and the crowd erupted in cheers, as if she'd just won a gold medal. Kat grabbed his face and puckered her lips, giving Nolan a big smack of a kiss. Nolan stood there, stock still as if trying to compute what was happening. "Anyone ever tell you that you kiss like a corpse? You need to work on that."

Before he could respond, Kat was already onto her next thought. "Hey, Tim. The next round is on the big guy here!"

"Keep your horse off my property or I'll be calling the glue factory come morning," Nolan said, and then walked off, refastening his belt without a backward glance.

"See ya, Milly," Lucas said and took a seat at the other end of the bar, where it looked as if he was joining a group of friends.

She expected her friends to give her a hard time, but when she looked back at them, they were staring down at the flip side of Kat's note. "What does it say?" she asked.

"She set up a college fund for Tessa," Kat said in disbelief. "Why would she do that?"

"Because she loved you. And you love Tessa," Milly said, referring to Kat's teenaged sister. Kat was practically raising Tessa after their grandpa passed a few years back. Kat moved home to help their dad with Tessa. Kat's mom was, well, unreliable, unaccountable, and unfit to be a mom and her dad was a cross-country truck driver who left Tessa alone most of the time. Which was why Tessa spent a lot of her time at Kat's. In fact, Kat was in the process of trying to gain custody of her sister. "She knew you were stressed about her college fund and wanted to help."

Kat tilted her head back and blinked up at the ceiling.

"Are you crying?" Gemma asked.

"You know I don't cry. It's just allergies." Kat wiped her face. "Your turn, Mills."

Milly knew about the start-up money and college fund, but she had no idea what her letter included.

"Okay, here goes nothing." Giving the urn a gentle glance, she opened her note and cleared the emotion from her throat. "*I dare you to do something for you and not what people expect you to do. Inside our hidey hole is a first-class ticket to anywhere you want to go. Chase happy.*"

"Oh my god." She had to place a hand to her chest to keep her heart intact. First, because Zoe knew how much Milly had dreamed about traveling. But there'd been college, then she'd landed her dream job straight out of grad school, and Dillon came along, quickly followed by a proposal, and then Zoe had been diagnosed. There was just never a good time.

Until now.

"Where are you going to go?" Kat asked.

"England," she said automatically. "I want to go visit all of the places Jane Austen wrote about."

"Your Downunder Mr. Darcy is smiling right now," Kat said.

"Yeah." And her sister was smiling too. Visiting England had long been a dream of Milly's. Although when she imagined it, her sister was there with her, making every memory that much brighter. "But before I start having an allergic reaction to all of the feels coursing through my body, I want to get to the other dare." She flipped the card. "*Love is Blind. Have a friend blindfold a cute guy, then you kiss him. See if he can guess who puckered up once the blindfold comes off.*"

"Lucas," her friends said in unison.

No was on the tip of her tongue, but then she thought of how Zoe would handle the dare and decided to go for it. It was all in the name of fun, right? What was the harm in asking? He could always decline, which would be a little embarrassing. But embarrassing was better than regret—and she didn't want to regret anything about tonight.

Tucking her note inside her purse for safekeeping, she adjusted her glasses and flagged Tim down. "Can I borrow a clean dish towel?"

"Sure thing."

When Tim returned with a dish towel the three ladies all strutted over to the other side of the bar. And Milly's strut was dialed to a ten. *Fake it till you make it, babe.* Not to mention Lucas was tracking her every move. It was as if they were completely aware of each other. The closer she got, the faster the pulse in her neck pounded, until she was nearing stroke levels.

Yes, she'd always had a tiny crush on him, but she'd never had this reaction before.

"Sadly, I'm not wearing a belt," he said when she walked up to him. "But I can borrow Nolan's."

"No belt needed. We came prepared." Milly held up the towel. The play was that Gemma would spin him around, Kat would caress his shoulders, then Milly would kiss him. Not a *kiss* kiss, just a quick peck on the lips.

"You open for a game of Love is Blind?" Kat asked, then explained the rules.

Once again, a crowd had gathered, and his buddies burst out laughing, followed by a series of catcalls.

"Didn't know you were into blindfolds, Macintyre," Nolan said, but Lucas didn't break eye contact with Milly. If he was embarrassed, he didn't show it. In fact, he looked intrigued.

"Are you sure? You don't have to do this if you don't want to," she said gently.

"Oh, I'm just waiting to see where this leads." The humor in his smile echoed his voice. He turned around and every female eye in the bar dropped to his butt and the way he filled out those slacks.

Milly tied the dishcloth around his head, then Gemma spun him in circles. "Okay, you have to guess which one of us kisses you," Gemma said.

"Challenge accepted."

Kat walked confidently into his personal space and ran her hands down his abs, and he smiled. Then Gemma tested his bicep and the guys whistled. Finally, it was Milly's turn and her stomach rioted with nerves. Was she really going to do this? Was she finally going to do something bold—like kiss Lucas Macintyre?

"I'm waiting," he said, and she went damp.

I'd better get seven years of mind-blowing orgasms for this, she mentally said to her sister.

Wanting to feel just how hard his body was, but not wanting to take things too far, Milly put her hands on his shoulders and went up on her toes. When she still wasn't tall enough, she threaded her fingers through his hair and pulled his head lower.

His lips split into a smile right before she brushed them with her own. He didn't grab her or take control, he just stood there with his elbows casually resting on the bar top behind him, letting her control the pace. She meant to make it a chaste kiss, she really did. But her mouth didn't seem to be listening, because one brush turned into two, and finally, by the time she pulled back, everyone was chanting, "Mac-in-ty-re." Milly felt like doing some chanting of her own. She'd broken out of her shell, kissed a sexy guy, and she'd had fun doing it.

"Hey, Mills," he breathed into her mouth.

"How did you know it was me?"

"Because you taste sweet and sexy," he said against her lips. "And the air seems to catch fire when you're around."

"Oh," was the only word she could form. She'd felt the fire, but she didn't know he had. The only men she knew who said those kinds of things were in the pages of a romance novel.

She started to lift the blindfold when he captured her hands, stilling them. "One more?" he asked roughly.

"This won't make things weird?"

"If it's weird then I'm doing something wrong," he said.

She let out a small chuckle, but she still needed to clarify what was happening. "This is just for fun. It won't change anything."

"Just for fun," he repeated. "Now, I need to hear you say it."

"One more."

She'd barely gotten the words out of her mouth when his hands came around her hips, possessive but gentle, and his lips took her in a kiss that was nowhere near chaste. It wasn't aggressive or over the top. It had just the right amount of pressure, the right amount of nibbling, and the right amount of heat. *Languorous* was the word that came to mind.

He pulled back and took the blindfold off. He squinted against the bright lights of the bar and blinked a few times before his gaze landed on Milly. And if she had to use another word it would be *scorching*.

He cupped her cheek and asked, "One more?"

"You've already had two," she said.

"Third time's the charm, angel."

"Angel?"

He tugged on her sash. She looked down, having completely forgotten what she was wearing. "My sister made me wear it," she said, and burst out laughing. How many times had Zoe forced her to dress up, go out for a night on the town? Nearly every time she came to New York for a visit. And this stupid sash was a total Zoe move. "She's actually down there, sitting on the bar." Lucas followed her gaze to the urn sparkling from the fairy lights wrapped around it. "Tonight is her Ghost-lorette. You know, kind of like a bachelorette party but with an urn. Zoe planned the whole thing, which is a total Zoe thing to do. She loved parties and people and all this kind of stuff. She'd made a whole party box and hid it in the attic, probably so my parents wouldn't find it and start crying. Which is why I'm relieved that I offered to go through her things alone because if my parents—" She stopped herself.

Why was she talking about this? Because he looked as if he were about ready to say he was sorry and she didn't want to be worried over tonight. She thought about Zoe and her dare: *Do something for you and not what other people expect you to do.*

What did Milly want? She wanted to have fun. With a sexy man. And not have to think about boxes or ashes or cancer. In fact, she didn't want to think at all.

"You know what? I don't want to talk about my family, I want you to kiss me."

"As the lady wishes." And then he did something that turned this from a fun dare into something heady, he kissed her like it was his vocation. They weren't just kissing, they were having a silent conversation while exchanging breaths.

He didn't take it too far, as if aware that two hundred sets of eyeballs were on them, but he still managed to blow her mind. When they came up for air, the entire bar was applauding and once again chanting his name.

But instead of enjoying the limelight, he waved off his friends, then took her hand and helped her onto the barstool next to his.

"What are you doing?"

"Well, I was kissing you, but if you have to ask then I guess I need a do-over."

She bit back a smile. "No, I mean you obviously came here to be with your buddies. I wouldn't want to intrude."

"I'd rather be with you." He looked down the bar to where her friends were once again sitting. "Unless you need to get back to *your* buddies."

She looked at her "buddies" who were waving her on. Kat even mouthed, *Touchdown!* And put her hands in the air again. Gemma was clapping as if the proud mama. Milly groaned with embarrassment.

"I think I've been banished from the group."

"Then let me buy you a drink," he said.

A buzz of activity and conversation surrounded them, but the longer they looked at each other the stronger the bubble around them became until it felt as if they were the only two people in the room.

"Do you think they have hot cocoa?"

Chapter Five

Take Life by the Balls
Without a bucket you can't score.

Jax stared at the pretty blonde sitting next to him, his lips still tingling from the touch of hers. He wondered what made her choose him, then decided it didn't matter. He'd chalk it up to him being one lucky SOB.

Women like Milly usually didn't spare him a second glance, preferring the safer of the twins, Lucas. But she was looking at Jax like he was just her type—and, *man*, that did something to his insides.

"So, Mr. Darcy, huh?" he asked.

"I didn't pick them out," she said with this enduring shyness to her voice. God, she was cute. "They were a gift. And, according to my sister, mandatory Ghost-lorette Party attire."

It was the first time she'd brought up her sister since earlier that evening. He didn't know the whole story and would never pry, but he could relate to losing someone too early. Although her loss was clearly still fresh.

He remembered her sister, Zoe. They occasionally hung out back in the day—partying, getting into trouble, giving their parents gray hair. Not his mom, but Peggy and Kent.

Looking back, Jax was shocked that the Carmichaels let him stay there at all. Without a dad, and their mom either drunk or at work, Jax and Lucas had been left to their own devices. Left to themselves, Jax had done some stupid-ass shit. Sneaking out, partying, pulling pranks—he ran with a wild crowd.

He still remembered the first time he'd been caught sneaking out—Brynn had been the weak link blabbing to her parents the moment Jax slipped out his bedroom window. He'd come home to find a worried Kent and Peggy waiting on his bed for him. They didn't get angry or yell, but they did lay down some ground rules:

1. If he'd been drinking, call—no matter the time. They'd pick him up no questions asked.
2. If he snuck out again, he'd be on dishes duty for the next month.
3. They loved him no matter what, but love was an action that went both ways.

Most teens would have rolled their eyes, but Jax had found it almost comforting. When he was at his mom's, there weren't any rules—or maybe there were but she just never enforced them. So when Jax wanted to party into the night he crashed at Cindy's place.

"Well, my undies are just black, so I guess I'd be kicked out of the party," he said.

"It's a girls-only kind of thing anyway."

"Girls only? My kind of party." His eyebrows shot up in amusement and she laughed. Damn, she had a beautiful laugh. Honest, real, and unabashed. While Jax lived his life with honesty, he wasn't used to a whole lot of real in his world, and tonight's unexpected date was refreshing as hell.

And when Jax had trekked down to the lodge's bar and grill he had been dreading being lectured by Nolan on why he still hadn't reached out to Lucas since yesterday's family dinner. Instead, he was sitting across from a stunner of a woman who had this sweet nature that got to him.

He normally wasn't into sweet or shy; he went for edgy and cocky. He knew what to do with that. But Milly? She was a mystery to him.

Gone was the padded snowsuit from the other day, and in its place was a little black dress—emphasis on the' little. Her golden blond hair was down and in shiny, slightly tousled waves that hung just past her shoulders. Her lipstick was slightly smudged, reminding him of their kiss. Scratch that: kisses—plural. Then there were her eyes, these gorgeous, dark-cocoa doe eyes. He'd never used the term before, but on her it was fitting.

"Although, I'm enjoying this party of two." He swiveled her stool so that it was facing him.

"Same." She bumped his knees with hers, looking up at him through her cute glasses.

Jax wasn't a master at nonverbal communication, but her *go* signal was impossible to mistake. So he rested his hands on her bare calves, his fingers sliding sensuously behind her knees, then tugged her forward until their legs were intertwined.

It was an idiotic move because flirting with Milly was a bad idea. She was clearly still healing from her sister's passing, which made her vulnerable. And if there was one thing Jax didn't touch, it was vulnerable. Especially since he was leaving in a less than a week and she wasn't a catch-and-release type of woman. Yet he couldn't seem to reel things in.

"How's the cocoa?"

"Delicious. But you didn't have to make it yourself. Tim could have handled it."

"Tim doesn't know Peggy's secret recipe." And Tim was a little too interested in Milly's neckline for Jax's liking. Not that he was jealous, he didn't mess with jealous—it never turned out well.

"Secret, huh?"

"It's the shot of chocolate schnapps. Not just any schnapps, but Godiva chocolate liqueur."

"I thought it was secret."

He leaned in close enough to graze the curve of her ear and, damn, she smelled good. Like a summer bouquet. "I think her secret is safe with you," he whispered.

"Oh no. I am the worst at keeping secrets. It used to drive Zoe nuts. She would deny, deny, deny to the end, but all my parents would have to do was stare at me and I'd crack like ice in spring. Even thinking about lying makes my skin itch."

"Brynn is the same. She ratted me out for every infraction."

Milly absently ran a finger around the rim of her mug. "You grew up with the Carmichaels. What was that like?"

"Comforting, I guess. My mom's house was a free-for-all, but Peggy ran a tight ship with a soft touch. There were rules and structure, but she was patient with me."

"And you needed patience?"

"Hell, I needed a keeper. When I first moved in with them, I was practically feral. I didn't trust easily and pushed back to test how long it would take before they snapped." Or if they'd figure out he was more trouble than he was worth.

"Did you live with them?" She held up a hand. "And if that's too personal, you don't have to answer."

He didn't usually talk to women—he flirted. He also didn't spill his guts—he charmed. But with Milly he was able to do all four.

"They never officially adopted us—my mom wouldn't give up custody—so I split time between houses. My brother spent nearly all his time at Peggy and Kent's."

"That must have been hard going back and forth."

"Not any harder than a divorced family." That was a lie.

As if she could read his mind, she rested a comforting hand on his, but the electricity that sparked was a hell of a lot more than comforting. It was like panty-ripping foreplay. He knew she felt it too because she looked at their hands and her mouth formed a perfect O of surprise. Then something changed. That spark became a flame, and he couldn't help himself.

"One more?" he said, bringing her hand to his mouth and nipping at her fingertips.

Her reply was to lean in and rest her palms on his thighs for balance, then she brushed her lips across his. If he thought she smelled good, she tasted even better. Then there was the little noise she made when he sucked on her lower lip.

Now, Jax wasn't into PDA, and he certainly wasn't open to the idea of the endless shit his buddies would give him if he didn't pull back. He could tell that, even though she was the one to initiate with that blindfold and dare, the attention they'd received after had made her uncomfortable. So even though he wanted nothing more than to take things from PG to PG-13, he wasn't going to open her up to his friends' hoots and hollers. He was surprised the catcalls hadn't already started.

He pulled back, slowly easing their lips apart. When her met her gaze, it was identical to his—lust-hazed.

She looked down the bar to where her friends sat, and he thought she was going to tell him his time was up. But then she shocked the hell out of him when she said, "Come home with me?"

It wasn't said in the cocky way the women he was used to would say. In fact, she looked like she'd shocked herself.

He chuckled. "Are you asking me or yourself?"

"Come home with me." This time it was a statement, her tone was nervous yet assured.

He tucked her hair behind her ear as if unable to stop touching her. "Isn't the rule three dates?"

"Rules aren't valid at a ghost-lorette party. Everyone knows that."

He cracked a smile meant to disarm her. "Everyone, huh?" She nodded. "I still want to take you on that date." *What the hell he was saying?* His desire to go home with her was stronger than it had been with any other women. But this wasn't any other woman, it was Milly.

She brought the mug to her lips and took a sip, dramatically setting it back down on the bar top. "You said a hot cocoa date. You made me hot cocoa and this feels like a date." Her confidence wavered. "Unless I'm reading this wrong."

"Mills, I've had my hands on your knees for the past twenty minutes, itching to get to your thighs. I just want you to be sure because my life is complicated and I don't have enough to offer more."

"I'm not looking for more. I'm just looking for some fun. I'm juggling too many plates as it is and if I'm not careful, they'd all come crashing to the floor." Her honesty exposed a part of his heart he tried to keep locked up tight.

"Is that what tonight's about? Fun?"

"Yes. And taking life by the balls."

He threw his head back and laughed. "Take life by the balls?"

"It's kind of Zoe's philosophy on life. When she got sick, she made me promise to do things that scared me, made me feel alive. We talked about things we wanted to do, places we wanted to visit, but we never got that far. She's been gone four months already, so I have some catching up to do. So, will you come home with me?"

A humdinger of an emotion slid through him. Interest. How much interest? Too much for a guy who did temporary.

Anything more serious than passing interest wouldn't work. Jax wasn't equipped for more. Casual was his natural state of being. From what he could tell about Milly, she went into things with her full heart. After losing his dad to suicide, then his mom to addiction, he wasn't sure where his heart was at half the time.

"Tonight is all I have to give," he said, wanting to make sure she knew the deal.

"I'm not asking for anything more than one night."

How could he say no to that? "As long as you're sure you won't regret this in the morning." Because the last thing he wanted to be for her was a regret.

"I won't. But my house is three miles away, so that gives me three miles to talk myself out of it."

"Then I guess I'll have to keep you busy."

Chapter Six

Take Life by the Balls

Have an orgasm.

Or two.

*L*ucas kept her busy all right.

The closer they got to her house, the higher up her thigh his hand went. And now that they were at her front door, nerves buzzed through her body—along with a potent mix of lust and hormones.

She shivered and he ran her hands down her arms. "Are you cold?"

"No, nervous," she said honestly.

"There's still time to change your mind."

The open way he communicated with her, reassuring her that they'd take it at her pace, was sexy as hell. He took his man-of-honor code seriously and that made her nipples dare her to take him inside.

"No, my mind is just a little scrambled by your smile," she said, and when the wattage on that smile beamed, butterfly wings tickled her belly. "Someone reminded me tonight that instead of doing what people expect, I should do something for me."

"And you want to do...?"

He was teasing her, and she liked this playful side. In fact, GQ Lucas was more easy-going out of the office. And she hadn't seen him outside of the office in years. Between college and her job on the other side of the country, she didn't make it to the cabin nearly as much as she'd like. Before Zoe's diagnosis, those visits were mainly just major holidays, and that time was spent with her family.

But she was seeing him now. And soon she'd be seeing *all* of him.

"You. I want to do—"

Before she could finish her sentence, his mouth crashed down on hers and she was lost in the sensation. One hand sifted through her hair while the other searched down her body until it found her Darcy-clad ass. Even through the thick wool of her coat she could feel his desire.

"Inside," he breathed into her mouth. "I need to get you inside so I get this coat off your body. Then I'm going to peel off that wet dream of a dress until you're in nothing but heels and skin."

"Inside works." Milly reached back to open the door and they both stumbled inside. Their bodies were pressed airtight, their mouths fused together through the whole maneuver as they crashed into walls and off the furniture.

She caught her heel on a box and would have fallen on her butt if he wasn't already holding it in his palm.

"It's like a minefield," he said, his lips never breaking contact.

"Work in progress."

His other hand slid down to her butt and he let out a frustrated grunt. "Coat. Lose the coat, Milly."

The syllables of her name came out like a caress, smooth and sensual.

Together they unbuttoned her coat, their fingers tangling as they both rushed to get it off. Finally, *finally*, it hit the floor and his hands were all over her. The curve of her lower back, her hips, her thighs—his thumbs slipping under the hem of her dress and inching high enough that he rubbed them back and forth on the undersides of her ass.

He kissed her as if it were the main event, something to be savored.

After what seemed like an eternity, his hands slid up her sides, rounding the hem of her dress and taking with it with him. Milly lifted her hands and, *poof*, she was left in her lingerie and heels.

He took a step back, flicked on the lights, and raked his eyes down her body. "Just what I imagined."

She covered her breasts. "What did you imagine?"

He took her hands and held them out to the side, giving a grunt of male appreciation. "That beneath that pink snowsuit you'd have a bombshell of a body."

"Thank you," she whispered. No one had ever looked at her like he did. As if she were the most delectable thing he'd ever seen. In the past, sex had been pretty vanilla. Missionary, in bed, lights off. But he wanted to see and suddenly she wanted to show him.

"Now it's my turn." She ran her fingers from his chest to his abs, then undid his shirt, button by button. "I like your shirt."

"I think I'd like it better draped over your naked, sated body."

Well, if that didn't curl her toes. "There's something about a pressed button-down and slacks that turns me on," she said, shoving it down his magnificent shoulders until it hit the floor. This time when she ran her hands down his abs, she watched mountains of muscle ripple beneath her touch.

She didn't stop there, sliding lower until she was at the waistband of his slacks. She toyed with the button. "Too bad you aren't wearing a belt, I bet I could beat Kat's time."

"I'm going to have to invest in one to test out this theory."

"Maybe save your money." She flicked his pants open and they slid all the way down. "This is easier access."

"A woman after my own heart." He stepped out of his pants, but not before removing a condom from his wallet, then walked her backward and down the hallway. "Room?"

"This one." She laced her fingers with his and led him to her bedroom. He took it from there, backing her up until her legs bumped the mattress.

As she started to sit down, he said, "One second." He masterfully unclasped her bra and her Mr. Darcy thong vanished. "I don't share well."

She spun them around and shoved him until he fell back on the bed. "Neither do I."

She wrapped her hand around his impressive erection and gave it a few strokes. Slow then fast, slow then fast. From base to tip and back down again.

"Much more of that and this will be over before I get the chance to taste you. All of you."

Oh my.

"Can I taste you, angel?" he asked, but he was already sitting up, cupping her hips and dragging her over him until she was on her knees and he was under her.

The position was new and erotic and made her feel alive. His mouth skimmed along her inner thigh, his teeth nibbling the sensitive flesh right below her slit sending her heart skittering into overdrive.

"Yes." The word came out in a rush. "Please." He passed over where she needed him most and started the same torture on her other thigh, again stopping just shy of the finish line. "Taste me now."

He chuckled against her and she could feel the warm puffs of breath on her skin. Then she felt his tongue—right up the center.

He tasted her again and again until her hips were bucking. If he hadn't been holding her thighs, she might have smothered him.

"I want to see you touch yourself," he said, and there was something about the quiet assuredness in his tone that spoke to her. Stole her breath.

She tiptoed her fingers down her body, circling her navel.

"That's it, angel. A little lower." Every word reverberated through her core, making her hotter and hotter.

He was still beneath her, his tongue doing delicious things to her when her fingers rubbed over her pleasure point. He grunted against her and that's when she realized he was watching her every move. Feeling exposed she nearly pulled back, but the hunger in his eyes overrode her nerves and had every thought tumbling out of her head. Instead of shying away from the unknown, she did what she'd always wanted to do but never had the confidence for—she took charge.

She brushed back and forth, pressing harder with each stroke, while his tongue was doing some stroking of its own. The deep pulls and barely-there strokes echoed throughout her body. It didn't take long for them to find a rhythm, for her body to tighten, and her thighs to quiver beneath her. And then she shot off like a firework on New Year's Eve. Flying high and exploding at the top before raining down.

When she was finally able to see through the sex-dazed haze, she was on her back and Lucas was over her, wrapped and ready. They both moaned when his length slid in. It felt amazing.

He felt amazing.

The heavy weight of his body, the way he stretched and filled her, the gentleness of his hand as he cupped her cheek right before he planted a mind-blowing kiss on her lips. She kissed him back with fervor and they both started moving, their bodies syncing almost immediately. It was unlike anything she'd ever felt. It was languid, sensual, erotic and gentle all at the same time.

The man knew what he was doing. He was skilled and prac-
ticed—a sex god. He knew just when to pick up the pace or slow
down until he had her right at the edge. And he brought her to
that point over and over until she was begging for release.

"Not yet. I want to feel you for as long as possible," he said.

"Possible is here." She arched against him. "And here." She
arched again, squeezing her core to create more friction. "And
here."

She could feel him smile against her neck. "How about
here?"

He gave a deep thrust and she cried out in pleasure. The next
time he came down on her, she gave a twist of the hips and he
was the one crying out. Game time clearly over, he got down to
business with a focus and determination that left her breathless.

They met each other thrust for thrust and before she knew
it, she was experiencing her very first vaginal orgasm—and, *holy
smokes*, she'd been missing out. Her entire sex history was erased
in a single man-made orgasm. Because that's what Lucas was—a
man.

She felt him tighten inside her and then he joined her,
groaning out her name and pumping all the way through their
release. When she opened her eyes, he was lying limp over her,
like a snuggly comforter. His face burrowed into the curve of
her neck, her hands on his ass, their legs twisted like a pretzel.

"Was that what you imagined?" she mumbled.

He lifted himself up. "Even better."

"Me too." She smiled and he dazzled her with a smile back.
"Once more?" she asked.

Chapter Seven

Take Life by the Balls
*Claim that morning-after
crown proudly.*

Milly was a peeper.

She couldn't help it. When she woke up next to a lightly snoring sex god, with the sheets hanging a scant inch from his flagpole—which was at full mast—leaving everything else visible, she snuck a peek. A long peek. Okay, she out-and-out ogled the guy.

But with his body on glorious display who could blame her. His messy, dark hair was standing on end, one arm was around her waist, the other holding her right butt cheek as if he owned it.

Always interested in the Laws of Attraction, Milly skated a finger down his chest, watching in fascination how the muscles rippled and bunched. His breaths, which rose and fell in a slow, steady rhythm, deepened whenever she touched him.

Knowing that this would be the only time she'd be able to look her fill, she explored the dark trail of hair that disappeared beneath the sheets. The man was built like some kind of Scottish warrior preparing for battle. She looked up to make sure he was still sleeping and lifted the covers and, *yowza,* ready for battle indeed.

Sure, she'd seen *it* last night. But not like this. Not when she had the luxury of admiring its beauty. This felt voyeuristic and a little naughty. And, if she were being honest with herself, naughty had never felt so good.

Naughty Milly had sex with Lucas Macintyre.

Lucas Macintyre!

That was a Take Life by the Balls–worthy adventure if she'd ever heard one. But now what? She'd never had a one-night stand and didn't know what the exact so-we-boned-three-times etiquette was. What was one supposed to say after a night like that? To her recollection, one-night stands were supposed to be gone by the time she woke up. Even her last boyfriend rarely stayed the night.

This was new territory for her. But new didn't have to mean bad or scary. New could be exciting and liberating if she chose. And she chose. She wasn't going to let uncertainty creep in and ruin her post-orgasmic glow. She was going to celebrate it—by pulling out a piece of paper and writing HAVE SEX WITH LUCAS MACINTYRE down just so she could tick off the box.

Huh, she'd have to write it down three times, since he was a three-time champion. She picked up her pillow and took a whiff, her eyes closing as the scent of fresh sweat and sex filled her nose. She took another sniff, this time putting an image to the scent. It was intoxicating.

She dropped the pillow and, in her sex-drunk state, went back to cataloging every inch of the male masterpiece lying in her bed. *Her bed!*

"Do you want your camera to take a picture?" a sleep-roughened voice asked.

Milly dropped the pillow like it was made of acid, then froze. She'd been caught snooping around his sword.

"Too late to go shy on me now," he said.

"Is it okay if I just lie here and pretend that didn't happen?"

"Nope, because if you pretend you weren't peeping," he said, giving her ass a cute squeeze and then a playful slap that forced a laugh to bubble up from her chest, "then you might want to pretend last night didn't happen and that doesn't work for me."

When she didn't move, he rolled her over, rising up between her legs. His hands on either side of her head, he slowly lowered himself, like some sort of Cross Fit plank champion going for the gold. He held steady, his biceps bulging, his stomach taut, his mouth inches from hers.

She slapped a hand over her lips. "I have morning breath."

"I don't give a shit." He nipped her knuckles. "Move your hands or I will tickle you until you do."

There was a genuine threat beneath the humor and since she was as ticklish as a jackrabbit, her arms instinctively flew to her belly, covering her ribs. His gaze followed and when it slid back up her body he smiled, the smile of someone who has dubious plans.

"I know about here." He descended just enough to run his nose along the curve of her neck, which was one of her *go* spots, and she bit her lip. "And here," he whispered, resting his weight on one arm to free up his right hand, which cupped her hip. His thumb skated lightly over her hip bone. Instead of giggling, she released a choppy breath. "Where else are you ticklish, angel?"

She pressed her lips in a *not telling* line.

"I see. I guess I'm just going to have to tickle every inch of you." His fingers slid across each rib slowly. Instead of squirming, she released several gasps. "Maybe I should go lower."

"Lower is good. I like lower."

"Like?" He rotated his hip so that his sword grazed her sensitive flesh. She shivered. "I think we can do better than *like*."

"Love. I love lower."

He waited until she met his gaze and when she did, something in her chest shifted. Maybe she was sex-brained, but she could swear that beneath the hunger and pulsing testosterone was something soft, almost tender. This time when he lowered his head she didn't care about awkward morning after or morning breath, all she cared about was finding out if morning sex with him was as great as nighttime sex.

She was willing to make the sacrifice.

With a groan of approval, he closed the distance between their bodies, so that all his good parts lined up with all her good parts and then his mouth was on her and—

His phone chirped.

Milly's lids flew open. "Do you need to get that?"

His answer was to deepen the kiss until Milly's leg swung over his hip all on its own. With a groan, he rolled over so that he was on his back, and she was straddling him—a position that, based on last night, he favored. He seemed to be an equal opportunity lover when it came to boobs and butt. He liked his hands on one while his mouth explored the other.

Ping.

She felt him hesitate, but then his hands plunged into her hair, yanking it slightly. Another thing she learned last night— Lucas Macintyre had a thing about her hair.

Ping. Ping. Ping.

"Jesus," he said, pressing their foreheads together as they listened to his phone blow up, chirping again like an angry mama bird defending her nest.

"It might be an emergency," she offered.

"Or it might be Nolan giving me shit for leaving him at the bar last night."

Milly gasped. "We left him at the bar?"

"He can find his way home." Jax flipped her over, trapping her beneath his big body and started nipping her neck. "He's a big boy."

Milly reached over and picked up his phone from the night-stand and pressed it to his chest. "Even so, you should always answer when it's family."

Because one day there won't be any more calls.

She didn't say it aloud, but she must have telegraphed through her expression because his eyes went soft. "I wasn't thinking, I'm sorr—"

She covered his mouth. "Please don't. I don't want this to end on a sorry."

A little part of her said she didn't want to end this at all. Which was ludicrous. She had a precious few weeks to go through her sister's things and build up the confidence to get to the top of Vista Peak without throwing up, passing out, or spiral-ing into panic. Then she'd have to figure out what to do with her life. Go back to New York and the city she adored? Move to San Francisco to be closer to her parents? Or stay in Sierra Vista? While she loved the city and carried this enormous weight to take care of her parents, there was something comforting about the cabin.

So while this Scotsman had jump-started her vagina, she'd have to let it sit idle for now.

"Check your messages and I'll go make us some coffee," she said, and before he could convince her to play a game of tongue tickle, she tried to squeeze out from under him with the blanket in tow. He didn't make it easy, the jerk. The moment she stood up, he yanked the sheet back, leaving them both naked.

Predictable Milly would have shrieked, but Naughty Milly didn't want to give him the satisfaction. She stood tall, shoulders back and, with the girls perky and up front, she sashayed around the bed. And instead of bundling up like she was headed out into a snowstorm, she picked up his shirt off the floor and slid it over her shoulders like it was red silk. She cocked a hip like she knew what she was doing and the material parted like curtains, giving him a peek of what was behind it.

"I fucking knew it." He ran a hand down his face and groaned with appreciation. "I say we skip the coffee and messages and you come back to bed so I can give you a proper good morning, slowly and thoroughly." He patted the space next to his very naked, very hard body, and she nearly wept.

"How about I start the coffee and after that we can see how fast you can unbutton this with your teeth." She buttoned the bottom two buttons.

Clearly comfortable in the buff, he stood in one fluid motion and came toward her like a hungry grizzly looking for its next meal.

"Or maybe we use this," he grabbed a scarf off the hook and slid it around her waist, pulling her to him until she was flush with his body, "as a blindfold and I get a little revenge."

She shivered. Revenge never sounded so good.

"Would there be kissing?"

"Angel, there'd be a hell of a lot more than ki—"

Ping.

He grunted. Frustration furrowed that cute crease in his forehead.

"Go." She encouraged. "This can wait."

"This can't." He cupped her ass and yanked her to him until his impressive erection was pressed against her belly.

Ping.

"Don't move." With an irritated grunt, he picked the phone up off the bed and read the screen. He looked up at the ceiling as if seeking divine intervention.

"Everything alright?"

"Just family," he said, a hint of exhaustion in his tone. "Seems my asshole brother called a mandatory meeting at the lodge. We all have to be there in thirty minutes."

"Oh." She pulled the shirt shut and suddenly everything came back to her. The bar, the night, the sex, the morning after which was destined to end, because that was the definition of a one-night stand—come sunup, the magic disappeared. "Why don't you use my shower to wash up and I'll fix you something quick to eat before you go."

His expression went carefully blank. She couldn't read a thing off him except that his shoulders had tensed. "You don't have to do that."

Was there some code about what a breakfast-after translated into that she was missing? Was she making what should be a breezy goodbye awkward? "I didn't mean anything by it. I just thought you might need some calories to fuel that big, muscly, manly body."

His smile was back, genuine and amused, curling as if always on the edge of laughter. "Muscly and manly, huh?"

She grabbed a towel from the closet and playfully threw it at him. "Go shower. I'll whip up some eggs. If you decide to eat them, cool. If not, then more for me."

She turned to leave, and he caught her hand. "Eggs sound perfect," he said, then placed the tenderest kiss on her lips.

She watched him walk into the bathroom, his glorious ass on display, and she didn't bother to hide her interest. And when he gave a little backside shimmy, the laugh that escaped was warm and full and free.

When was the last time she'd felt so free?"

With a little shimmy of her own, she headed toward the kitchen. As always, the first thing to draw her attention was a collage of family photos stuck to the refrigerator door with magnets from every state they'd visited together—including Hawaii where they learned to surf. Well, Zoe learned. For Milly it was more of a man-overboard kind of experience. Instead of sorrow, her heart warmed with memories. Some sad, but most of them happy.

When Zoe had received the tragic diagnosis, she'd decided she wanted to live her life full of adventure and low on regret. Zoe being Zoe, she had come up with adventurous things she wanted to accomplish before she passed, like ski-diving naked or hitting the slopes dressed like Snow-Bunny Barbie—a task Milly was determined to get right. Zoe wanted to do anything that involved heights, which terrified Milly. But she was determined to finish every single one in honor of her sister. Like hiking Vista Peak.

Gah, she didn't even want to think about that yet. It made her belly flip—and not in a good way. But she'd figure it out. That's what Milly did, her life depended on her ability to figure things out. Like how to live in Manhattan on a junior logistic coordinator's salary, how to get her boss what she needed before she knew she needed it, how to convince her parents that she was living her best life and not wallowing in the aftermath of losing her sister and fiancé only a few months apart. Milly managed so many daily how-to's for so many people, she rarely had time to think about fun how-to's.

Like, how to best have sex with Lucas on the kitchen counter or how to have as many orgasms one person could have in a twenty-four-hour period. Those were problems she'd like to solve. Sadly, she thought as she opened the cupboard, the most pressing two how-to's at the moment had to do with a) how to cook a proper breakfast without burning it—cooking was a how-to she had yet to master—and b) how to make coffee with her parents' ancient and temperamental coffee machine. The thing came from the era of paper newspapers, landlines, and freeze-dried grounds.

Humming to herself, Milly grabbed the bread from the cabinet, dropped four slices in the toaster, and sashayed back across the kitchen to the refrigerator. She opened it and grabbed the eggs, her bootie bopping in rhythm to the song in her head.

She turned toward the stove and the entire carton of eggs went crashing to the floor, because there, looking road-trip rumpled, stood her parents, Howard and Gennie.

"Mom? Dad? What are you doing here?" she croaked, haphazardly buttoning the shirt all the way to the collar. *Lucas's shirt!*

"It is our house, dear," Gennie said.

God, she'd had freaky-deaky sex in her parents' house. She threw up in her mouth a little.

"I know, but you're supposed to be at home. Healing."

"Seven days of staring at the television and I needed a change of scenery," Howard said, stepping over the broken eggs and pulling Milly into his arms in a hug that nearly knocked the wind out of her. Where Milly was vertically challenged, her dad stood at a steady six foot two. Big arms, big belly, and an even bigger heart.

"Netflix is a crucial part of the healing process," Milly said. "A guy can only take so many episodes of *Bridgerton*."

"You know your dad can't stay in one place very long," Gennie said. "I caught him geared up for a hike just yesterday morning."

Zoe had inherited her curious side from their dad. Where Zoe was a nature photographer—an adventurer by trade— Howard was an attorney during the week and an outdoorsman on the weekends. He liked hiking, bird watching, and anything that placed him in the wild.

Gennie's idea of outdoorsmanship was pruning her roses, but she obliged her husband and oldest daughter by going on weekend outings. Zoe's idea of outdoors was scaling a mountain. Her dad would hike it, her mom would remind everyone to stay on the trail, and Milly would be back at base camp staring cluelessly at the map.

Growing up, her parents worried that Zoe would come home with a broken bone—or worse. When it came to Milly, her parents had worried that she'd never leave home. Zoe couldn't be corralled, and Milly couldn't be convinced that there was anything worth risking life and limb for. But her hermit habit sometimes concerned her parents as much as Zoe's daredevil lifestyle.

"We wanted to check in on you," her dad said carefully, then glanced over her shoulder at the unopened boxes blanketing the front room. "Make sure you weren't holed up in the house in your pajamas."

"Oh, Howard," her mom admonished. "We've been here all of two minutes and already you're smothering." Gennie grabbed Milly by the hands and pulled her arms out to the side, taking her in. Thankfully, the shirt fell to her knees. "I mean look at her. Up and about, in the kitchen, looking fantastic. I mean she's positively glowing. What's your secret?"

Her secret was multiple orgasms in a single night.

"How are you handling things, Milly Rae?" her dad asked as if only the stone-cold truth were an option.

Milly winced. That first and middle name combo was only used when he was in lecture mode or worried. And right then he was worried—about her state of mind.

"I'm fine. Really."

Howard folded his arms over his big belly. "We both know what *fine* means."

"I know what you're thinking. But I've been so busy catching up with Gemma and Kat," who were going to have an encyclopedia of questions later, "that I've barely had time to breathe. In fact, just last night we went to Bigfoot's Brews." Which had led to sex with her childhood crush. "I even went skiing." Into said crush.

Her dad's eyes tracked the room and all the untouched boxes of her sister's things. "I knew I shouldn't have left you to do this alone."

"Dad, I need to do this alone."

"Why?"

"Because I need closure. You were there to say goodbye in her last moments, and I wasn't. Plus, I doubt your doctors would approve of you lifting any boxes."

"My doctor's an idiot. I bet he isn't even old enough for his balls to have dropped."

"He's the top cardiologist in the county."

Howard opened his mouth to argue, then snapped it shut, his face going pale while his ears turned red. "Where is she?" He walked toward the mantel over the fireplace and touched the empty spot where Zoe's urn used to sit.

Shit, the urn! She hoped Gemma and Kat hadn't had too much fun at the bar and left her behind. How could she have forgotten her sister? How could she have been so irresponsible? She'd been baited by the promise of an orgasm, that's how. She would call Kat as soon as her parents were out of snooping range.

"Did you remember to lock the doors? Did someone take her? I knew it was a mistake to get such an expensive urn," her father said.

Her mom's hand flew to her chest, her face going pale. "Honey, where's Zoe?"

"No one stole her," Milly rushed to say. "She's, uh, sleeping over at Kat's."

Her mom released a relieved breath. "See, Howard, she's fine. She's just having a sleepover at her friend's house," Gennie said as if this were a normal reason for her daughter's urn to be missing.

Her dad looked as if he had more to say on the topic, but at that precise moment the floor creaked behind her. Panic hit so quickly she thought she might be the next one to stroke out.

"What was that?" Howard asked.

"What?" She scratched her wrist.

Creak.

"That."

Her dad moved toward the hallway, but Milly stepped in front of him. "Why don't you two go out to breakfast. I know how much you like the Brown Bear Diner."

"I was going to make you breakfast here." Her mom looked at the dented carton and demolished eggs on the floor. "But we might need to go to the store."

"Yes! The store!" Milly nearly shouted. "Why don't you two go to the store and I will shower. Then we can have a nice family breakfast. Just the three of us."

That would give her enough time to get rid of Lucas, clean up the proof of hook-up alley, and put some clothes on. But before she could put her plan into action, her mom's eyes went wide and her mouth dropped into a perfect O of shock and awe.

Milly knew the look. She'd worn it herself for the past eighteen hours.

"Or, I'm guessing it will be a breakfast of four?" her mom said, and Milly didn't have to turn around to know who the fourth was. She could smell the testosterone fill the room.

She closed her eyes and prayed, *Please be dressed. Pleased be dressed.* She turned around and FML, he was dressed in only his slacks, no shoes, no shirt—right, she had his shirt. He was truly the sexiest guy she'd ever seen, much less slept with. But all she could think about was that this *was* going to be the most awkward morning after ever.

"Who are you?" her dad demanded to know, puffing out his chest and staring down Lucas as if challenging him to a dual—of fists.

"Howard, don't be rude," Gennie admonished. "This must be the man you've been so secretive about."

Right, the fake man she'd been seeing for a big fat fake two months.

Lucas met her gaze with a lifted a brow.

"I promise, this isn't what you think," she whispered to Lucas.

There was no secret man. In fact, the only thing secret about her secret man was that he didn't exist. Milly had made him up the moment word of Dillon's engagement reached her parents. Of course, Gennie had gone into mother-hen mode, telling Milly it would be alright, while Howard went into protective mode, convinced the only way things would be okay was if he pummeled Dillon. So Milly mentioned that she'd started dating a nice guy in Sierra Vista. Gennie, the eternal romantic, took Milly's single post-Dillon date to mean that she was in a relationship. And Milly had never corrected her.

Her father met Milly's gaze and she saw the seriousness in his eyes.

She considered telling them that she'd hired a professional mover to help with the boxes and as a joke she'd hired a shirtless moving company. Except she was the worst at lies and her dad would see right through her.

She scratched her wrist, and her dad lifted a parental brow. Shit, he knew.

"Mom, Dad, um, this is Lucas."

There was a long pause where she felt Lucas's gaze bore into her. Her stomach twisted when she looked at him and he shot sparks at her. His expression was dialed to *pissed*. She didn't blame him. Who met the parents on the first date?

He stepped past her, his woodsy scent lingering. He offered his hand. "Lucas's brother, Jaxon," he said. "Nice to see you again, Mr. Smartt."

Her heart pounded against her ribs, robbing her of breath.

Oh!

My!

God!

No. It couldn't be. He had to be joking, right? In her rush to jump off the FOMO train, had she accidentally slept with a guy and didn't even have the right name? Even worse, the right brother? No, it had to be Lucas. He'd been wearing slacks. A button-down. His shoes were so polished they reflected the overhead lights.

If it was Jax, and by the look on his face she had a good idea it was, then had he known from the start that she thought he was Lucas and played along like it was some kind of joke? *Ha-ha, wrong twin!* And more importantly, what did she say now? To him. To her parents. And what did *he* have to say for himself?

Apparently nothing since he was staying tight-lipped on the subject. Her mom was confused, her dad looked homicidal, and Milly was equal parts embarrassed and angry. She didn't like being played. She'd been there before and wound up with a broken heart.

The problem was she didn't know if he was an innocent bystander or guilty of catfishing her. Either way she had a precious few seconds to fix this and prevent her father's second heart attack. The wheels in her brain were spinning so fast they might strip a gear.

Fix it, Milly. The problem was she wasn't sure how to convince her parents she wasn't making rash decisions. Because while sleeping with Lucas—um, Jaxon—was a spur of the moment thing, it hadn't felt rash. It felt right.

He'd come along at the right moment in her life and they'd shared something amazing. Or so she thought.

"Jax?" she laughed, elbowing him in the gut, willing him to say *just kidding* and laugh with her.

He didn't laugh. He stood tall and straight like a towering pine. The very way he held his posture told her he was livid.

As if smelling the tension wafting off them in waves, her dad demanded, "What the hell is going on here?" Then he sent her *the* look and Milly's wrist itched and her lungs felt as if they were being strangled. She'd seen that look, but never aimed at her.

She looked at Jax who was looking back, something inquiring burning in his eyes, which were clearly transmitting a message: *Yeah, what is going on?*

How should she know? She'd swiped right and look where it landed her. In a total Zoe situation—standing in her parents' kitchen with a half-naked mystery man. And Milly had spent her entire life trying not to add stress to her parents' plate. She loved her sister with every fiber of her being, but Zoe had been a magnet for trouble and chaos—and was responsible for every gray hair on her dad's head. And the last thing Milly wanted was to have her parents thinking she was as reckless as her sister in bringing home the wrong man—or as desperate as to make up a fake boyfriend out of thin air.

"I know who you are," Gennie said. "You were friends with my Zoe."

She *knows my name,* Jax's expression seemed to say. But when he spoke to her mom, his tone was tender and warm. "I was sorry to hear about Zoe, Ms. Smartt."

"Why, thank you." Gennie gave Jax a pat on the arm, then squeezed his bicep before looking him up and down. "Well, didn't you fill out nicely. Snowboarding really agrees with you."

"Mom!"

"So you two are dating," Gennie said, a warm smile slowly spreading across her face. "Oh, Milly, we're so proud you've put yourself back out there and found a nice man. Isn't that right, Howard?"

Howard snorted like a bull to the matador.

"I mean after everything that happened with Dillon and the news that he is now—"

"Mom!" Milly said again. Today was embarrassing enough without Jax knowing that the man who had loved her enough to get down on one knee had dropped to his knee yet again, proposing to another woman just months after breaking Milly's heart.

This was a disaster. A complete disaster. She could already tell by the challenge in her dad's expression that he wasn't about to buy what she was thinking of selling.

So her story had to be nothing too elaborate. Keep it simple, to the point and as close to the truth as possible. Except when she got nervous, she rambled and rambling led to spilling the beans. And these particular beans needed to stay in the can. At least until she and Jax had a conversation about what the hell was going on.

Until she was proven differently, she was blaming Jax for this whole mess. Yes, he'd never said his name and, no, not a single one of his buddies called him by anything other than Macintyre, but he'd been in slacks. And acting like a responsible adult. And if this was some kind of switch-a-roo, then she'd fallen for it hook, line, and sinker.

Milly didn't make a habit of running from confrontation, but then she thought back to her sister's letter about finding her happy. She really wanted her family to think she was happy and holding on instead of being worried about her all the time. So she held on all right, taking Jax's hand in hers, lacing their fingers, and in a moment of desperation, blurted out, "We kind of crashed into each other and nostalgia just kicked in." Which was the truth, the whole truth, and . . . Oh hell, who was she kidding? She was a big fat liar.

"Did you hear that, Howard? Nostalgia kicked in," her mom said with an excited hand clasp to the chest.

Jax's lips thinned and his eyes blazed with something that pierced her heart—hurt—but then he smiled up at her parents and said, "Yeah, nostalgia can be pretty surprising sometimes."

"Well, when did this all happen?" Gennie asked, practically glowing with joy.

Milly's brain farted and her mouth betrayed her good sense. "It's new," she said, her smile too bright.

Jax froze and so did Milly. She couldn't believe the lies that were spewing out of her mouth. For someone who broke out in a rash when they lied, she'd just jumped neck deep into it.

She looked up at Jax, her eyes pleading with him to go along with her plan. He crossed his arms in an *Are you serious?* stance that had her blanching. Then she saw the moment he decided to play along. His eyes went from blazing to irritated but with a hint of *You so owe me.*

"It almost seemed to happen overnight," he said.

Chapter Eight

Take Life by the Balls
Get through today.

Jax's day had turned to shit.

First off, Milly had slept with him thinking he was his brother. Sure, he and his brother had swapped places a time or two growing up, when Lucas took a math test for him or Jax would cover a shift at work for his brother, but this was the first time someone had switched things up on him. And yes, Jax was used to sleeping with women and not exchanging much personal information. But this was different.

He knew Milly from growing up around town, so he'd just assumed that when she'd said hi to him that first day that she knew which brother she'd been talking to. Hell, he and Lucas might be twins, but they were like night and day. Where Lucas was always destined for the Ivy League, Jax was the athlete. Cerebral versus cunning.

There was a time when Jax had constantly tried to fight his way out from beneath Lucas's shadow. But he'd learned a long time ago there was no point in trying since he was never going to measure up. It was a fact he'd accepted, but it was hard to move past. It was why he'd taken a different path in life, using his talent to travel the world. And he'd been pretty damn successful at it too. But hearing Milly call him Lucas this morning really burned. It brought up feelings he'd worked hard to tamp down.

To make his day worse, he'd been summoned by the golden boy to appear at the palace for a mandatory family meeting. Jax wondered if he should feel honored that he was actually included on the "family" text thread or irritated that Lucas had once again kept something so big to himself. Something that became apparent the moment he'd stepped into the boardroom to find everyone arguing.

Lucas sat back in his chair, arms folded, body language reading proud and unmovable. Brynn, on the other hand, was on her feet, palms placed against the round conference table, leaning halfway across the thing, steam blowing out the top of her head. She might look like the sweet girl-next-door, but when riled she could argue with a pack of gum.

The Carmichaels loved as fiercely as they fought and with Lucas accepting the Carmichaels as his kin from the word go, he didn't shy away from situating himself right in the middle and rarely backed down. As much as Jax wished he could have integrated into the family so easily, his trust issues came between him and the one thing he craved—acceptance.

Jax walked into the room and it fell silent; not a single person moved. Well, not a single brother moved. Brynn huffed out a sigh and sat back in her chair.

"Thank god you're here," she said. "Your brother is being an idiot."

"I second that," Harris said with his hand in the air like he was in elementary school.

"Lucas has a few good points," Nolan ventured carefully. "I think we should hear him out."

"Wait. Are you on his side?" Brynn asked.

Nolan held up a neutral hand. "There are no sides. We're just having a discussion."

"Sounds more like World War Three," Jax said, eyeballing his designated seat, which was next to his twin. Lucas didn't give a single indication if Jax should take it or let the door hit him in the ass on the way out.

Right. World War Three.

Jax knew that he had allies. Just like Lucas knew he was on the losing side. Didn't mean his brother wouldn't fight dirty.

Jax took his seat at the table and his past and present collided. The day he'd turned twenty-one, Peggy and Kent had placed him on the board, like he was one of their kids. He'd sat there many times, but this time felt different. It felt significant.

"What did I miss?" he asked.

Nolan checked out Jax's rumpled walk-of-shame clothes and grinned. "You tell us."

Irritation coursed through him. Instead of riding the high of a spectacular night, he was still reeling from the morning after. Then there was the way Lucas was looking at him, as if Jax was just pulling another Jax, and that pissed him off. "No comment."

Lucas looked at Jax. "I wasn't sure you'd come."

The statement set Jax's teeth on edge "Why? Did you mean to text the other text thread?"

"This just isn't your scene."

"I figure we're here to talk about the lodge so, yeah, it's my scene."

Jax had spent the entire drive over thinking about how to save the Sierra Vista Lodge from going to a conglomerate while still giving Peggy and Kent their dream of living on the beach. He'd listened to what they'd said, but he'd also read between the lines. They were as unsettled about selling as the rest of them were. Giving up one dream to chase another was always scary. Which, if Lucas had listened, he'd know.

Lucas's phone rang. He checked the screen and something flickered in his expression. Exhaustion. He sent it to voicemail and pocketed it.

"Was that Mom?" Jax asked. It was a cheap shot, but he wasn't feeling all that forgiving today.

Lucas understood he was asking about their mom, Cindy. "That was one time, a year ago. Haven't spoken to her since, which you'd know if you'd stuck around."

The comment cut deep and Jax felt as if a fist was trying to punch through his sternum. He wasn't the one who'd had a clandestine meeting with their mom. Wasn't the one who'd made a decision to keep Jax out of the loop. After five years, their mom had actually reached out for help and Lucas singlehandedly turned her away.

Jax only found out because he'd heard through the grapevine that Lucas and Cindy had coffee at Coffee Run.

"Why stick around? Mom shut me out. You shut me out." He saw anger banked in his twin's eyes and Jax met it with equal force. "Seems like I've been shut out on a lot."

"We didn't shut you out," Nolan said. "We just didn't want to bother you with day-to-day things."

"While this family reunion is sweet, I've got to pick up Emma in twenty minutes, so can we get this argument over with?" Harris said.

Jax let out a breath. "I didn't come to argue. I came to hear what you guys thought about the decision to sell, because I think it's a mistake."

"So do we," Brynn said, waving a hand between herself and Harris. Then she nailed Nolan with a look. "And I'm pretty sure you do too."

"I do, but Lucas is right in that Mom and Dad deserve to live their life the way they want. We've all left the nest to move on to our next chapters. Maybe it's their time."

"I'm not questioning that. I'm just wondering why we all can't pitch in. It's not like we all didn't grow up working here. Between the five of us we know the ins and outs of this place," Jax said.

Over the years each of them held numerous jobs at the lodge, ranging from teaching lessons to doing maintenance on the ski lifts, chopping wood for the firepits to tending bar. When they were kids, it was considered chores, but as they got older, they'd held down actual jobs. It was a rite of passage.

Lucas's expression stayed even. "And the house in Santa Barbara?"

Here came the part of his ten-minute-ride-to-the-lodge plan that made his stomach churn with uncertainty. "Maybe I buy their Sierra Vista home off them?"

Once again, silence blanketed the room.

"Does that mean you're staying?" Brynn asked quietly.

Jax ran a hand down his face, the stubble a not-so-subtle reminder of how his mind-blowing night had ended. "I need a place when I visit, and Peggy and Kent will too."

"You can't just throw money at problems and expect them to magically fix themselves," Lucas said, and Jax knew he wasn't just talking about the house. He was talking about how Jax gave their mom money a couple of times when Cindy had popped back into his life.

"Why not?" Jax argued. "Peggy and Kent want to retire. They need money to do that. Correct?"

"They need support." Lucas's body language was as frigid as his tone. "And if you'd been around, you'd see why they made that decision."

"I could see in Peggy's eyes that she felt trapped between two options."

"Jax is right. Can you imagine how she's going to feel when she sees what a chain hotel will do to the lodge? It will break her heart," Brynn said. "But we can't ask you to buy their house."

"You didn't ask. I'm offering." Jax wasn't rich by any means, but he'd done well for himself on the circuit. Plus, his finance guy has been on him to get some write-offs.

"I can pitch in," Harris said. "I bet we can all throw some money into the pot."

"Even if we could get them the house in Santa Barbara, do you guys have any idea how much work goes into running this place?" Lucas said. "I do. I'm here every day, all day, making sure this place runs. Making sure things don't fall through the cracks. We have the Sierra Vista Cup coming up in four weeks. Do any of you know how many hours go into planning this one event? And it's just the first of the season."

"If you need help, then just ask," Harris said. "It's called words, bro, use them."

"Here's a word." Lucas flipped him the bird.

"Seriously, where can we fill in the gaps?" Nolan asked.

"You guys pitching in a few hours a week won't cut it. There's vendors, competitors, spectators, security, staff, sponsors, maintenance inspections. Because of a competing event in Colorado, enrollment for our event is at its lowest. David in business development quit, some sponsors have pulled out—"

"Which is why we can hire people and train them," Jax said.

"I do have people. An army of people. Guess who oversees them all? Me," Lucas told them. "I mean, the Sierra Vista Cup alone is a full-time job. Every year, I have to hire enough temp employees to cover the event, but they need to be babysat."

"Outsource some of the responsibility to the managers," Jax said.

"I do, but they report back to me. If there's a problem, I have to make sure it's fixed. If someone calls in sick, I have to step in. If there aren't enough hours to get the job done, I stay here until it is."

"Micromanage much?" Brynn asked.

"I don't micromanage, I lead by example and sometimes that means working alongside the employees."

"So you're micromanaging," Brynn repeated.

This was going nowhere fast. His brother loved to talk, but was a shit listener. He was seven minutes, a mere four-hundred-twenty seconds, older and the guy thought it entitled him to be right every time. And that drove Jax crazy.

"You need help," Jax pointed out. "Let us help."

"You don't need to be here for this," Lucas said to Jax.

"But *they* do?" Jax said, regarding everyone else at the table. Lucas's silence said everything Jax needed to know about his brother's stance on how little Jax's input meant. "Until Peggy and Kent say differently, I have a seat at this table. You want me to leave, you're going to have to remove me yourself."

They might be identical twins, but Jax had more bulk. His size came from years of honing his craft, making his body a machine. But he wouldn't count his brother out. In a fight, they were well matched. Something they'd learned during their one and only fight last year.

"I can handle all aspects of security that day," Nolan said like he was yard duty, and the twins were errant children. If he'd had a whistle, he would have used it. "I can even get a few off-duty agents to help with crowd management."

"And I can manage Ski Patrol," Brynn offered. Being a chopper pilot for the National Guard, she'd had enough medical training to perform open heart surgery from ten-thousand feet up and knew how to put guys twice her size in their place.

"I can act as general contractor on the various structures you'll need," Harris offered.

"What about Emma?" Lucas asked.

"I'll get Mom and Dad to babysit over the next few weekends. No biggie."

But the whole table knew it was a big deal. Balancing being a business owner and a single dad wasn't easy, so Harris's weekends were his most treasured time with his daughter. He didn't date, rarely went out, and spent his free time volunteering for various parent-y things—like hosting scrapbooking night, planning fundraisers for Emma's preschool, going to Mommy and Me dance class.

Lucas looked bowled over by the offers and Jax started to see what his brother was talking about. In the past, the whole family chipped in on these bigger events. When had that changed? How long had Lucas been shouldering the burden alone? And how had Jax not noticed the strain?

Trying to juggle separate homebases, between Vail and New Zealand—and his fallout with Lucas—he'd been gone most of the last few years. Had he been that disconnected from his twin?

He wondered just how much Lucas had on his plate. Then he wondered how he could help. The event was four weeks off and the Xtreme games were in two. Not only would he be in Wyoming for the event, he liked to get into town a few days beforehand so he could get in the right mindset, clear out the clutter and gain some of that laser focus he was known for. He wasn't getting any younger and his time in the pros was limited. His knees had two, maybe three, more seasons.

He was already missing a competition because of Peggy's birthday; he couldn't afford to miss another. So while his offer to help had been genuine, the reality of the situation was more complicated.

And what a hell of a time for their through-the-ether way of communicating to kick back in.

That's what I thought, Lucas's smug expression said. His brother looked at the rest of the table, purposefully not including Jax when he said, "I'll take you up on your offers. But I need to tell you that it's not just Mom and Dad who want to move on to the next chapter. I want out too."

It was like the oxygen was sucked out of the room. And for the first time since coming home Jax saw the exhaustion on his brother's face.

"But you love working here," Brynn said quietly.

"I did. When we were all here together," Lucas said. "Once Mom and Dad leave, it will be just me. That's a lot to take on."

"Then we hire someone to replace you," Jax said, and immediately regretted it. Lucas's smile was a ghost and he sat back as if Jax had just punched him in the throat. And whatever his twin felt was nothing compared to the twisting in Jax's stomach.

Growing up, they'd been replaced a lot. By age seven, they'd both learned that they were on their own. It was them against the world. Now it was as if they were continents apart. And Jax hated that. He just didn't know how to fix it.

"That was a shit thing to say," Jax said.

Lucas ignored his attempt at an apology. "That's up to you guys." He stood. "Take this as my notice. I'll finish the rest of the season and then I'm out."

Chapter Nine

Take Life by the Balls
Do something that scares you.

This was a disaster.

Realizing that she wasn't cut out for balancing two different boards that always seemed to go in opposite directions, Milly had decided a single surface was safer. Which was how she found herself with a snowboard attached to her left foot, her right foot quaking in her boot.

She was dressed in another one of Zoe's fashion-forward pink snowsuits with a fluffy white scarf and matching earmuffs. It wasn't cold enough for earmuffs, in fact the sun was shining bright enough to make the snowcapped peaks look like they were covered in diamonds, but when she'd looked up Ski-Bunny Barbie online, the ensemble included white earmuffs. So she'd stopped by the lodge's boutique and bought the fluffiest white earmuffs she could find.

What she didn't find was Jax, who hadn't returned a single one of her texts since the weekend. She'd apologized so many times she had carpal tunnel, leading her to believe she was the villain of this short-lived romance. She only compounded the problem by lying to her parents—and she still hadn't come clean.

She'd stayed in Sierra Vista to Marie Kondo the house and wound up making a mess of everything. It was time to make a change. Take responsibility for her life. Which was how she found herself standing in line for the ski lift, ready to take life by the balls.

Only she was pretty sure this adventure would cost her her life. The closer she got to the front of the line, the more convinced she became that she was going to die. If not from the contraption itself, then certainly from a coronary.

"Miss," someone said.

Milly looked up to realize that no one was in front of her any longer. It was just her. She'd been so distracted thinking about how to resolve this problem with Jax that she didn't even notice how fast the line was moving. Now she was looking up at a hundred-and-eighty-degree view of the Sierra Nevada mountains looming in front of her in all their snow-blanketed imposing beauty, and the awaiting bench, shifting in the breeze. All she had to do was climb on.

Held together by nothing more than a chain, a pole, and a prayer, the red metal ski lift was big enough for three. But unlike the people who had been in front of her, Milly was a party of one. No ski buddy to tell her it was okay. No one to hold her hand. No one to plummet to her death with.

Milly found happiness in safe, manageable doses, whereas Zoe found happiness in over-the-top adventures—like scaling North Face or setting up a tent on the side of a cliff to capture a photo of an American bald eagle—that defied the odds,. But in the end, she lost. Milly's entire family had. But today would be an all-around win—Milly would make certain.

"You got this," she whispered to herself. She bent to take a step forward and instead found herself stepping off to the side, dragging her snowboard with her, before smacking right into a hard wall.

"Whoa." Steady hands gripped her hips right before she would have tumbled ass over teakettle into the snow. Correction, they didn't grip, they possessed, with a familiarity of someone who had seen said ass and teakettle sans the snowsuit.

She looked up into the greenest eyes ever, but instead of warm they were—well, she wasn't sure, but she missed the way he'd looked at her the other morning. Even so she was rendered momentarily speechless by the magnitude of swagger and testosterone. He was, hands down, the sexiest man she'd ever kissed. And he was all man. Six feet plus of hard muscle and intoxicating confidence, with this graceful athleticism that turned her tongue to dust.

"Jax," she breathed.

"Was there a question mark on the end of that?"

She grimaced. "That's fair. But for the record, you didn't tell me your name."

"You never asked."

"Because I thought you were Lucas! You were in slacks and loafers and had this whole Boardroom Babe thing going on."

"Dress shoes. Only a stuffed suit would wear loafers and, angel, I am no loafer. I think I proved that the other night."

He'd proved it over and over. Milly's thighs quivered at the memory.

"Then what was with playing dress-up?"

"I had just taken Peggy to dinner for her birthday, and I know how she loves it when I wear a suit. Then Nolan called, and I said I'd meet him for a drink. Then you blindfolded me."

His answers made sense. And now that she thought about it, how had she ever confused the two? Yes, they looked identical, although Jax was bigger and broader, but their personalities were polar opposite. Lucas would have never been as spontaneous as to play a silly bar game and Lucas would have never gone home with her—because it would be highly unprofessional.

Zoe, what have you gotten me into?

"So, you didn't try to trick me?" She had no idea how much that thought had been bothering her until she voiced it.

A flicker of hurt passed through his eyes, then it was gone. "I'd like to remind you that *you* kissed *me.*"

"That was a dare. What came after, was you."

"You were there too." There was a hint of defensiveness to his four crisp words. She couldn't even imagine what it must have felt like after the night they'd shared for her to have called him by the wrong name. "Do you really think I'd take a dare that far?"

She didn't even have to think about it—knew in her gut that he wouldn't. He might be a flirt, but he wasn't cruel. "No. No, you wouldn't." Not in a million years, she realized. "I just haven't seen you around town since I've been back, so I assumed... It's really true what they say about assuming. I was a total ass, Jax. I'm sorry."

"At least you got the name right this time."

She grimaced. "I may have thought you were him, but you were you, and you looked nice. Handsome."

"You called me *dashing*," he said, and the tiniest bit of a smile cracked through.

"Did you know you have pink glitter in your hair?"

He ran a hand through his dark locks and gave them a shake. A clump of glitter floated to the ground.

"I was playing prince and princess with my niece. Guess who got to be the princess?"

She laughed. "Pink is your color."

"I was going to say the same."

Milly knew she looked ridiculous in her loud, pink, could-be-seen-from-outer-space getup but that's what happened when one's sister was a prankster. "You should see the rainbow one my sister wore for Pride. It has hearts over the"—she looked down at her breasts—"you knows."

"Oh, I know," he said in a tone that people used when they'd seen each other naked. Suddenly, all the playfulness drained out of his face and that easy nature vanished as quickly as it had come on. "So you took me home thinking I was him?"

"I took you home because you were sweet and funny and made me feel seen."

"One more night and I promise you, you'll know you picked the right twin," he said, and she laughed nervously. He did not. Nope, the man was dead serious.

A vaguely sensuous light passed between them, and her nipples responded. She took a fortifying breath, so deep icicles formed in her lungs, and pulled herself together.

"When I think of that night, I think of us."

"You mean the 'us' where you thought I was Lucas."

She wanted to say no, but the whole night was a big messy blur. Lucas—Jax. Sensible—outgoing. Serious—playful. Compatible—different from any guy Milly's ever been with. Maybe that's why their night had been so surprising and exhilarating. In fact, Milly couldn't remember the last time she'd has as much fun with a man.

But fun didn't translate into the kind of relationship she wanted for herself. *Record scratch*—back that up. Since when was she thinking about relationships?

She'd already lost a chunk of her heart when Zoe passed, another over her broken engagement, not to mention the marks her dad's heart attack left behind. She wasn't about to give even a molecule of herself to an emotionally unavailable man—even if he did kiss like a Mr. Darcy.

Side-stepping the topic all together, she said, "I've apologized for the mistake, and I am sorry. I'm also sorry for how things went down the morning after. I never meant to pull you into a lie."

His brow pulled into itself in confusion. "Then why did you?"

"I told my parents I was dating someone so they wouldn't worry about me. But I'm not. In fact, the other night was the closest thing that I've had to a date in nearly a year." She grimaced. "Anyway, I was trying to figure out how to handle the morning after when they walked in. My dad had a heart attack last week and had to be air lifted out, so he was supposed to be home healing, not at the cabin. If I'd known they were coming, I never would have put you in that position. But I panicked."

"Ah."

"If they found out that I slept with a guy whose name I got wrong…" She pressed her palm to her forehead to chase off the impending headache. "This is why I don't lie. It starts out small and then grows from me moving on with my life to having a fake boyfriend, who morphs into a real-life fake boyfriend."

If he had an opinion, he remained silent on the topic.

"I don't want to worry my dad with anything more right now. He's still coming to terms with my sister being gone." She sighed. "I just couldn't stomach them looking at me the same way they used to look at my sister when she made an impulsive decision. Or lied."

"You don't like being compared to your sister." It wasn't a question; it was a statement and something about the way he said it told her he'd been compared to his brother and come up short. Which made her feel even worse.

"I didn't handle my sister's diagnosis all that well and they noticed. In the middle of all of that, my fiancé called things off, I quit my job, and then I decided to relocate to Sierra Vista for the time being. Now my ex is somebody else's fiancé and…" She covered her face. "My life is a complete mess, but I don't want them to know. I'm the daughter who always held it together. And right now I need them to think I've got it all under control so they won't add more worry to their pile, but instead I'm losing my shit. I mean, I made up a boyfriend and then brought you into my lie."

"What now?"

"Now, I fix this. That's the right thing to do. My dad's got a doctor's appointment on Friday and then they'll be back in San Francisco. Once I hear that everything is fine and he gets clearance from his doctor, I'll clear this up."

"What are you going to tell them?"

Good point. Coming clean would worry them more than if she'd just told the truth. Keeping her lie made her itch. "What if I tell them that we broke up?"

"Now you're breaking up with me?"

"It is the easiest way to explain things that won't upset my parents further. And, well . . . " She tried to think of another reasonable excuse for tacking on another lie to the first. She couldn't think of a one. She shrugged. "That's all I've got."

"Are you asking me to keep your charade until they leave town?"

She blew out a breath; here came the hard part. "If you wouldn't mind. I mean I'm not asking you to lie, just not to say anything to anyone. And if you see my parents before I do, maybe hide." *Hide?* God, she sounded like a teenage girl asking her boyfriend to hop out the window. Then again, isn't that what she'd done the other morning? "It will only be a couple of days, but if you're not comfortable with it I completely understand."

He took a long beat, and she could tell he was carefully weighing the options. "You know, if my brothers find out about this, they'll never let me live it down."

She frowned. "Because I'm me?"

Guys like Jax never looked at women like Milly. Not that he was *her* usual type. She liked them polished and primped, and Jax was rugged and rough around the edges. But, *lordy*, those edges were sexy.

For the first time since she'd called him by the wrong name, he softened. "No, angel, because I'm me and I got caught sneaking out of a girl's bedroom by her parents."

"I promise no one will find out. And I will fix this."

He blew out a breath. "Your secret is safe with me."

"Thank you," she whispered. "And I'm really sorry about everything."

His brow creased questionably. "Everything?"

"Not everything, but how it ended."

"Me too."

Those two words were spoken with such finality—as if her apology was accepted and she was forgiven but he'd never forget—and it made her stomach pinch. "Does that mean you don't want to be my friend?"

His smile was back. "Do you want me to be your friend?"

"Very much."

She didn't know what his grunt meant, but his eyes tracked down her body before stopping at her feet. "Is something wrong with your binding?"

"There's something wrong with my brain. It won't let me get on the lift."

"Here, I'll help you." He slung his arm around her waist, practically carrying her back to the front of the line, and the next thing she knew her feet were swinging in the breeze. She clutched the seat of the chair, terror snapping along her spine like a rubber band.

"Oh my god. This is even worse than I remember," she said, slamming her eyes shut.

"Are you afraid of heights?"

"No. Of course not. I'm a grown woman. That would be silly."

He chuckled. "Then why are you climbing me like a tree?"

When had that happened? She forced herself to scooch back to her side. "I'm feeling much better now."

He looked at her hand still squeezing his bicep. "You really are a terrible liar. Now, you want to tell me why you're afraid of heights?"

"Do you promise you won't judge me?"

"I'd never judge you," he said quietly, genuinely, and without a trace of humor.

"Believe it or not, I used to ski with my family. But one time, when I was five, my dad and I were partnered up. We got to the lift and the tip of his ski caught in the snow and he pitched forward, hard. My mom and Zoe stepped aside to help him. I was so scared that my dad was hurt it took me a moment to realize I was on the lift by myself. I don't know why but, midway up, the lift just stopped."

"Someone must have been moving too much. If there's too much movement the safety switch is activated, and the lift will stop."

"We stayed stopped for what felt like an eternity. I remember being too terrified to even cry. I sat there stone-still, strangling the pole." The panic she had felt when she looked down at the treetops beneath her and realized just how far up she was, was still fresh in her mind. "By the time I made it to the top I was too worked up to even budge a muscle, so they had to stop the lift and help me off. The operator was kind and held my hand while I waited from someone to come and get me. By the time my mom arrived I was hysterical. I couldn't even ski down, so I scooted on my butt the whole way back to the lodge. Thankfully we were on a green run, but it still felt like I was standing at the top of the Sierras."

"I'm sorry you went through that," he said, and she felt his warm body press up against hers. His arm slid around her, carefully tugging her closer into his strength. His breathing was slow and steady and, suddenly, her heart started to match his pace. "Why did you decide to do this alone then?"

"I'm trying to face something that I'm afraid of. And that includes dressing up like Ski-Bunny Barbie and hitting the slopes. Or at least trying to. Today is Ski-Bunny Barbie 2.0."

"Ski-Bunny Barbie, huh?"

She met his gaze, which was twinkling with amusement. "It was all Zoe's idea. She was the one who was supposed to be up here living her best life, but her time ran out, so now I'm going to do it for her."

"Take life by the balls?" he guessed.

"Yeah. According to my sister, taking life by the balls includes dressing up like—" She accidently looked down and gulped.

"I got you." He gave her a reassuring squeeze.

She buried her face into his neck and breathed him in. She'd always thought Lucas was the steady rock, but it turned out Jax had this bold confidence about him that made her feel safe. Even when she was twenty feet up without a net. But everything about this was complicated.

She'd had a crush on Lucas, slept with Jax, and now her parents thought they were dating.

"That's the sweet spot, right there," Jax said.

Having helped her off the ski lift, he now stood directly behind Milly, his hands cupping her hips, his nose itching to nuzzle the sweet curve of her neck—which, because her hair was tucked up under that hat, was completely exposed. Just begging to be nipped.

Unable to help himself, he moved in until his mouth was nearly pressed against her skin—close, but not touching. "Now, relax," he whispered, his breath causing bumps to appear on her flesh.

Sweet spot indeed.

"It's hard to relax when I'm staring down inevitable death," she said with a shiver—that wasn't a result of the cold temperatures. She was thinking about the other night. Had been since the second they'd locked gazes.

That made two of them. Crazy as it made him, even when he was mad at her he wanted to be around her. It was the only reason that accounted for this impromptu little game of teacher and student.

"Don't look down just yet." He wrapped his arms around her waist. "Just close your eyes and listen to the sound of my voice while you get used to the feel of the board beneath your feet."

She looked at him over her shoulder, her beautiful brown eyes so wide with mistrust it nearly leveled him. "Is this like one of those 'trust me' and then you get tossed into the pool games? Only the pool in this case is a forty-five-degree slope?"

"More like six degrees. And I would never do that to you, angle."

He wasn't sure what kind of assholes she'd been hanging around, but she clearly didn't trust easily. Not that he was any better with trust. Besides Lucas and the Carmichaels, Jax didn't let people get close enough to hurt him. That didn't mean that he couldn't be there for her when she needed someone to have her back.

His finger gently traced the line of her cheekbone and jaw. "You and I are going to make it down this mountain together. Got me?"

"Like holding hands?" she asked, and back was that shyness in her voice that stoked him.

When he'd seen her standing in line at the ski lift, his first thought was to ignore her. Just walk right on past. Jax didn't do drama, which was why he had a hard-and-fast one-night-only policy—one that didn't include showering or breakfast. And it sure as shit didn't include the parents. Or made-up conversations where they talked out their feelings. Wasn't that the point of no strings?

Feelings weren't a part of the equation. For some reason, this crazy cutie had him feeling all kinds of complicated emotions. Frustration being at the top of that mountain.

Childhood crush aside, Grown-up Milly wasn't his type and he sure as shit wasn't hers. They had nothing in common and their timing couldn't have been more off. But, man, how he couldn't stop thinking about that night. Stop thinking about what would have happened if her parents hadn't crashed the party.

Jax would have had the entire weekend to get her out of his system. As it stood now, he'd only gotten a taste and he wanted more. Plus, there was the whole mistaken identity thing that still burned. He wasn't just attracted to her; a part of him wanted to prove that he wasn't the second-choice brother. And not just to her, but to himself.

Which was the only logical reason he could come up with for why, instead of walking the other way like he should have, he somehow managed to walk straight into her arms—where they hugged it out. Now, he was practically spooning her while fantasizing about what kind of thong she had on under that snowsuit.

In high school, Jax used to give lessons after class to make some extra cash, so this wasn't uncharted territory. But never once, in the thousands of lessons he'd taught, had he started with his hands all over the student.

"If holding hands will make you feel better," he said, ignoring how difficult *that* was going to be. He didn't have a board or the right boots or even a ski jacket. He was in jeans and a sweatshirt, both of which were covered with glitter. After his playdate with

Emma, he'd been headed back to his room, not out for a ski date. But Jax had made a career out of changing direction on a dime. Only this particular dime had his mind going every which way.

He placed her hands on her hips, trapping them beneath his own.

"I'm going to move you forward, so you get used to the feel of the snow beneath your board," he said, giving a little squeeze of reassurance when her whole body went rigid.

"I swear I'm not a 'fraidy cat," she said on a self-conscious laugh. Her fingers were digging into her hips, her gaze lasered in on her boots. "This is just more of a Zoe thing. I didn't have to worry about any ski lifts in Manhattan."

Her statement gave him pause. "You gave up your job and life in New York to take care of your sister?"

"She's my sister," she said, as if everyone would make the same sacrifices as she.

"And she was lucky to have you. You put her before your own needs and dreams, which is damn inspiring. But then you invented a boyfriend to make your parents happy. You're up on a mountain in an outfit you clearly wouldn't pick, even if it was the only clean thing in your closet, just to make Zoe happy. Now, you're about to spend your day doing something to make someone else happy. What would make you happy? What would be your thing to do on a snowy day?"

She twisted her upper body toward him. "I think that's the problem," she said honestly. "I don't know what makes me happy anymore. The things I used to want seem silly now and the things that used to be important seem trivial. Before Zoe's cancer I had this very clear map of where my life was going. I had a job I liked, a promotion right around the corner, a fiancé I loved, an apartment that was the size of a cereal box, but it was mine. I was living my big-city dream."

"You make it sound like you can't go back."

She shrugged. "I can. I mean, I want to. But what if it doesn't feel the same? What if when I get there I still feel as lost as I do now?"

"I can't even imagine the pain of losing a sibling, but I know how life-altering loss can be. When Lucas and I were kids, my dad committed suicide. My mom came home from work to find him in his recliner, the Niners playing on the television, and a gun on the floor."

"Oh my god." She touched his jaw. "That must have been awful for her. I can't even imagine the shock and heartache."

"I don't remember a lot from before the suicide, but I do remember my mom had this bright, contagious laugh that would fill the house. Her laugh died with my dad. It was as if all the light had been extinguished." Looking at photos of his mom when they'd been kids was like looking at a stranger.

"That's what I'm afraid will happen to my parents. Even though we had time to prepare, Zoe's death shattered them. My mom went into a deep depression, my dad had a heart attack. For Gemma, who'd lost a baby, it reopened old wounds. And Kat lost her best friend."

Milly was so busy holding everyone else together it was as if she hadn't given herself permission to mourn. "You're allowed to reclaim your life and chase those dreams again."

She blinked several times as if what he'd said didn't compute. "Then who will pick up all the other pieces?" she asked as if she honestly didn't know. How isolating it must be to assume responsibility for everything and everyone in her life.

Was this how Lucas felt? Like it was up to him to shoulder all the burden for the entire family? Maybe, just like Milly, Lucas had found himself trapped between what he wanted and the needs of others.

"How about for today, you let me carry the pieces," he offered.

"I have a lot of pieces. We're talking a fleet of suitcases."

He held his arms out to his sides. "I've got big arms."

A smile broke through that was so genuine it had something shifting in his chest. "So, you're saying that if I fall, you'd catch me?"

Before he could answer she pulled him to a secluded area off the ski path and knocked him back in the snow and fell on top of him. He broke their fall, rolling her to the side. She flipped on her back and started moving her arms and legs.

"What are you doing?" he asked.

"You asked me what I would do on a snowy day. I'd make snow angels." She made a snowball and pegged him in the shoulder. "Come on. Get those big arms moving!"

Jax did as he was told and by the time they'd made a circle of angels, Jax's clothes were soaked straight through, his ass was frozen, and they were both laughing. Damn, it felt good. All of the frustration and stress from the past few days vanished.

"Way better than breaking the speed of light on a one-legged sleigh," she said.

Jax rolled his head to the side and was met with bright, sparkling eyes and a set of dimples that turned him on. He'd never noticed a woman's dimples, unless they were on her lower back, but there was something about this woman and those dimples that did him in.

"Oh, we're going to get you and that one-legged sleigh down the hill. With me holding you the whole way."

She licked her lips, while staring at his. "That might be a little difficult."

He leaned up on his elbow so that his face was within kissing distance of hers. But he didn't go in for the kill. That would turn this friendly lesson into something a hell of a lot closer to a date. And Jax didn't have the time nor the inclination to date.

He didn't do relationships. At all. Hard stop. He wasn't enough for his dad to stay or his mom to get clean, and he'd never felt like enough to be a real Carmichael. That was his theory anyway, and he wasn't willing to put it to the test—in case he was right.

Yet, there he was, playing with fire. "I'm sure we can figure it out."

"Then how about we up the difficulty factor. I mean, if we're going to face death, we might as well have some fun."

Before he could ask what fun was, her mouth was fused to his. No gentle exploration or a simple reacquaintance. Oh no. Milly's mittened fingers were in his hair, her tongue in his mouth, and her knees dug in the snow on either side, straddling him.

And he was holding her. An ass cheek in each palm, plastering her against his body. They were creating more heat than global warming—like melt-the-polar-ice-caps temperatures.

In one fluid movement, he had her board unclipped and flipped them over, pinning her hands above her head. Even through her bulky snow pants he was certain she could feel his hard-on because when he pressed into her, she moaned.

He kissed his way down her neck which had been taunting him for the past hour and she wrapped her legs around his waist, tight enough to knock the wind right out of him. God, she was sexy.

He licked and kissed as far down as he could before being blocked by her scarf, then nibbled his way back up to her mouth, which he took without apology.

Jax had had his share of kisses. In fact, he considered himself a kiss connoisseur of sorts. He'd started young, Nicole Waverly in the third grade, and quickly rose the ranks to dating college girls when in high school and cougars when he was in college.

But kissing Milly was on a whole other level. The way her tongue moved with his was more erotic than the act of sex. And that was saying a lot because in their one night they'd covered every letter in the word erotic—some of them twice.

She moaned into his mouth and he opened his eyes. And that's when he realized she was watching them kiss. Her gaze was hazy, her glasses a little fogged up from the heavy breathing, and her thighs were squeezing his middle.

Damn, what a turn on.

Holding her gaze, he nipped and nibbled, putting his entire body into the kiss. Her hands ran the length of his torso, not stopping to pass go, she cupped him through his jeans.

· He gasped.

Resting on one elbow to free up a hand, he fisted his fingers in her hair and gave a gentle but stern tug, pulling her head to the side. This time she gasped.

He looked into her eyes to check in, when she smiled a mischievous smile before tilting her head to the side so he could get a taste of the spot where the neck meets the shoulder. That sensual, elegant slope that was begging for his mark.

He ran his tongue over her pulse, which was pounding with need. And he wanted to fill that need so he—

"Get a room!" someone hollered as they skied by.

Behind her cute glasses, Milly's eyes startled wide, her hands flew to her mouth and, just when he thought she was going to shove him off, she burst into laughter. "Why does this keep happening?"

He kissed her nose. "It's called animal magnetism."

"Then you need to stop"—she poked his chest—"being"—*poke*—"so"—*poke*—"sexy."

The last word was punctuated with a long, lazy kiss that seemed to go on and on. It wasn't hungry or hurried, it was sweet and tender. The kind of sweet and tender that could get a guy in trouble.

Shit.

"Jax?" she whispered, making him realize he'd stopped. "Are you okay?"

No, he wasn't. This was foreign territory and he needed to take a step back—for both their sakes.

He cupped her face. "I don't want to complicate this or mislead you. I'm leaving in a few days."

The smile she gave him was open and understanding and complicating as hell. "It's just animal magnetism, remember? We're friends who find each other attractive. It happens. But like you said, you're leaving, and my life is up in the air. So friends it is."

Chapter Ten

Take Life by the Balls
Don't tiptoe into the cold water.
Go for the Polar Plunge.

Jax walked into Bigfoot's Brews after one hell of a day. His calves were burning, his nose was still frozen from the icy winds, and he had snow stuck to every eyebrow and eyelash.

He'd worked out for about two hours, ran the treadmill for another, then hit the slopes to take advantage of the fresh powder that had arrived overnight. It had been the first time since last year's Sierra Vista Cup that he'd boarded down Vista Peak, the hardest run in the Sierra Nevadas, and he had to admit it felt different. For competitions, he played to win. Today he was out there playing for the fun of it. He'd finally called it a day when he couldn't feel his legs any longer.

His head was still buzzing from the high.

Or maybe that was the recurring dream he'd been having about a particular Ski-Bunny Barbie, with her warm, curvy body and lush lips.

It was a weeknight, so instead of wall-to-wall tourists, the bar was humming with locals and familiar faces. Including the four hanging out by the pool tables in the back room. Nolan had texted him earlier that day about joining him for some billiards and beer, but he'd failed to mention Lucas would be there.

Maybe it was a good thing. When Jax hadn't been thinking about his situation with Milly, he'd been thinking about how he could help with the Sierra Vista Cup. How he could be a part of things again. Seeing his family, no matter how strained things were, filled this void he hadn't even known existed.

His brother was at the pool table, stick in hand, ready to make a shot, when he paused. As if sensing his arrival, Lucas turned and looked right at Jax. He hadn't seen Lucas since the board meeting and he wasn't sure what his brother's reception would be.

It was a quick jerk of the head followed by Lucas going back to his game. It wasn't the warmest brotherly welcome, but there weren't any fists thrown. Progress.

Nolan caught Jax's eye and, with a big-ass smile, waved him over. Jax started toward the table. By the time he got there Harris and Brynn were arguing over who would be the next Bachelor.

"Glad you made it." Nolan clapped him on the back. "Lucas here is kicking everyone's ass and you're the only one who can put him in his place."

"You want to rack 'em up?" Lucas said to Jax with an impersonal nod.

No pleasantries or greeting, just that same indifferent attitude that he'd had the other morning at the board meeting. Jax would prefer irritation or even anger. This apathetic bullshit was getting old. He couldn't think of a better way to blow off some steam than to get a rise out of Lucas by kicking his ass in a game of pool.

"Game on, bro." Jax racked the balls, then picked up a stick. Lucas chalked his, gesturing for Jax to go first.

"I racked. You go first. That's the rules," Jax said.

"Since when do you follow rules?"

Jax might like to let loose some of the time, but he was no longer that wild kid. And Lucas knew it. "My livelihood depends on following the rules. In fact, I'm a gold medal rule follower."

"You push the rules to the limit, blur them when necessary. That's your livelihood."

"I don't know," Nolan said. "He was following the rules pretty well the other night."

Jax shot Nolan a look that would make most men wet their pants. Nolan just smiled.

"Are you talking about how he was kissing his girlfriend blindfolded?" Brynn said.

He froze at the comment. "Where did you hear that?"

"That you were kissing Milly? There's a video of the whole thing on Instagram," Brynn said.

"It's pretty incriminating," Harris added.

"I heard there was a second sighting. On the bunny slope," Nolan said.

"No, I mean, how did you hear about her being my girlfriend?"

"Mom. She said you have to bring Milly to her birthday party." At Brynn's comment, Lucas jerked back and missed his shot.

"Jesus," Jax said, not sure how Peggy found out, but thought it probably had something do with Gennie. And if Gennie was talking, that meant Milly hadn't come clean. He was already on the lookout for the Smartts, he didn't need to add anyone else to the People to Avoid list. "Can't everyone just mind their own business?"

"That's called being a part of a family," Brynn said, wrapping her arms around his waist. She was built like Peggy, small and slight. Her fingers didn't even touch behind Jax's back. "Get used to it."

"Back up. You're sleeping with Milly Smartt?" Lucas asked, his eyes full of fury, disbelief in his tone. Disbelief that a woman like Milly would go for a man like Jax.

Jax's hackles rose. "It's none of your business. And why wouldn't a woman like her be into a guy like me?"

"You're not her type."

Jax wasn't about to give his brother the satisfaction that he was right. He'd take the mistaken identity fiasco to the grave. And he hoped to hell Milly did as well. "Clearly, you're wrong. Again."

"I don't give two shits about your sex life, unless you're sleeping with an employee. Christ, she's our logistics coordinator and I can't afford to lose her when she realizes you aren't the long-term bet."

Jax didn't have the words to tell his brother where to shove it because he was left speechless by this news.

Milly worked for Lucas? Jax gripped the back of his neck. How had he not known this? And how did he feel about Milly being in close quarters with the man she thought she'd slept with? Strangely, the idea irritated his chest.

Lucas's expression was one of suspicion. "You didn't even know she was working with us on the Sierra Vista Cup, did you?"

No. No, he did not. Jax loved to weave a good story, loved being part of the con, but he'd never conned his brother. And even though he was pissed beyond hell about his brother's duplicitous act with their mom, he was caught between a con and crazy cutie. The best course of action would be to tell Lucas to go screw himself, then change the subject, but instead he surprised himself by saying, "I was actually looking forward to helping her with the event."

Lucas laughed. "You're always *in* the competition. You've never planned one. It's like being a bridesmaid versus the bride. One puts on a dress and walks down the aisle. The other plans for months and months. You're in the middle of a season and when you're not on the slopes, you're in the gym."

"I can handle it," Jax said.

"Isn't the Xtreme Games this weekend?"

"I can fly out and fly back."

"You don't do flyout, flybacks. You get there days ahead of time and spend hours on the mountain, then schmooze with brands and sponsors."

Frustration began to twist its way through Jax's body until he felt like snapping. He wrung the neck of the pool stick. "Well, this time I am. I leave Friday and I'll be back Monday morning, so I'll be here for the week."

"And what about the next week?"

A twinge of anger and frustration worked its way along his spine. Why was his brother digging in so hard? Jax might not have planned an event before, but he wasn't incompetent. In fact, he was quick on his feet, knew when to pivot, and never shied away from a difficult situation. He took them head-on. It was how he'd managed to dominate the slopes even though he was one of the more senior athletes on the circuit.

Jax liked to think of himself as the Tom Brady of the snowboarding world. He'd decide when he was past his prime. In his opinion, his age gave him a leg up on the competition. And being on the flip side of these kind of events would give him a fresh perspective that could be invaluable.

"Do you need help or not?"

"Yes, I need help. But it would take me longer to catch you up to speed than just doing it myself."

"Which is why I'll be working with our logistics coordinator closely."

What was he saying? He and Milly had just agreed to stick to being friends and here he was putting himself in the line of fire, where one misstep with Milly could end in disaster.

"You can't commit to a year lease," Lucas said. "Let alone the stick-to-it-ness it would take to pull off an event this size."

Jax's jaw flexed. "Is that a challenge?"

"Mom and Dad are fighting again," Harris said.

"You guys are more dramatic than Mom's book club," Brynn said. "And for the record, Milly isn't an employee. She's a contractor. Big difference."

Jax didn't give a shit either way. He didn't like to be told what he could and couldn't do. But that didn't explain his reaction to his brother acting as if Jax wasn't good enough for Milly. It was the truth, but hearing that she was off-limits ticked him off. "Seriously, I can help with sponsors and the competitors. Who knows what they want better than one of their own? As for the rest, Milly can catch me up."

Lucas schooled his expression, which meant he was trying to come up with a reason why this wouldn't work. Jax had witnessed this particular look many times before, but never aimed at him. He knew things between them were strained, and for good reason, but would Lucas take it as far as to not let him help with what had always been a family event?

Sure, Jax didn't know the ins and outs, but how hard could it be? He had some major sponsors on speed dial, knew some up-and-comers who would love to come and show off their talent. And when he made a decision, he went after it with a singular focus.

"What can I take off your hands?" he asked.

"We've been doing this event for five years and you've never helped once. Why now?" Lucas asked.

"You seriously have to ask?" That they'd gotten to this point in the relationship scared Jax. "It's because you need help and no matter what's going on between us, we're still brothers."

Lucas seemed to mull that over, then nodded. "Drop by the office tomorrow and then we can take a look at what you come up with." He picked up his stick. "Now, are we going to play pool or what?"

Chapter Eleven

Take Life by the Balls
Be a queen.

Milly was buried eyeball deep in Zoe's closet engaged in a game of "*Does it bring you joy.*" There was the Keep Pile, the Give Pile and the Maybe Pile. The Keep Pile was overflowing while Give consisted of a headband, a collection of Justin Bieber T-shirts, and two tubes of lip gloss. The Maybe Pile was empty.

Milly might be too sentimental when it came to parting with her sister's things, but she was decisive.

Keep.

Keep.

Keep.

Um... she held up a plastic MVP award from when Zoe had been six and decided to turn in her cleats for pompoms... *I am overcome with joy. Keeping.*

How was she supposed to just give her sister's personal effects to a stranger, when every item felt like a connection to her sister?

She pulled out a cocktail dress that Zoe had worn to Gemma's engagement party. Milly held it up to her torso and admired the metallic material shimmering beneath the bright sun that flickered through the window.

Mother Nature was showing off today. With temperatures in the high forties and clear skies, the view from her sister's window was breathtaking. It was the kind of day that Zoe would be out photographing. She'd have awoken before dawn, bundled up, and hiked to one of the many peaks to capture the sunrise cresting over the mountains.

Milly turned toward the mirror and swayed side to side, watching the material swish around her thighs. It was bronze, bold, pro-cleavage, and short enough to challenge the line between sex pistol and sophisticated. In a word, it was Zoe. And Milly needed a little Zoe in her day.

"Mom? Dad?" she called out.

They'd headed back from San Francisco after her dad's cardiology appointment and weren't expected to arrive until early evening, but that never stopped them from surprise visits. The other morning wasn't an abnormal occurrence in the Smartt household. Her parents were masters at the surprise drop by. The last thing she needed was for them to show up early and witness the tornado that had struck Zoe's room.

When no one responded, she stripped down and tugged on the dress and, *wow*, it was magical. Kind of like *Sisterhood of the Traveling Pants*. Even though Zoe was taller and had a whole cup size on Milly's basic B's, the dress fit like a glove.

Grabbing a tube of red silk lip gloss from the Give Pile—what was she thinking, giving away a perfectly new lip gloss—she broke the seal, puckered up and swiped it on, giving a little kissy face in the mirror. Next came the heels—black, pointy, and mile-high.

She smoothed her hands down the lux fabric and, adopting a little Zoe into her attitude, she popped out a hip. "Looking smart, Smartt."

She was about to do a runway strut down the hallway when her phone pinged. She looked at the screen and a trill of panic tiptoed down her spine.

Gemma: Did you really have sex with Jax Macintyre?

Milly threw the phone on the bed as if it were on fire. It pinged again. And again. Knowing that if she didn't respond she'd have two more witnesses to her box problem, Milly picked up the phone and swiped the screen. It came to life.

Kat: Hello?

Gemma: You can't avoid us forever!

Kat: You have two seconds to answer and then we're coming to you. And before you think you're safe remember I know where the hide-a-key is. And if you try to leave the state I have you on my Find My Friends app.

Milly took a deep breath and responded.

Milly: How do you know I slept with him? He might have just driven me home because I had too much to drink.

Kat: Right. Because driving under the influence of hot cocoa is so dangerous.

Gemma: Spill the beans Milly. And before you try to fib your way out of this know that Ms. Tilden saw him sneaking off the next morning.

Alarm slid its way up Milly's back. If Ms. Tilden had seen them, her secret would be all around town by the time her parents returned home. And that meant even more lies to tell.

Milly glanced out the window to Ms. Tilden's house next door and rolled her eyes. Ms. Tilden was the nosiest neighbor in the neighborhood. She even set up a surveillance camera on the side of her house to make sure Milly's parents weren't renting the cabin out as an Airbnb.

Milly: Fine. We slept together.

Kat: I knew it! You owe me a drink Gemma.

Milly: You were betting on my sex life?

Kat: Well duh? You finally have a sex life to bet on. We couldn't resist.

Milly knew the feeling. Her lack of a sex life had made it hard to resist Jax. So she'd un-resisted three times, then mauled him on the slopes.

Kat: So Jax huh?

Gemma: Yeah what about Lucas? Is this some kind of Sabrina in reverse?

Milly: I thought he was Lucas!

Her screen went dead. Where were those three little dots flashing in judgment? She held her breath waiting for a response, and when one never come, she texted:

Milly: You were the ones who pointed him out and said he was Lucas!

Gemma: He was wearing slacks and a button-down. He looked very Lucas-esque.

Milly: That's what I said! And it was an accident. I told you I crashed into him.

She texted, repeating the lie she told her parents—and what had become her new mantra.

Gemma: It must have been some crash because you went home with him and you've been avoiding us for days. So it was either really good or really bad. Spill.

Life altering was more accurate. Sex with Jax was like being reborn in the form of a sex goddess. His mouth alone was a lethal weapon.

Kat: Rumor has it that you two are lining together.

Gemma: What did your parents say?

Milly: OMG we aren't living together. And where did you hear that?

Kat: Tessa heard it at school. Two of the teachers were talking about your ski date, where you were making a snow angel on top of him the other day.

Gemma: So is it true? Are you dating?

This had gotten so out of hand. Milly was going to kill her mom. Because while Ms. Tilden was nosy, Gennie was a champion gossip.

Milly was about to answer that they were, in fact, *not dating*, when a knock sounded at the door. Rolling her eyes, she tossed her phone on the bed and went to let her friends in.

"You have no idea what I'm going to do to you," she called out, starting for the door.

"That sounds promising," the response came. Her heart screamed into her throat.

Jax.

She went still. Trying to make as little noise as possible, she tiptoed to the door and looked through the peephole. *Good lord*, the man was beautiful. He was wearing a black ski jacket, a matching beanie, and enough scruff to make her legs buckle. She remembered that scruff. Still had a few burn marks on the inside of her thighs, a keepsake of just what he can do with that scruff.

He looked like a ski bum and *Sports Illustrated* spread collided.

She glanced down at herself and panicked. She looked like a pageant queen turned sex worker and he looked . . . perfect. And purposeful.

Had he come here to make sure she'd cleared the air with her parents? She hadn't. Her parents had stayed in San Francisco for another night. They were supposed to be here yesterday, but her dad had been tired from his doctor's appointment and needed to rest before heading up. Then there had been the questions her mom peppered her with about Jax.

How long have you been dating?

Not long.

How did you meet?

I told you. While skiing.

Skiing? Isn't that wonderful how he's getting you out of the house. Does he like meat loaf?

I don't know.

Honey, this is something you should know. Every woman needs to know if their man likes meat loaf.

Is that some kind of unwritten rule?

It's just common sense. If you're going to invite a man to dinner and I'm serving meat loaf, then I need to know if he likes meat loaf. You know, a lot of these athletes now eat whole-food, plant-based diets. Could you imagine, never eating meat loaf again?

Before her mom could force her to commit to an official dinner date, Milly managed to get off the call, citing her sister's unpacked boxes as an excuse.

Something to add to the Lie Pile. She hadn't touched a single box since last weekend. Which was why she was going through the closet now. If she could clean out enough room to hide a few boxes, her parents wouldn't know the difference.

Her Lie Pile was growing by the second. So what was another little white lie? Was pretending you weren't home really a lie, or had it become a standard practice in the times of texting before you call?

Standard practice, she decided. Then, so as not to make a sound, Milly skulked away. She got as far as the landing when another knock sounded. She jumped back like her designer dress was on fire and clutched her hand over her breasts that were saying, *Look at me. Look at me.*

Was she ever in trouble. There was a door and a good ten feet between them, but her body was reacting as if they were naked, setting the sheets on fire. Letting him in would be a miscalculation on her part.

"I know you're home, angel."

She crept closer to the door and looked back out the peephole. He was leaning casually against the railing, flakes of snow clinging to his long, thick lashes. If he was here to break up with her and end their fake relationship while she was playing dress-up, she'd die.

"You're thinking about this too hard," he said. "I can smell the smoke from here."

"I wasn't thinking about you all," she called out through the door. And this was what happened when she lied. She had to compound that lie with another even less convincing lie until she couldn't keep her lies straight.

His grin was dangerous. "Really? Because you seem to be checking me out."

She jumped back once again, her traitorous heels ratting her out as they clicked on the slate floor of the mud room.

"I can stand out here all day, but if I get frostbite you'll have to use your body temperature to warm me up."

She cracked the door, just enough to stick her nose out. The frigid air was at polar ice cap levels, but Jax's heated gaze melted right through it. Nerves rioted in her stomach. At least that was what she told herself it was—certainly not butterflies

"Before I open the door you have to promise not to laugh at me."

"Scout's honor." He even gave the little salute, which looked legit enough.

With a sigh, she opened the door and his lips curled at the corners, as if holding back humor. "I said no laughing."

His eyes tracked her from lips to toes. "Angel, there is nothing funny about you in that dress." After that a small smile crossed his face. "You going to invite me in?"

Her mind flashed back to the last time she'd invited him in.

Okay, so it was definitely butterfly wings.

A flicker of movement came from Ms. Tilden's window. Milly squinted to find two beady eyes spying on them. Then a phone appeared, clearly videoing the entire incident.

Milly grabbed Jax by the jacket and yanked him inside, slamming the door, then barricading it by leaning against it. She sagged with dread. First, the morning after and now he was back, looking sexy as ever. Ms. Tilden was going to have enough fodder to get her through bingo and bunco.

He was looking around her family room and she knew what he saw. Untouched boxes. "I'm making progress in her bedroom."

"There's no clock ticking." His voice was deep and eyes were filled with compassion.

"Tell that to my parents."

He stepped closer, so close she could smell his rugged male scent, and the winter breeze on his skin. "Maybe you should."

And explain to her parents that she needed another year or two to get used to the idea that Zoe was gone? No way. This timeline wasn't about Milly, it was about giving her parents permission to move on from the grief. A stage Milly was still struggling to move past.

"What are you doing here?" she asked. "Are you breaking up with me?"

"Depends," he said, and a little flutter of disappointment touched her chest. "Have you told your parents the truth?"

She grimaced. How many things had she inadvertently lied to her parents about? Implying they were an item, not correcting them when she had the chance was about as responsible as it was intelligent. "No. They stayed an extra day in San Francisco so I haven't had a chance."

He looked relieved. Talk about confusing. He shouldn't be relieved. He should be pissed. With her. She'd promised him it would be cleared up by the weekend and the weekend had come and gone. And now rumors were spreading like wildfire through town. According to Tessa, it had even reached the high school.

"Everyone knows about us," she said, and he pondered that for a moment but didn't look surprised. "You already knew."

"My sister may have mentioned something."

She swallowed hard. "Your sister?"

"And my brothers. Apparently, your mom ran into Peggy at the market and they're hoping for a summer wedding."

Milly laughed and when he remained silent, she let out a long, tired sigh. She was going to kill her mom.

"What did you say to your family?"

"I kept it vague," he said calmly, the exact opposite of what she was feeling.

Milly had dragged him into her lie, begged him to keep her secret, and he had. Even when pressed by his family, he'd remained loyal to his word.

"This has gotten so out of hand. Misleading my parents was one thing. Now my friends think we're living together, and the whole town is talking. When they find out I made it up, people are going to think I've really lost it. Or I'm really desperate."

"What if we let them talk?" he said.

"What do you mean '*Let them talk*'? Talk about what? How crazy I am?"

He stalked closer and she took a step back, bumping into the door. "Talk about how you kissed me as a part of that dare in the bar. How I kissed you back. We had a ski date. And now we are dating."

Had she heard him correctly? Maybe the heels were giving her altitude sickness and she was imagining things. "Say that again?"

"We let people go on thinking that we're a thing. It solves the problem with your parents, and I don't have to break it to *my* family that I was part of a dating conspiracy."

"Conspiracy? That sounds dramatic."

"You thought I was Lucas," he pointed out with no heat. "I don't think it gets any more soap opera-y that that. You have to admit, it's a fair proposition."

Her body heated. "A proposition got us into this mess in the first place."

His green eyes smiled, then fell to her cleavage. "I like where your mind went, but I was thinking about your predicament and thought, What the hell?"

She folded her arms, putting it up as a barrier between them. "I'm not going to sleep with you again to make a point to my parents, if that's what you're thinking."

"When you sleep with me again it will be because you want to." His voice was low and seductive, like verbal foreplay.

"That's not going to happen. Look at how it turned out last time?"

"We blew the roof off this place." He cupped her jaw and ran the pad of his thumb across her lower lip. "We were both there, angel," he whispered. "And we both know it will happen again. Just look at the other day. This kind of chemistry is impossible to ignore." The sheer conviction behind his statement made her body quiver. Traitorous body! "And when it does, you're going to be screaming *my* name."

She swallowed. "What do you get out of this?"

"Wow, that hurts," he feigned, as if it cut deep when they both knew it did not. She leveled him with a look. "Fine. I need to prove to my family that I'm not a selfish asshole."

"How does dating me accomplish that?"

"I told my brother that I could help with the Sierra Vista Cup. He clearly thinks I can't do it, and then Lucas sent over this file, and it only took two pages to realize I'm in over my head. You're the logistics expert. I'm a fast learner, I just need a coach." The flirty playboy was replaced by a seriousness that felt incredibly intimate. "If you help me pull this event off, I will help you convince your parents that you're moving on."

"You don't even live in Sierra Vista. How would this work?"

"I'll be around for the next few weeks."

That gave her pause. "What about your season? I thought you were leaving tomorrow?"

"I have a couple of competitions over the next two weekends, and I pulled out of the smaller competitions. That gives us plenty of time to make it look real."

"So when you leave, people will just think we're doing the long-distance thing?"

"If that's what you want."

What did she want? Lying felt wrong, but not as wrong as making her parents worry. Her dad needed to be healing and the doctors said that meant no stress. The amount of worry she'd cause by confessing didn't seem to outweigh the impact of them discovering on their own that she'd made the whole thing up.

"I tried long distance and it doesn't work." Dillon taught her that heartbreaking lesson. "Long distance would worry my parents. Not that it will be real," she added quickly. "I mean, this would be an arrangement for convenience, nothing more." She couldn't believe she was giving this serious consideration. "And I'm a horrible liar. How would we even convince people this is real?"

"We haven't even gone on a real date and already people are planning our wedding. I think we can keep up pretenses for a few weeks."

He was right. It had already gotten so out of hand, at this point corralling it would be like trying to wrangle the wind. "If I agree to this fake romance, then there would have to be guidelines so we both know what's up and nobody gets hurt."

"I've never been good at staying within the boundaries."

"You'd better learn." She mentally went through every romance novel she'd ever read and made a list of how someone might successfully navigate a faux-mance. "There will be no behind the scenes flirting, no verbal foreplay, and no sex. This is a faux-mance, nothing more."

"Does that mean when we're not behind the scenes, we can have sex?"

She poked him in the chest and her finger bounced back. There was absolutely no body fat there. He was sinew, muscle, and bad decisions all rolled up into one.

"And, for that matter, no kissing."

"You were all into making it believable a moment ago. And if people are to believe us, kissing stays."

"Fine. Kisses can stay. On the cheek."

"Lips."

With him a kiss would lead to sex and that might lead to feelings. Her heart was too vulnerable to engage in feelings right now. They had to make it look real without it feeling real. Zoe had wanted her to enjoy herself, not get her heart broken by an unavailable man.

"This isn't a negotiation. But you're right, cheek kisses won't cut it, so I'll agree to lips. But even a hint of tongue and the arrangement is over."

His mouth twitched as if choking down a laugh. "Is there anything you *are* open to?"

"In addition to our work meetings, which will stay professional, I'm open to hand holding and a weekly hot cocoa date."

"I like the sound of that."

"No sex."

"I *don't* like the sound of that." He made a face. "Because of you I have to live a sex-free existence."

"Tough. Do you have anything to add?"

A flash of something vulnerable flickered in those intense green eyes, so fast she wasn't certain she saw it.

He wiped a masculine hand down his face. "My mom's birthday is coming up. My whole family, not to mention a bazillion friends, will be there. If I show up stag, people will talk."

Pretending from a distance was one thing. Pretending up close and personal? She wasn't sure she could convincingly pull that off. "We don't know the first thing about each other."

He stepped into her, one hand cupping her hip. "I know that you're fiercely loyal, you have a big heart, so big that you put your loved ones' needs over your own. All things I can relate to. I like you, Milly, there's nothing fake about that." He gave her a tummy-flipping grin. It was slow and sensual. "I think you like me too. And before you deny it, remember the only way this will work is if we're honest with each other."

Did she like him? Like *like* him? The answer scared her.

"No comment. As for the party, I agree. It would be suspicious if we didn't show up together." She drew a circle around his face with her finger. "But just remember the rules."

"That's a lot of guidelines and not enough romance," he said.

"That's the point. No romance." Because romance led to feelings, and she couldn't afford to grow feelings for this guy. He was leaving, she didn't know which direction her life was taking, and that was an equation for disaster. Not to mention that while they were compatible in bed, they weren't compatible in real life.

"You aren't the catch-and-release kind of woman. If I'm not romancing you, people will begin to wonder."

Her heart swooned a little. Stupid heart. No man had ever said something so sweet to her before. She'd never been romanced or wooed. Her relationships had been based on compatibility and mutual respect. Not the kind of nuclear reactor attraction that sparked between them every time they were within the same vicinity. It was like his body was made of metal and her lips were a giant magnet, being pulled by the forces of nature.

"We'll be spending a lot of time working together on the event," she said, reminding herself that this situation could quickly become dangerous—to her mind, body, and soul.

"All work and no play doesn't make for a fun faux-mance." She snorted. "Your whole life is fun."

"Looks can be deceiving. I spend most of my life on the slopes, in the gym, or alone in a hotel room. Don't get me wrong, I love what I do, but it's still my job. And while I love my job, it might be nice to live outside of my job for a while."

Maybe she wasn't the only one who'd lost something precious in the game of life. There seemed to be two sides to Jax. The flirty, play-it-fast-and-loose side, which he let people see. But then there was this other side, a deeper side, that was vulnerable and lonely. That was the side that drew her in.

"A date a week," she agreed. "That will be held in public." Because lord knew what would happen if they holed up in a cozy cabin.

Orgasms. That's what.

"Public?" he asked, his eyes smiling. "Is this where the flirting and tongue comes in?"

"This is serious."

He raised his hands over his head to grip the frame of the doorway that separated the mudroom from the family room. His mountain of a body blocked her escape. "When it comes to tongue, I'm always serious."

She shoved at him, but he didn't budge, so she walked under his arm and escaped to the family room, where she paced. Her mind went through every pitfall and possible problem, and the results were overwhelming. But the reverse was even more problematic.

"We date until the Sierra Vista Cup," she said. "Then we break up and if it's okay with you'd, I'd like to do the breaking because if I have another man walk out on me, my parents will hover again. I can't handle any more hovering."

He seemed to consider this, then shrugged as if he didn't care what people thought about him. What a luxury that would be. "I've got one guideline to add," he said.

"That's fair."

"Remember how you said this was fake? I need you to promise that no one loses sight of that fact. I'm leaving. I always leave and I don't want to hurt you."

"I barely have time for fake let alone real." Not to mention she lacked the bandwidth to worry about yet another person. She spent so much time caring for others she couldn't remember the last time she'd cared about herself.

"I need to hear you say that you understand."

"I understand and I promise not to fall for you, Mr. Cocky."

"If that's settled, let's get to know each other better and, while we're at it, take life by the balls. Snowmobiling is a great place to start, and I happen to know an excellent snowmobiler."

She looked behind her at the stacks and stacks of boxes that she'd rather chew yellow snow than sort through. Then back to the grinning sex-on-a-stick man in front of her, and her belly quivered. Just like the way it did on that damn ski lift. But the quivering, she was pretty sure, had to do with her snowmobiling partner and not fear.

"I don't like going fast."

"You don't like heights and you don't like speed. Have you ever had any fun?"

"You sound like my family."

"And you sound like Lucas." He took her hand and laced their fingers. "Now, let's give this town something to talk about."

How hard could it be? A few appearances? Maybe a date or two? Easy-peasy. It's not like he was hard to look at. All she had to do is resist falling into bed with him.

Chapter Twelve

Take Life by the Balls
Accept a challenge that scares you.

"You're incredible," Jax said, looking at the spreadsheet Milly had compiled. It had each vendor, what they were delivering, when they were delivering, and how many units were ordered, all catalogued into one tidy file. "You have it down to the hour of each drop off."

"I've found that if everything arrives at once things get misplaced or overlooked, and it adds more stress to an already stressful day. So I staggered them over the three days leading up to the event."

"Smart." She was beyond smart. She was efficient, brilliant at her job, and had the organizational skills of a COO at a Fortune 500 level. She'd not only helped Jax understand how an event like this worked, but she'd also gone above and beyond laying out what the different departments handle. And there was more than a handful of departments to get to know and manage.

Lucas wasn't exaggerating about the magnitude of workload. Jax had only uncovered a fraction of what this competition needed. On top of the Sierra Vista Cup, his brother was also overseeing the day-to-day responsibilities of running a lodge. The gift shop, equipment rentals, Bigfoot's Brew, lodging, guest services, ski patrol, security, and the list went on. Not to mention being CEO, which meant he was the authority on long term strategies, driving profitability, and communicating with the board. That was a lot to tackle, but Lucas had shouldered all of it, which made Jax ashamed and angry all at the same time.

He was both ashamed that he'd been so Jax-centric he hadn't seen the signs of burnout and angry Lucas hadn't been honest with him. Sure, he could blame Lucas for the distance over the past twelve months, but Lucas had started running the show not long after he'd graduated college. Jax wasn't a time traveler, so he couldn't fix the past, but he could help now by supporting his brother.

Not that he supported Lucas's viewpoint on selling the lodge, but he needed to respect Lucas's stance. Opposing opinions on how to manage their mom's addiction and recovery had already damaged their relationship. They didn't need one more obstacle between them if they wanted a shot at repairing things. And deep down Jax wanted to fix things so they could go back to being thick as thieves. He just wasn't sure how to do that. But this event felt like a step in the right direction.

Which was why Jax had asked Milly to meet at Coffee Run, an upscale coffee shop downtown situated on the corner of Sequoia Lane and Main Street, and across from Town Square. With its massive windows, the café was the most visible location in town. This little meet-up accomplished two things: help with the event and to bring some validity to their fake relationship in the eyes of the public.

If he were being honest, it also accomplished a third thing—his desire to lay his eyes on Milly. Something that was quickly becoming a pastime.

Jax cleared his throat and scanned the list of companies she'd compiled. Everything from swag bags to snowboard wax to travel plans for the VIP competitors. He recognized several of the companies and an idea bloomed.

"Are any on these vendors sponsoring the event?"

"I don't know. I only handle point A to point B and back to point A. But I have all the invoices in this file." She pointed to a folder on her laptop.

"Can you send that to me? I'm betting I can get some of these companies to sponsor the event and supply the items at no cost to us."

"Sure." Nibbling at her lower lip, Milly pushed her glasses up the bridge of her nose.

Jax's body reacted as if she were nibbling on *his* lower lip, which made no sense. Even though she was dressed in a simple pair of faded jeans, boots with fur on the trim, and a soft gray sweater, his mind was scrambled.

Her face was fresh of makeup and her hair was pulled back into a messy bun that was secured with a ballpoint pen. Then there were her sexy-librarian glasses, perched on her petite nose and playing into the girl-next-door vibe that was becoming harder to resist by the minute.

She made a big show of punching the Enter button on her laptop. "Sent!" The smile she flashed him had his heart skipping a few beats. "Now, I think we should talk about the new athletes you got to sign up."

"How do you know I was behind it?"

She grinned with an all-knowing glint in her eye. "Because they were all VIPs and I imagined that someone who requires the pampered package wouldn't sign up this late unless another VIP asked them to."

"Are you saying I'm a pampered athlete?"

"Are you denying it? And before you answer, know that I called the spa to see if there were any openings for these new VIPers and noticed *you* have a massage booked for nearly every day the week leading up to the Cup."

"Keeping my body limber and fine-tuned is part of the job."

She stretched her neck from side to side. "Where do I sign up for that?"

Jax looked at his phone and noted the time. It was nearly nine, the sun had long ago blended into the horizon and dipped behind the mountains, bathing the evening sky in hues of pink and mango. Now all that lit the sky were a million dazzling stars and the full moon.

Most of the café had already cleared out, leaving only a few stragglers behind. They'd been sitting there working for over three hours. That was in addition to a full workday for Milly. He knew because she'd answered his email to meet well before six that morning.

"You angling for a massage, angel?" He hooked his foot around the leg of her chair and yanked until their thighs were bumping.

She squeaked. "What are you doing?"

"Giving my girlfriend a massage after a long day's work." Taking her waist, he scooted her backward until her body was between his spread legs.

"You don't have to do that."

She tried to wiggle free, but he slid a hand around her waist. "I want to."

"Seriously, you don't—" Before she could squirm away, he sank his thumbs into the lower part of her neck and worked them up her spine. When he reached the base of her skull and applied pressure, she groaned.

"I like that sound falling from your lips."

He worked his fingers back down, his thumbs sliding beneath the back of her sweater, to the bare, silky skin beneath.

"Jax," she breathed.

He leaned in until his lips brushed the sensitive skin behind her ear. "I like that sound even better," he whispered, then he feathered a kiss to the column of her neck. She moaned again and he kissed her a little lower—his hands slipping further beneath her sweater, kneading out every last bit of stress.

"What about the rules?" she murmured.

Jax smiled against her neck because, even as she was reminding him of the rules, she'd tilted her head to the side, ever so slightly but enough to give him better access—which he used.

"We're in public, so it would be natural for me to give you a massage after you helped me for over three hours."

"Three hours?" she asked, but didn't seem all that alarmed. In fact, her body was relaxing under his touch and sinking back against his chest. "I hadn't even noticed."

Neither had he. Even though they were talking about numbers and dollars and cents, it had somehow felt intimate. Now this, touching her, felt even more erotic than when he'd taken her from behind. Damn, his brain was scrambled.

He laid on some more gentle kisses, but when his mouth reached that sweet curve of neck he couldn't help himself—he gave a little nip.

"No tongue, remember?"

"That wasn't my tongue. That was my teeth." And to prove it, he gave another nip. This time she hummed, then her neck fell all the way to the side. He sank his finger in deeper, really working out the tension at the base of her neck as he rained kisses down and around her throat to the other side.

"What if someone sees us?" she asked, but didn't sound too concerned. Nope, she sounded thoroughly turned on.

"Isn't that the point?" he asked, dragging his thumbs all the way down her spine until he found the bottom hem of her sweater. He tugged it up so that he could get his hands on her lower back, then dug his fingers in and she let out the same kind of moan she'd made that night right before she came.

"To be seen?" There was a hint of demureness to her voice, as if she was intrigued by the idea of an audience. When she'd approached him at the bar, her kisses had been bold, packed with a brazen bravado, even when it became clear that they had spectators. He'd chalked it up to adrenaline from a good game of Truth or Dare. But then there was the ski lesson turned make-out session. Maybe she had a little more kink than he'd originally thought.

He'd file that fact away to explore at a later date.

"Any other reason behind those sexy little moans of yours?"

"Just playing the part," she lied. And he knew it was a lie because, while she might cling to those rules, she wanted him—he was certain of it.

"For someone who claimed she's a terrible liar, you're pretty damn convincing."

"I said I wasn't good at keeping secrets."

"That's okay. You're good at other things." He nipped her earlobe. "Amazing, actually. So you might want to keep up the good work, because my sister's friend is two tables behind us."

"Is she watching?"

"Has been since she walked in. I think she may have even snapped a picture to send to Brynn."

He felt Milly swallow. "What do you think the text would say?"

"Maybe it would say the town bachelor had found his person. Or maybe she's asking Brynn if the rumors are true. Maybe she is placing bets on if we're going home in one car or two. Or maybe she just thinks I'm telling you about my day." He moved his hands around the front, letting his fingers dip down to her collarbone. He loved the feeling of her skin beneath his fingers.

She swallowed again—this time harder. "Why don't you tell me about your day, then," she said on a long exhale.

"Babe, I've got my hands all over you and you want to know about my day?"

Over her shoulder, she shot him a mischievous grin. "It's what a girlfriend would ask her boyfriend. You were gone all weekend, it's only natural I'd be curious. So, how was your weekend, *babe*?"

Had she asked him that question when he'd first walked into the café, he would have said long. After two days of competing, pushing his body to the limit, and being "on" in a never-ending circle of hanging with the fellas and meeting fans, he was burned-out. Then there'd been the long trek from Wyoming back to Sierra Vista. His first flight had been delayed so he missed his connection, leaving him stranded in Boise for six hours. He'd tried to catch up on some sleep last night but, frustratingly enough, his brain was fixated on family drama.

He couldn't get the look on Lucas's face out of his head when Jax had offered to plan the event. It had been disbelief. Not disbelief in the way that Lucas didn't believe he'd offered, but disbelief as if he'd had a hard time picturing Jax delivering on his promise. And while Jax might be stubborn and occasionally a hothead, he'd only ever defaulted on one promise.

That had been to his mom and the decision had been ripped out of his hands.

Milly must have mistaken his silence for indifference because she cleared her throat and looked back at him. "I didn't mean to push. I was just curious."

"Because of our arrangement?"

"Because we're friends. Right?" Her eyes darted to the side, but before they did he saw a hint of confusion and uncertainty.

He crooked a finger beneath her chin, tilting her head until she met his gaze. "Of course, we're friends. And you weren't pushing. I've just got road-trip hangover. I left from Wyoming around six this morning and because of weather delays I arrived back here right before meeting you."

"You could have canceled. I would have understood."

"I know." There was no chance he'd have canceled on Milly. Even though the cocoa meeting included spreadsheets and the exact number of folding chairs ordered, it was the thing he'd been the most excited to get back for. Something he didn't want to examine too carefully. "Now, ask away."

Her smile broadened in approval, then she turned back around.

"Let's start with your competition. How did that go?" She patted her shoulders, as in *Get back to work*. He chuckled.

"It went okay." More like, he'd been okay. Wyoming was one of his favorite places to board and the Xtreme Games was one of the top competitions of the season. The event didn't fail to impress. The weather had been great, the powder perfectly packed, and some of his closest buddies had been there. But he'd been distracted. Between the idea of Peggy and Kent selling the lodge and thinking about his relationship with Lucas, his head hadn't been in the game.

"*Okay* is a pretty broad word. Plus, you placed fifth. Out of a hundred people!" She twisted slightly in her seat. Not enough for him to stop massaging but enough to where she could meet his gaze. "That puts you in the top five percent!"

"Last year I was in the top one percent," he said, noting that the frustration he'd felt earlier over his placement wasn't as strong. "You been googling me, angel?"

"I may have heard it around town," she said, the little liar. "And besides the ranking, which you should be totally proud of, what would have made your trip better?"

He moved his hands a little higher, his fingers wrapping around the front. Her head fell back against his shoulder. "This," he whispered and realized that it was true. When she'd walked into that café he'd snapped out of his funk. He pressed his lips to her temple. "And this."

He kissed her until he reached the start of her hairline. He breathed her in. "God, you smell good. What is that?"

"My conditioner."

"I need to switch conditioners," he whispered into her ear. "So that when I'm taking my morning shower, I can coat my hand with it. Then when I'm pumping into it the room will smell like you."

She met his gaze through her lashes. "I haven't washed the pillowcase you used and at night I smell it."

He let out a low growl. "What else do you do with it?"

Her face pinkened but she still held his gaze. "Verbal foreplay is off-limits."

"Damn, baby." He slid his hands around to her belly and she sucked in a breath. He allowed himself exactly five seconds to dream about what it would feel like if he slipped his hands into her jeans, then pulled them out from under her sweater and tugged the hem back down.

"What are you doing?" she asked.

"If I asked you to come back to my place, what would you say?"

"That I don't think we'd make it farther than the car."

His dick agreed. Which was why... "While I want to take you home and massage every inch of your body, I made you a promise and I never go back on my word. Which means I need to walk you to your car and then go back to the lodge in mine."

Chapter Thirteen

Take Life by the Balls
Shout from the mountain top.

"Don't ruin it by opening your mouth."

Jax had just hung up with three different companies, all of whom committed to either a sponsorship or donation, and he was feeling damn proud of himself. He'd officially taken on the Sierra Vista Cup three days ago and he'd already increased the family pot by thirty grand.

"You want to tell me why Brandon Turner from Samson Ski Wax just called me to ask why our order has been canceled?" Lucas asked from the doorway to Jax's office. Well, it wasn't really Jax's office—he didn't have one—it was on loan from the events manager who'd gone on maternity leave last month.

"You want to close the door before lecturing me?" Jax said. "I'm not sure ski patrol heard you from the top of the mountain."

His brother gave him a long, even look. And while Lucas would have Jax believing that he was calm and collected, Jax knew better. His twin was in a mood. So while he stepped in the office and closed the door behind him, he didn't take a seat, instead standing with his legs in a wide stance and arms crossed in irritation.

"Samson Ski Wax has been our supplier since the first year of the Cup."

"Samson Ski Wax is a shit brand," Jax explained. "They're overpriced and targeted toward wannabes who don't know any better."

"While that would have been helpful information to know last year when the board decided to go with Brandon's company again, it doesn't do us a whole lot of good now. Which is why I had him put the order back in."

Now it was Jax's turn to shout. "Without consulting me?"

"You didn't consult me when you dumped our wax company."

"Because it isn't your job anymore. It's my job now. And for the record, I didn't make some last-minute decisions to change suppliers for shits and giggles. I have a close contact at a competing company, whose product is far superior, and I got them to commit to not only give us enough units to fill every swag bag, but they're also sponsoring the event."

"How much?"

Jax rattled off a number that had Lucas looking impressed. "You got all this done since our talk last week?"

"It's not rocket science. And Milly helped." She hadn't made any of the calls, Jax had done that, but she'd identified some of the vendors they could approach and vendors that they had to stick with due to the event being just weeks away. "Look, I understand the limitations we're under with the time constraint, but I'm going to do what I can to help. However, I can't make things happen with you micromanaging me." Jax stopped, a sudden thought crossing his mind.

"Are you trying to find mistakes so that you can point out what a disappointment I am?" Jax asked.

Lucas's eyes went wide with surprise. "Do you really think I'd do that?"

"Shit, man, I don't know what to think."

The look on his brother's face was a familiar one, one he remembered from the day Jax had caught Lucas in the biggest lie of his life. "For the record, I'd never do that. I got the call from Brandon and wanted to double check to see what was going on. Looking at the invoices, I noticed that we'd canceled accounts with two other vendors."

Feeling the impending frustration that came with someone undermining him, deliberately or not, Jax scratched at his face, the scruff reminding him that he hadn't had more than a handful of hours sleep since Monday. And that was on the back of an exhausting weekend.

"Both of those vendors I met in Wyoming last weekend. I mentioned the Sierra Vista Cup to a group of buddies, whom I convinced to sign up by the way, and there happened to be the owner of a new snowboarding goggles company there. He wanted to talk about carrying them in our ski shop and I said we were looking for sponsors for the Cup."

"You make it sound as if we don't already have sponsors," Lucas said.

"We do, but it's the same people we've been working with since the event started. It's grown and so should we."

Lucas let out a tired sigh. "I hired a business development guy last year and six months in his wife left him and, well, things fell through the cracks," Lucas admitted. "I was lucky I was able to get any donations for the swag bags."

"That's the thing, we shouldn't be relying on donations. They should be paying *us* to feature their products and services."

"You say it as if I don't already know this. When the biz-dev guy quit, he left us in a lurch. The kind of connections you're talking about rely on cultivating relationships—relationships I don't have the time for right now. Which is another reason Mom and Dad want to sell."

"You're so stuck on selling this place that you can't see another point of view," Jax argued. "I've always admired your ability to laser focus on something and take it from an idea to a success, but sometimes it hinders your ability to see the bigger picture." Lucas could be bullheaded sometimes, but he usually wasn't so black and white. "You don't have the time to cultivate relationships. I do. Plus, I'm shoulder to shoulder with those guys six months out of every year. What you do in the boardroom, I can do over a beer."

He could see the wheels moving in his brother's head. He could also see resignation and stubbornness waging a war, and Jax didn't like either outcome.

"Maybe you aren't just the bridesmaid," Lucas teased, then pulled out the chair and took a seat across from Jax. "I appreciate everything you're doing and, honestly, I like how the family has come together. I really do. It feels like the old days."

It wasn't a truce by any means, but a door had been cracked. All Jax had to do was step inside. Be the bigger man.

Jax was just opening his mouth to respond when Lucas said, in his *brother knows best* tone, "But the time for all of this was last year." And there went being the bigger man—right out the window. Lucas sighed. "That was a shit thing to say. It's just that with Mom and Dad taking a step back, these past twelve months have been brutal. I'm doing the best that I can, but I feel like I'm about to go under."

The vulnerable honesty in his brother's voice sucked the wind out of Jax's chest. "When I implied that we could just replace you I was being an ass. You run this company and you're doing a damn fine job. But if there's a way to keep the lodge and get the house in Santa Barbara, isn't it worth a try?"

"What do you mean?"

"When you got your panties in a bunch over me offering to give them the down payment for a house, I looked into what it would take to have the company purchase the house. And before you cite the financial state of the company, I've already thought of that."

Lucas took a beat. "You went through the company's financials?"

"I know. It surprised me too."

"You paid me a hundred bucks to take all of your math tests in high school."

"Just because I hate numbers doesn't mean I don't understand them. But I wanted all the information before I brought it to the family, so I met with our CPA yesterday and she walked me through things. I think between sponsors for the Cup and getting people to pay us to endorse their products, we can make enough additional money to help with the down payment. And maybe next year we can pay off the house. Peggy and Kent would have their dream retirement and the lodge stays in the family."

Instead of Lucas vetoing the idea right away, he went quiet—Lucas's MO for life. When faced with a problem, Jax used others as a sounding board, it was what made him such a competitive athlete. He knew when to seek outside expertise and didn't have a difficult time asking for direction. Lucas was more introspective and tended to troubleshoot solo. It had always been that way. Even throughout school the difference between their approaches to life had been stark. Jax used every resource at his disposal, whereas Lucas would rather read an entire textbook by himself.

Jax knew why his brother was hesitant to let people inside his circle. It was hard to rely on others when they couldn't even rely on their own mother. But, even as isolated as he made himself, Lucas had always trusted Jax—with everything. That was why the past year had gutted him. Lucas hadn't just kept things, important things, from Jax; had he not been caught, Jax wondered whether he'd ever have learned of the meet-ups with their mom.

And when it came to his twin he never wanted to have to wonder.

"Be straight with me," Jax said quietly. "What's the real reason you want to sell?" Jax held up a hand, silencing Lucas. "And before you pin this all on Peggy and Kent, I know something else is going on."

With a deep inhale, Lucas placed his elbows on his knees, making a platform to rest his forehead. He sat like that so long Jax was convinced he wasn't going to get what he wanted—the truth. Then Lucas looked up and his uncertain expression was one of complete disillusionment.

"My heart isn't in it anymore."

The space between Jax's ribs froze, causing his chest to seize. How the hell could his brother's heart not be in this place? The lodge and the Carmichaels' house had healed their hearts. Made them the men they were today.

"Even saying it makes me sound like a selfish asshole," Lucas said. "But it's how I feel. I've tried everything to get my head back into the lodge, but nothing seems to work. When Kent confided in me about considering an offer, all I felt was relief." Lucas took a deep, pained breath and closed his eyes. "Relief. The Carmichaels invited us into their family, their home, trusted me with their legacy, and I couldn't even muster up the words to tell Kent that they could walk away, that I'd handle everything, that I've got their back."

"You're just burned-out, bro," Jax said. "After a week in your shoes—more like a lace of a single shoe—I'm exhausted. So I started delegating and relying on the team and that exhaustion turned into excitement."

"Even if we hire someone to replace me, you know damn well that Kent will want to have his nose in everything. He won't be able to help himself. He'll have one foot in the business and the other in retirement. That spells disaster to all parties involved."

"And if we sell the lodge, Peggy and Kent won't be able to stomach coming back to Sierra Vista. I give it a couple of months before they sell the family home here."

"They already have a Realtor."

"Christ, man, I know you're an island of one but at least let me on the beach."

Lucas's eyes locked on Jax. Neither of them spoke for a long moment but a whole conversation played out without uttering a single word. Lucas was in a bad way.

"I'm stuck, man," Lucas finally said. "I've *been* stuck. Here in Sierra Vista while you all have been out living your life."

"Running your own business was your goal and here you are running a multimillion-dollar business."

"But it's not *mine*. I stepped in to fill a vacancy, help out where I could. But that vacancy got larger and larger until it took over my whole life. I love this place, just like the rest of you, but I don't get to enjoy it on the weekends, or when the rest of you pop in for a family visit. We're halfway through the season and I haven't had the time to even hit the slopes. Not once."

"Okay, so more time. What else do you need to make this feel like yours?"

Lucas tipped the back of his neck to look skyward. "In the beginning, I felt as if I was actually running the company. Then Kent became less and less involved and now I'm the CEO, president, GP, and a god-damned therapist all rolled into one." Lucas's gaze held steady, concerningly intense. "I had to walk away from AvalancheEx."

Jax froze, cemented to his seat, beyond boggled about why his brother would make that kind of decision. He'd put every-thing he had into AvalancheEx, an adventure company that specialized in extended excursions for extreme athletes and executives. During grad school, Lucas landed an internship with a successful excursion company and discovered he was a natural for identifying challenging and team-building courses. His thesis was a business plan for AvalancheEx and not only did it earn him the highest marks, but it also caught the eye of a few investors.

Lucas had invested his time, his heart and, to Jax's knowledge, his cut of the life insurance policy from their dad.

Jax's gut clenched. In comparison, he'd left his hometown and family behind without ever looking back. Maybe he was a selfish asshole. He knew the lodge had struggled after their long-standing general manager left for a job in Aspen. He'd just assumed that Lucas wanted the position. He'd never said differently.

Then again, Jax had never asked.

"You told me the investor backed out." Lucas shifted uncomfortably in his seat and that was all Jax needed to know. "That was your dream. You've talked non-stop about it since we were kids."

"Exactly. We were kids. Some of us have to adult for a living."

Implying that Jax spent his days playing in the snow. Which was as far from the truth as it could get, and Lucas knew that. Jax's first impulse was to tell Lucas to go screw himself, but he pushed down his frustration and tuned into what his brother was really saying. He'd given up his dream so that someone else could live theirs. And Jax hadn't even offered to help.

"Do Peggy and Kent know?" Jax asked.

"Nobody knows, and I'd like to keep it that way."

"Why didn't you tell me?"

Lucas laughed humorlessly. "When was I supposed to do that? When you got your first sponsor or when you won your first medal?"

"The moment you started considering backing out of your deal. We're brothers, you should have told me no matter what was going on in my life."

149

"What would it have changed?"

"I would have had your back. I'd have helped you find a new general manager."

"Finding a GM isn't the problem. Keeping them is. Over the past two years, I've hired three, all of whom quit and all of whom stated on their exit interview that they weren't allowed to properly do their job because Kent can't let go. So unless you want to tell Kent that he isn't welcome at the table, then I don't see a solution." Lucas paused, as if reading the room. "You want to talk about Cindy?"

Jax shook his head. "I'm kind of enjoying being on your island and I don't want to have to punch you."

Chapter Fourteen

Take Life by the Balls
Don't be stingy with hugs.

It was after ten when Milly finally plopped down on the couch. She'd reconfirmed delivery times and dates, sent out itineraries to VIP guests, and had back-to-back meetings with her staff. The only other person she wanted to meet with by day's end was Jax.

Bright and early, he'd greeted her with the perfect good morning faux peck and a hot cocoa. He'd kissed her when they'd bumped into each other in the hallway—for onlookers, of course. Even sat next to her during all three of their meetings, so close their thighs brushed whenever she shifted in her chair.

She'd shifted a lot. And he'd noticed. He'd also noticed when her gaze fell to his crotch. Milly had turned bright red. Jax had winked. Then, about midday, everything changed. He vanished into his office for a meeting with his brother and when he reappeared that contagious smile of his had also vanished.

Milly waited for an appropriate time to check in on him, but she couldn't find even a spare minute. It was as if he were avoiding her. She tried to stuff down the doubts that began to swirl around, but it was impossible. Which was why she was curled up in her pj's, on the couch, eating pickles. Some people sobbed into a bowl of ice cream when they did stupid things—such as engage in a fake relationship with a guy who puts his career above all else. Milly ate pickles.

And watched Mr. Darcy, who at that precise moment was dashing around on his horse. Because that's what dashing men did—they dashed this way and that. Jax had been dashing that morning, then he'd just been disillusioned. And that bothered her—more than it should.

"It's because you're friends," Milly told herself. "And friends worry about each other when one of them is struggling. So this overwhelming sense of solicitude is normal."

She blew out a breath and leaned back, trying to forget the sensation of his hands on her, his mouth on her. They hadn't talked about the other night in the café. But that was the problem, when she was around him, she didn't want to talk. She wanted to kiss, and touch, and if there were any sounds, she wanted it to be moaning. Lots of moaning.

Then when I'm pumping into it the shower will smell like you.

She wondered if he had actually done it. The idea dampened her panties.

"This is bad," she whispered. "Really bad."

He was right. This thing brewing between them wasn't going away anytime soon. Thank goodness *he* was going away. How far could feelings cement in a couple of weeks?

Milly was trying to come up with a mathematical equation to determine the risk factor involved in a faux-mance with someone who had the potential to ruin her for all men when there came a knock.

Following Morning-After-Gate, Milly had established some boundaries with her parents. One of them being, as long as Milly was residing at the cabin they had to give twenty-four hours' notice prior to visits. Not that Milly was planning on having any other sleepovers between now and Jax leaving—but precautions must be taken.

Just in case, a little voice whispered.

Her parents had agreed, but their quick and easy compliance had only added to Milly's skepticism. So she wasn't surprised when, after only two weeks, Howard and Gennie had infringed on their arrangement.

Patting herself on the back for donating four boxes of Zoe's things, she set the jar of pickles on the coffee table and walked to the mudroom.

She opened the door and stopped mid-lecture. It was Jax. Dressed in jeans and a dark-green shirt that emphasized those broad shoulders and impressive biceps she'd had her hands all over. It also matched his eyes—which were haunted with a solemness that had her going still.

"Jax?"

"Hey," he said quietly, resting a shoulder against the door-jamb. His eyes ran the length of her. She was in blue pinstriped bottoms with a matching Mr. Darcy top, which read, I PRE-FER TO BE UNSOCIABLE AND TACITURN. A small smile crossed his mouth. "I thought I made it clear that I don't share well."

"You spent the entire afternoon avoiding me, so Mr. Darcy came out to keep me company."

His smile vanished. "About that."

So, he had been avoiding her. Those swirling doubts turned into a fast-acting tornado. A chill blew through the house and cut through her pajamas, so she stepped aside to let him in. When he hesitated, she asked, "Did I do something wrong?"

"No." He looked genuinely shocked by her assumption, then he stepped inside the doorway and, kicking the door shut behind him, he cupped her jaw. "And I'm sorry if I made you feel that way."

"You didn't make me feel that way," she admitted. "This whole pretend thing was easier when it was just the two of us concocting a plan. Being in the office, around everyone, it gets confusing. Am I giving too much, or not enough, or...?" Her gaze moved to his chest.

Milly had never mastered the art of dating. Dillon had claimed that she was a relationship strangler, smothering him with so much love that he couldn't breathe. Then she'd turned that attention onto Zoe and Dillon had accused her of being emotionally unavailable. He wasn't the only boyfriend to point this out.

It seemed that Milly's love was either too big or not enough. She just couldn't seem to get it right.

"Never mind, I'm just being silly."

He didn't move, didn't speak until she was looking at his eyes. "You never have to worry about any of that with me. You're as perfect as they come."

Milly didn't even blink. The need to be still and let the relief sink in was too great. No man had ever said words to her like those.

"Thank you." Her voice was barely audible through the emotion.

"It's the truth." The pad of his thumb grazed her lower lip and then he dropped his hand. She immediately missed the intimacy. "Did I wake you?"

"No. I was just eating pickles."

"Pickles, huh?"

"Don't deflect with that smile," Milly said, crossing her arms over her very distracted nipples. "Tell me what's wrong?"

His answer was to scrape a hand through his hair.

"Jax, you didn't come here in the middle of the night to discuss pickles."

"I'm always up for a good pickle debate." Milly lifted a brow and he let out a sigh. "Some things are hard to talk about."

"In my experience, those are the things that should be talked about the most."

"Am I a selfish prick?" he suddenly asked, and she could tell that he believed it to be true.

"You are the exact opposite of a selfish prick." He didn't believe her. "You walked away from your season to help with your family's event. You've stepped into a project mid-way, which means that you either have a second life as a corporate bulldog or you're spending all your free time researching how to become one." She took his hands. "Jax, you are helping me with my parent problem *and* my sister's wish that I go after fun. Those are not the actions of a selfish man."

"But I should have been helping my family all along. And you and I made a deal, which is more beneficial to me than you. And I offered to help with the fun because I want to get in your pants again."

Want. Present tense.

She led him to the couch and sat, pulling him down next to her. "You're not fooling me, Macintyre. And where is this all coming from? I could tell something was up today."

"The entire office knew something was up."

Sensing he needed someone to hold on to, she laced their fingers and rested them in her lap. "Siblings argue. Siblings who work together, I imagine, argue more. And things that are said during a sibling argument don't count. That was one of Zoe's rules since she was the shout-first-and-think-later one in the family."

"Well, I'm the shout-first-and-think-later one of my family. And the last time I shouted at Lucas it was so loud it's still echoing a year later."

"You guys haven't spoken in a year?"

"Angel, I haven't been home in a year," he said, resting his head against the couch back and closing his eyes. "And besides talking with him about family and work stuff, and then today, we haven't spoken at all."

Before Zoe's death, Milly couldn't imagine not speaking to her sister for an entire week let alone an entire year. The whole town knew Jax and Lucas were inseparable. What could have been so horrific to sever that kind of bond?

She turned her body and tucked a foot beneath her, so that she was facing Jax fully. "You want to start with what happened today?"

"Today I learned that while I've been off acting stubborn and sanctimonious, counting all the ways my brother wronged me, he's been here in Sierra Vista holding the family lodge together. Pretty much all by himself. As kids, it was the two of us against the world and we promised to always have each other's backs. I didn't live up to my end of the bargain."

"That must have been hard to hear."

"I used to accuse him of not listening but, as it turns out, I'm just as bad." He rolled his head to meet her gaze. "Peggy and Kent got an offer on the lodge and they want to take the deal."

Milly didn't know how to respond. The Carmichaels were Sierra Vista and Sierra Vista was the Carmichaels. She couldn't imagine a situation where they'd want to sell. Then again, she'd never imagined that Lucas and Jax would have gone an entire year without speaking.

"I know deep down they don't want to sell, but in order for them to retire, they'd need to. My siblings are on board to find a way to keep the lodge in the family. All except Lucas. At first, I thought it was because he wasn't getting the bigger picture, but today I realized that he gets it more than any of us ever could. He's been running the lodge *by himself* for the past year. He even walked away from ... I promised him I wouldn't share his business, so all I can say is that it was something important to him and he gave it all up to run the lodge."

"Is that why the Cup is so important to you? Because it might be the last?"

"I want to say yes. I want to say that I'm doing it to help the family and prove to Lucas that he doesn't have to carry all the weight all the time. But what if I did it just to stick it to my golden-boy brother? Prove to him that I could do it better?" He dropped her hand and leaned forward, resting his elbows on his knees, his head dropped to his chest. "Does that make me a selfish prick?"

She wove her fingers into the hair at the base of his neck, using her nails to gently scratch his scalp in a soothing rhythm. "It makes you human. But I don't think that's the reason you're doing it. I think that this is your way of showing the Carmichaels that you love them. Of showing your brother that, even though you aren't on the best of terms and you are on opposing sides of a big decision, you have his back. Did you ever think that this could be about reconnecting with your life here?"

"I wouldn't have to reconnect if I'd never left in the first place." He gave her a sidelong glance and the anguish swimming in his eyes broke her heart. "My mom wasn't the most present parent. After my dad died, she couldn't cope and became an alcoholic. She'd promised us so many times she'd get sober, to make amends, and I always believed her. Lucas gave up on her not long after the Carmichaels took us in. I just couldn't let go of the hope that one day she'd get it right. All it takes is getting it right once and then the past doesn't matter."

Milly's stomach sank at the idea of a young Jax struggling to get it right, afraid that when he did it would be too late for the people who mattered.

"No matter how often I blew it or purposefully shoved their love back in their faces, Peggy and Kent always gave me a second chance."

She noticed the way he called them by their first names, whereas Lucas referred to them as Mom and Dad. She wondered if Jax knew that part of the reason he put distance between himself and home and the people he loved was because he was afraid that, somehow, he'd ruin things and lose it all.

"I don't want to let them down. I know they will regret selling, so I've been thinking about a solution that benefits everyone. If I go to the Carmichaels with my idea, it will be like I'm going against my twin. But if I don't speak up, the lodge gets sold and there will be a lot of broken hearts."

"So it's a good-for-all, bad-for-one kind of situation."

"Yeah."

Milly made strokes with her nails, starting at the base of his neck and going up to the crown of his head. Beneath her hands she felt him relax slightly.

"What would you do?" he asked.

"I think that having all of the information before making a big decision is best."

He leaned his head back and gazed into her eyes. "Even if you knew that it would piss off Zoe?"

Milly cupped his jaw. "All you can do is present your idea, what the Carmichaels or Lucas does with that is on them."

"Being one of the Carmichaels without Lucas on my side is new and I don't know how to navigate it."

"I know the feeling," she said softly. "Did the Carmichaels adopt you?"

"In every way that mattered. My mom refused to give up custody. Lucas said it was because she wanted the tax write-off, but I always thought it was because she loved us too much to give up entirely. She isn't a bad person; she's sick, and that sickness made her a bad mom."

How many times had he said those exact words to himself? How many times did a young Jax stay up worried that maybe he'd gotten it wrong and she didn't love them?

"When she comes around, I give her money to get back on her feet, to get in rehab. Whatever support she needs. It drives Lucas nuts, which is why, last year, when she'd reached back out, Lucas intercepted the call and met with her behind my back. She needed help and he made the unilateral decision to send her packing."

She could only imagine how much that must have crushed a man like Jax, who was so terrified of love, he'd rather walk away than run the risk of getting hurt. Even when it came to his twin. A fact that she needed to remember.

"Do you think maybe he was protecting you?"

He lifted a broad shoulder. "His why doesn't matter. If he doesn't want a relationship with her, fine. But he made my decision for me."

"Love makes us do pretty crazy things sometimes," she said, a sliver of guilt making its way through her chest. "I never told you why I'm dragging my heels on deciding what I want to do or where I want to go."

He straightened, causing her hand to fall from his neck. "I thought it was to sort out your sister's affairs."

"That's part of it." He took her hand and that's when she realized they were trembling. "Losing Zoe made me realize I really need to re-evaluate the things in my life and what I really want. And I need to make the right choices so my parents don't worry. The last thing I need is for my dad to have another heart attack. I can't lose him too."

They sat there, their hearts, their fears and all their emotions raw and heavy in the air. Milly could see the exhaustion and vulnerability in his eyes and before she knew what she was doing she stood, tugging him up with her.

She laced their fingers and started toward her bedroom.

"Where are we going?"

"To bed."

"Angel, there is nothing I want more than to take you to bed and spend all night making you smile. But I made a promise to you. No sex. And even though it will likely kill me," he stopped, slowly pulling her against him until her back was plastered to his front—until she could feel what was killing him pressed firmly against her bottom. "I won't break that promise."

She looked over her shoulder, bringing her lips within kissing distance. Right before their lips touched she whispered, "Don't worry, there won't be any promises broken tonight. I just figured that we could both use a little cuddle therapy."

He chuckled. "You're asking me to cuddle?"

"As soon as you feel my cuddling prowess, you'll be asking me."

Chapter Fifteen

Take Life by the Balls
Say yes to the dress.

"*I* want you."

Milly's towel dropped to the ground as she pressed her phone firmly against her ear to make sure she was hearing her old boss correctly. "But you already filled my position." A position she'd loved. A position that was supposed to be a stepping stone to the next chapter in her life.

Milly picked up the towel and wrapped it around her body. She'd just come out of the shower when her phone had rung. When she saw Leah's number she'd assumed it was a social call, but it was clearly a business call.

"I'm not talking about your old position," Leah said. "There is an opening for a senior logistics coordinator in the author relations and events department, and I think you'd be perfect."

Oh my god! Author relations would be her dream job. Her last job was basically just making sure the manuscript got to the printer and that the printer got the books to the distributor. In her new position, she'd be dealing directly with the authors—authors she'd read and loved—shipping books out to conferences and managing signing events. She'd even get to go to some of the conferences to ensure everything went smoothly.

"You'd report directly to me, but you'd have complete control over how you want to manage and arrange your team," Leah said, and Milly couldn't help the smile that overtook her face.

Leah wasn't just her boss, she was also a good friend. One of Milly's closest New York friends. She'd picked Milly out of a sea of interns and given her a shot at something greater—and Milly had rocked it. She'd love to work with Leah again.

But she already had a job with Sierra Vista. *It's just a contract job*, she reminded herself. A contract that would expire in a month.

"If I took the job, when would it start?" she asked.

Leah snorted. "What do you mean *if*? This is what you've wanted."

It was what she wanted. It was the kind of job she'd shine in. The kind of job she'd dreamed about when she'd decided her major in college. So why wasn't she jumping at the offer?

"It's just that I'm contracting with another company right now."

"I can hold the position for a month. Six weeks tops. There is a big romance writers conference happening in New York in three months and you'll need to have a team in place and be up and running," Leah said. "Have I mentioned the pay?" Leah rattled off an obscene number and Milly's mouth fell open. With that kind of salary she could pay off her student loans in a year or two. Maybe even save for a place of her own.

But if she took the job, she would have to put her trip to England on hold. She'd also have to leave Sierra Vista, and Zoe's wish would remain unfulfilled for likely another year. "Can I think on it?"

Leah went silent. "Absolutely. But don't think too long. If you pass, I have to find someone else."

Milly hung up and sat on the edge of the bed, holding her phone to her chest. With a squeal she fell back on the mattress and stared at the ceiling.

A six-figure dream job had just been placed in her lap. A six-figure job! This kind of opportunity didn't come along all that often, yet she'd hesitated. Why?

Before she could dive down that rabbit hole, her alarm went off. She glanced at her phone and sprang up. Tonight was Peggy's birthday party and Jax was picking her up in exactly one hour and she was still in a towel looking like a drowned kitty.

"Get a move on," she said, walking across the hall to Zoe's room. She didn't need to riffle through the closet for what she was going to wear. She'd already decided on the dress. The shimmery one she'd been wearing when Jax had come to the door last week.

She knew she was playing with fire, but she didn't mind getting a little toasty.

Milly was kissing him.

It was a barely-there feather of her lips against his. Nothing to warrant how his heart was pounding, or his blood was surging through his body. By the way his dick was standing at attention, he'd think they were executing a series of naked frontside one-eighties.

Her hands were looped around his neck and his were inches from her ass. All he had to do was follow the curve down and around. And man, did he want to go down and around and down some more until his fingers grazed bare skin.

He quickly ran through her list of no-no's.

1. No verbal foreplay—*whoops.*
2. No tongue—*so far so good.*
3. No sex—*why did he make that promise? Right, so no one's heart gets involved.*

Problem here was that his heart was inching toward involved. Not that he'd cross that line. Addiction ran deep in his family. He was no better than his mom, only his vice was his profession. But he had a feeling this fake relationship was going to blur a few things. Like how much he was coming to care for Milly.

To care about her feelings, her thoughts, her opinion of him, and not hurting her. He couldn't hurt her. The second he felt like that was a possibility, he'd call things off. Period.

But right now, he was going to enjoy this surprise-of-all-surprises, out-of-nowhere, match-to-gasoline kiss. That she'd initiated.

Milly slowly pulled away and he leaned further into it, trying to fill the growing space between their lips. He opened his eyes, and she was staring back, the deep, brown pools of hers filled with confusion.

That makes two of us.

Maybe if he played his cards right, she'd ask him to cuddle again. Jesus! Did he even possess a man card anymore?

"There you two are," a distant voice said. A voice that sounded strangely like Milly's mom. "Everyone, the happy couple is here."

Milly dropped her hands and stepped back. Not like they'd been caught, but as if she knew they were being watched all along. Which meant that kiss wasn't impromptu—it was for show. Which was the point of tonight, to show their parents that this was real. So then, what was that twinge of disappointment deep in his stomach?

"Don't you look handsome," Gennie said, straightening Jax's collar in a maternal way that he'd never received from his own mother.

Jax was suddenly nervous. There was a lot riding on tonight. Not only would it be the first time he'd seen Lucas since their "talk," it was the first time Jax and Milly would be together in front of his family and friends—and apparently her parents.

"Mom, what are you doing here?" Milly asked, as confused at her mom's presence as he was that Gennie was answering Peggy's door.

"Surprise," Gennie said, making fireworks with her fingers.

"We talked about surprises. We vetoed surprises."

"Oh, don't blame Gennie," Peggy said, coming to loop an arm through Gennie's. "I asked her to keep it a surprise. I didn't want to make you feel obligated to come and if you knew your parents were coming, you might feel pressured to make an appearance."

"Of course I wanted to come." Milly held out a bouquet of flowers she'd already had when Jax picked her up. Sexy and thoughtful. "These are for you, Ms. Carmichael. Happy birthday."

"Well, isn't that sweet." Peggy gave an encouraging smile. "Isn't that sweet, Jax?"

"Oh," Milly jumped in. "They're from the both of us."

"From the both of them." An independent look passed between Peggy and Gennie. But their smile was conspiratorial and dialed up to *We already have the Save the Date cards picked out.*

Lord, help him.

"Come in, before you both freeze." Peggy waved them inside.

"We'll hang up our coats and meet you both inside," Jax said to Peggy, who gave him a sly wink and took Gennie by the arm before the two women left together.

"You okay?" he asked.

She nodded back at him without speaking, but her hand reached up to scratch her wrist. A sign, he was coming to learn, that meant she was nervous or lying. She'd been rubbing the same spot the entire way to the Carmichaels.

"Are you sure you want to do this?" he asked.

"A deal's a deal," Milly said, the set of her chin suggesting a stubborn streak. That wasn't the answer he was looking for.

"That deal didn't include me forcing my family on you. They're a lot. Peggy will hammer you with questions, Brynn will be eavesdropping so she can needle me later, Nolan will make some comment about the dare, my niece Emma will probably ask if we're getting married, and Lucas will grunt a lot. It will be like the Spanish Inquisition and *Meet the Fockers* collided. So let me reiterate, they're a lot."

"Have you met my parents? 'A lot' is a quiet night at our house."

He chuckled. "I wouldn't blame you if you wanted to leave."

"Do you *want* me to leave?" she asked quietly. "Because if you're uncomfortable with—" Her hand fluttered to her mouth in realization. "Is this about the kiss?" she asked. "I knew it was too much. It was too much, right? It wasn't premeditated, I swear. I just heard someone coming and…well, I panicked."

For some reason, he always found her rambling adorable. "So you kissed me?"

"We hadn't really talked about how we were going to meet everyone, and I figured if I didn't have my mouth doing something else, I'd end up blabbing the whole story out before we even made it through the front door."

"I'm glad I could help you keep your mouth busy," he said. "And I want you to be here. But only if you want to be."

She fiddled with a button on his shirt, then smoothed out a nonexistent wrinkle with her hand. "I want to be here, Jax. I'm just nervous I'm going to blow it."

He took her by the hip and tugged her to him. She met his gaze with a shyness that had the soft underbelly of his heart rolling over. "I'm nervous too."

Not about blowing it with his family. But about blowing it with Milly, which made no sense. He wasn't the kind of guy who remained friends with his exes or turned flings into a friendship. Hell, he barely had enough time in his schedule for flings. These past two weeks were the first time, in what seemed like forever, that Jax had felt as if both feet were firmly rooted in the same place for any given period of time.

"You? You're the King of Cool. Here I am breaking out in hives, while you look like you're about to slay a social gathering."

"You're the one slaying it." He looked down at her dress and whistled. She was in that same shimmery number, that showed just enough cleavage to make a man stupid, and hugged every one of her curves. And the woman had curves. "Have I told you how beautiful you look?"

She bit back a smile. "You told me when you picked me up. When you opened my door. When you helped me out of the car. And right before I kissed you."

He gave her another once-over and had to admit his decision-making skills were in serious jeopardy.

It started with the other night. The second Milly pulled him in the direction of her bedroom he should have protested. And when she'd pulled back the covers, he should have tucked her in and called it a night. But he hadn't.

Nope, he and Milly had slept together. As in *slept* in each other's arms the entire night. No sex, no kissing, just cuddling. Then there was the morning-after breakfast, where he'd made omelets while she baked blueberry muffins. All things that were a first for him.

When it came to women, Jax avoided moments that could be misconstrued as a door opening to something more. He didn't know a whole lot about strings. Hell, he had a habit of doing things that severed any chances of strings forming. But he was forming something, all right. He was forming a serious habit for a cute blonde with whiskey-colored eyes, whose curves and silky skin made her the perfect cuddling partner. Which was the only reason he could come up with for saying, "What I haven't told you … was that the other night … well, thank you."

A beautiful smile lit her face. "Is that an admission that my cuddling prowess is ninja level?"

"That's my way of telling you that you are truly amazing."

"Your dad and I are just so proud of each one of you kids," Peggy said, looping her arm through Jax's and walking him through the crowd to a quiet corner of the room.

Jax worked hard to swallow. He couldn't think of the last time someone had been proud of him for something other than winning a trophy. "We're just doing what you taught us."

"What you're doing goes above and beyond anything we taught you." Peggy paused as if pondering what she was going to say next, then reached up and cupped Jax's face. "I know that you're the one who rallied the troops to keep the lodge in the family."

"Is that what you and Kent envisioned? To keep the lodge in the family?" he asked. "Or do you want to sell? Because I want you to have the life you've worked so hard for, and I will support your decision no matter what."

"We know that, sweetie. It was such a hard decision. We went back and forth for nearly a year and in the end, we couldn't figure out how to manage the lodge without putting all the responsibility on your brother. He'd take on the world for this family and that's a lot to carry," Peggy said. "The idea of some big chain coming in and turning my family's lodge into impersonal, cooperate housing tore me to pieces."

"What if there was a way for you to have both. Your home in Santa Barbara and the lodge in the family? I mean, I have enough money in the bank that I could—"

"Absolutely not," Peggy admonished. "That's your money and we won't touch a penny of it."

Damn, he hated it when his twin was right. Especially when they were at odds.

"Okay, then what if the company buys the Santa Barbara house as an investment." In his mind, it was a win-win. Peggy and Kent end up with their dream and the lodge would stay in the family. "Companies do it all the time. And before you veto the idea, I really think that this year's Cup is going to bring in a lot of unanticipated cash."

Peggy's eyes lit with possibilities. "We hadn't even thought about that. I'd have to talk to Kent. Your idea might help us accomplish both of our dreams. Travel the world while having our own little world here to come home to. I mean, just watching you kids rally around Lucas, knowing that if we didn't sell, he wouldn't be alone in it, it all goes a long way."

Peggy's heart might be lighter, but Jax's had become heavier. While Peggy listed off all the reasons she wanted to keep the lodge, Jax's mind raced, mentally urging him to tell the truth. But how could he do that without betraying his brother's confidence.

"How do you think Kent would handle us hiring a president for the company? Someone to handle the day-to-day managing and operations?"

Peggy's poorly concealed grin told Jax she knew exactly what he was getting at. "Do you mean, would he be a busybody and stick his nose into places he's not needed?"

"Something like that."

"We'd have a long, lay-it-all-out-there conversation where I made it crystal clear that if we're passing the torch on to you kids, then we'll let you kids keep it burning."

"Do you think he'd agree?"

"Oh, he wouldn't have a choice," she said, and Jax laughed. He could already picture the stern look she would give Kent. Jax had been on the receiving end of that look a few times. "With frostbitten winters and a two-hour airplane ride between him and the lodge, it would be impossible for him to 'drop by' the office every ten minutes." Peggy smiled. "The lodge needs some fresh air, new energy. That's what you kids are doing. You're bringing this place back to life, rejuvenating something that had become stagnant, and that might give him the assuredness he needs to open a new chapter. One that might be even more exciting than the last."

Chapter Sixteen

Take Life by the Balls

Go commando.

"You suck," Kat said, shooting Milly a mock glare over the rim of her wine glass. "That Gemma and I had to get an invite to this shindig from her super sexy neighbor is a disgrace to Girl Codes everywhere."

"We didn't get an invitation," Gemma hissed. "You told Harris we were coming and to give his mom proper planning time." Gemma sent Milly a distressed look. "Kat considered proper planning time to be the night of the event."

Unfazed, Kat sat back further into the couch. "You act like you've never crashed a party before."

"I've never crashed a party before!" Gemma snagged the glass of wine out of Kat's hot little hands.

"Rude much?" Kat said.

"I need a drink." Gemma finished it in a single gulp. "It's not like you have to go back and face *your* neighbor."

Kat looked over her shoulder to where the four sexy men stood in conversation with each other. All of them had a wide stance, even wider biceps, and mouth-watering butts.

"Like that would be a hardship," Kat said.

"Well, your neighbor is over there too." Gemma openly pointed at Nolan. "You could have asked him."

"My neighbor has a stick up his ass, while yours is a funny, charming contractor who has the whole sexy single dad thing going for him."

A laugh erupted from the men and Milly looked back at the group. She wasn't sure what they were talking about, but when Jax had approached the group, Lucas didn't leave. He hadn't given Jax the same open and warm greeting as the other siblings, it was more of a brisk nod, and she wondered if Jax was okay.

As if sensing her attention, he turned and immediately met her gaze. It had been like that all night. She'd feel this pull and look up to find Jax looking back, and vice versa. Only this time he'd caught her ogling his butt and he let her know by giving her an *I caught ya* wink.

"I can practically smell your clothes melting off," Kat said loud enough that Jax heard.

"Can you keep your voice down," Milly asked. "The last thing I need is for you encouraging my mom. She already mentioned to Jax what beautiful grandbabies we'd make. I know she's just being her eccentric self but..."

"But what?" Gemma asked.

But what if her mom knows something's off? What if Milly wasn't as convincing as she thought?

She didn't know if she was spending too much time with Jax or not enough. She looked over at her dad, who did look much improved. Were they pulling this whole "dating" charade off? And when did this charade start to feel too close to something real?

Milly said none of those things because it would only lead to more questions. Questions she couldn't answer honestly, and she hated lying to her friends.

She pressed a palm to her forehead to ward off the impending headache. In trying to placate her parents with a simple white lie, she'd made it more complicated than string theory.

"Just that Zoe would know how to handle this situation."

"Are you kidding?" Kat asked. "You're killing at life right now. You've got this new hot boyfriend, you're getting laid, and you seem happy."

"I am happy," Milly said and realized she meant it. She hadn't allowed herself much happy since Zoe's diagnosis because it felt wrong to be happy when her sister was dying. And then after Zoe passed, guilt felt less complicated. But these last couple of weeks with Jax had made her begin to wonder if grief didn't have to be the final destination.

"I'm so happy you're happy," Gemma said, but she didn't look like she meant it. "I'm just worried about you moving so fast. Jax is not a commitment kind of guy and he's leaving."

Kat nudged Gemma in the ribs. "Why do you want to shit on her happy?"

"I don't want to. I am so happy she's happy. I just know how bad heartbreak is when someone leaves." She looked at Milly. "You've had enough heartbreak for a lifetime and you're not a casual person."

Milly already knew this—hence the rules. She also knew that when it came to feelings, rules didn't apply.

"Maybe that's been the problem. I've always been so invested that I get hurt. Maybe I just want to have fun and we all know he's the perfect guy for that."

Kat and Gemma exchanged glances. "Are you sure you aren't just using this as a distraction?"

"Of course I'm not sure. I don't know what I'm doing. I don't even know if I'm staying," Milly said, and both of her friends shared a look. "What? I don't. When my contract with Sierra Vista is up, I have no idea what I'm going to do. Do I go back to New York? Move to San Francisco to be closer to my parents? Stay here in Sierra Vista to be near you guys? Or maybe follow a different opportunity. I don't know what the answer is, but right now I just want to enjoy the happy."

Both of her friends went silent, and Milly knew, before turning around, that a new party had joined the conversation. Someone whose woodsy and manly scent wove its way around her.

Milly tilted her head back and found herself staring up at Jax. His smile was dialed to devastating, his charm at a million, but the twinkle in his eyes held a hint of concern—for her. Her immediate reaction was relief, that he'd come to save her from spewing more lies.

He rested his hands on her shoulders and gave them a little squeeze and it brought her back to the café, which brought her body's core temperature to simmering.

"Am I interrupting?" he asked, sliding his palms down her arms. That extra slice of birthday cake Milly had eaten somersaulted in her stomach.

"Nope," Kat said. "Not at all. In fact, she's all yours. Take her and do what you wish."

"Lucky guy," he said, taking her hand and tugging her to her feet. And then, like one of those cute couples in a rom-com, he twirled her around the couch and into his arms, giving her a cute little dip, before pressing her into his body. "Can I borrow you for a second?"

"I'll give you two."

"Then I better make them count."

He placed a firm hand on her lower back—a possessive move that both confused her and turned her on—and led her through the crowd and toward the stairs, not slowing down until they were past the landing and down a small hallway that led to a row of doors.

When they found themselves alone, she asked, "Where are we going?"

"Somewhere that we can talk and not be overheard."

"That sounds mysterious," she said.

"Come on," he tugged her further down the hallway, then stopped. "I want to show you something."

"If it's in your pants, I already went to that party."

He stopped right outside of a bedroom. It had some snowboarding stickers and a big CAUTION, SNOWBOARDER CROSSING sign stuck to the door. "Is this the infamous Jax Macintyre's bedroom?" A giddy feeling exploded through her at the idea of seeing something from his childhood.

She opened the door and she bit back a laugh at the poster covering one wall. It had snowboarding goggles and a message in a Star Wars font. "May the snow be with you?" she teased.

"I had a thing for Princess Leia."

"I bet you did."

"I think it was the hair."

"Something else you seem to have a thing for."

His eyes took in her hair, which was twisted into a messy bun at the base of her neck, and he flashed a sexy grin. "I also have a thing for necks, and sometimes I have to give the hair a little tug to get my mouth on it."

Her insides turned into a heated pool of goo. "I think that falls into the category of verbal foreplay." To resist the urge to give her own hair a tug to expose her neck, she walked to the window to take in the stunning view.

His room overlooked a small pond, which had frozen over and resembled a mini–ice rink with the twinkle lights strung around it. In the distance was a forest of pines, reaching toward the inky sky, the ice on their branches glimmering under the glow of the full moon.

The sky didn't have stars like this in San Francisco or New York. Nor did those cities bring the peace of being surrounded by nature and the comfort of being surrounded by good friends. Sierra Vista had always claimed a special space in her heart, but lately that space was expanding to include so much more.

She looked over her shoulder at Jax, who was watching her intently. "Is this the window Teen Jax would sneak girls in and out of?"

He came up behind her, resting his hands on the sill, caging her in. "You're the first girl I've ever snuck in here."

That came as a shock to her. Every summer growing up, Jax had a new girl or sometimes he'd start off the summer with one and end up with another. "How come you never dated Zoe?"

"Because I liked her sister."

Utter shock slid through her. She looked at him over her shoulder to see if he was joking. He was dead serious. "I didn't even think you knew I existed."

"Right back at ya, angel. In fact, you were so busy making cow eyes at Lucas, I didn't think I stood a chance."

Uncertainty flickered in his eyes, and she knew he was thinking back to when she'd mistook him for his brother and that caused her heart to sink. "Looking back, Lucas was the safe crush. You seemed like trouble and Zoe was all about trouble."

"I was trouble," he said. "I'm still trouble."

Her heart went out to the boy who was abandoned by the two people who were supposed to nurture him—and the man who still carried those scars.

Turning in his arms, she rested a hand on his chest. "You're not trouble, Jax." She gave those words the space they needed to settle. "Earlier tonight, I had a long conversation with Lucas."

"I noticed." His tone told her he didn't like it and for some reason that gave her a tiny thrill.

"Do you know what I was thinking the entire time? That I wished I was talking to you." She rested a hand over his heart—which, she could feel, was pounding. "You're funny and charming and thoughtful and you love what you do. You went after your happy and accomplished it. Don't you see, your world is just too big to be fenced in. You don't sit around waiting for approval, you go after what you want. It was the thing I admired most about Zoe, and the same thing I admire about you."

He rested his hand over hers. "Is that what you're doing? Waiting for approval?"

"What do you mean?" she asked, even though she knew exactly what he was referring to. That she made up this huge story instead of just telling her parents the truth because she was afraid of their disappointment.

Milly had always been too scared to ask for forgiveness, so she'd never acted at all. She made the responsible choices. Earned the responsible degree. Accepted the responsible job. Said yes to the responsible type of man. Did the responsible thing when Zoe became sick—not that she'd make a different decision, even though it cost her a lot.

"Your parents want you to move to San Francisco. You friends want you to stay in Sierra Vista. And it sounds like New York is an option."

"It is," she admitted. "I got a call from my old boss tonight, right before you came. She offered me a great position at the company. It's an opportunity I thought I'd lost out on when I came here to take care of Zoe. The offer comes with a huge raise, and a change in title that gets me one step closer to VP of logistics."

"That's incredible."

"It is. I'd essentially be running my own team and my own projects, which has been a dream of mine since college. I love city living. The people, the energy, the vibrations. When I was there it was just about me. It was the last time I truly felt free. But—"

"But what?' he asked gently.

But that dream didn't seem so bright any longer and she didn't know why. "Going to New York means leaving everyone else behind."

"You've spent your whole life worrying about everyone else." He cupped her cheek and ran his thumb down her jawline. "Have you ever stopped to ask yourself what you want?"

There were too many cooks in Milly's kitchen for her to even think about what she wanted, and she was so afraid to disappoint everyone that she couldn't remember the last time she done something just for herself. Except her night with Jax, she realized. That first kiss might have been part of a dare, but the rest was a conscious decision. And that night felt as if it set a part of her, a part she'd suppressed for far too long, free.

She placed her other hand on his pec, the muscles under his blue button-down quickened her pulse. "This." She gripped the starched collar of his shirt and tugged him down. "I want this." And then she kissed him.

It was more of a coming together, with her lips cradling his lower one. When they pulled apart, only to come back together, their mouths changed positions, and his hands slipped to the lower curve of her back, holding firm but sensual, in an authoritative way that made her feel protected.

They held still, breathing the same air; their bodies melding into one another. Never breaking their hold, she walked him backward to the bed and pushed him onto the mattress. His powerful, muscled body moved with the easy grace of an athlete.

She crawled onto his lap—one knee on either side of his sturdy thighs.

The skirt of her dress inhibited her ability to fully lower herself down, so she tugged at the material.

"Let me help with that," he said, his hands sliding up her legs and under the silky fabric. She moaned at the feeling of his rough palms against her skin.

The hem reached as high as it could go, and he stilled completely. "Angel, are you commando right now?"

She bit her lower lip. "The dress is a little too tight, and it showed panty lines."

"This dress is the perfect amount of tight, and if this is your way of testing my ability to follow rules, know that I'm going to fail epically."

Milly pushed back into his palms. "You do everything epically, if I remember correctly."

His eyes glowed with a savage inner fire. "And what do you remember?"

"Every touch, every caress, every time you … " She rose up on her knees and, plastering her body to his, slid back down in a position that ensured her core would connect with the bulge in his pants. "I could go on, but anything else would constitute verbal foreplay."

"What the hell do you call all of those little moans you're making?"

"The natural exhalation of air from my lungs."

"There isn't anything natural about this." He rolled up against her and she caught fire. "Chemistry is too benign a word to explain how our bodies react around one another. I can feel the pulse from across the room."

"I can feel the pulse from across town," she admitted. "All I have to do is think of you and my resolve starts to crumble."

She took a nip of his lower lip and, when he nipped back, she slid her tongue across the seam of his mouth.

He pulled back and, *whoa baby*, he was sexy. His hair was messy from digging her nails through it, his shirt was wrinkle-free but untucked from his slacks, and those green eyes were dark with desire.

"What happened to no tongue?"

"I'm working on corralling my hormones."

"Then why are you grinding on me?"

She looked down and she was pressed against him like she as a cat and he was made of catnip. "My body hasn't received the signal from my brain."

"I guess I'm just going to have to distract you enough that your brain shuts down completely." The determination in his voice matched his expression.

"Then it's your job to remind my hormones that this dress is the only thing between me and rescinding the ban on sex."

"Honey, at the rate you're going I'm not even going to have to take off your clothes. In fact, my hands won't even budge an inch."

His fingers spanned to cup each one of her entirely bare butt cheeks, and he yanked her fully against his impressive arousal.

"Mmm," she moaned, her fingers flirting their way down the buttons of his shirt. She fiddled with the first one, easily sliding it through the hole.

Jax shook his head. "I made a promise to be the brains of the operation, but I'm already having a hard time keeping the blood flowing to the right head."

"A *hard* time?" she mused, sliding back up his ridge, but when she started to descend, he squeezed her butt and slowly lowered her down, holding her to him so that the delicious friction created was verging on orgasmic levels. He lifted her up and made the same pass and that's when she realized what he was doing.

Jax Macintyre was on a mission to give her an orgasm. "Oh."

"O, is right." His eyes twinkled with mischief. "No hands, no tongue, no verbal foreplay, but, Mills, you're going to come apart in my arms."

"I think that constitutes verbal foreplay."

"No, that's just me stating the facts."

"Well, then..." With a flick of the wrist her hair broke free from the tie and came tumbling down. She threaded her fingers through the strands and gave a not-so-gentle tug. Her head dropped to the side, exposing her neck. "*Fact* away, Jax."

Reclaiming her lips with his, he crushed her to him, her calm shattering with every lust-filled kiss. With a surge of sheer greed, she ran her hands all over him, taking in every inch of his body, then clinging to his yard-wide shoulders that were made of bronze.

Replacing his hands on her ass, he guided her up and down his erection, the texture of his fabric on her bare skin, the snugness of their bodies as they moved in tandem.

Milly didn't think it was possible, but Jax was driving her higher and higher with just his lips and body. Pushing, pulling, grinding, she rode him hard and fast.

"Jax, I'm going to..." she trailed off into a moan.

"Me too," he said against her neck, where his teeth were gently scraping down the column.

"I mean, I'm right there."

"Then let go." He drove up against her while at the same moment sliding her down and onto his lap with enough force to shatter her. Her vision went dark, her head began to swim, and every muscle inside her coiled and clenched.

"Jesus, angel," he said, and she felt him stiffen beneath her touch. The sound of him igniting set her free.

Free to tumble. Free to feel. And free to let go.

This was what she wanted. He was what she wanted.

Only he wasn't hers to claim.

Chapter Seventeen

Take Life by the Balls
Go for the jelly-filled.

Milly thought long and hard about what she was about to do. She didn't take promises lightly, but she was afraid she'd already broken one promise, so what was another?

Last night with Jax had left her confused and scared and she desperately needed advice. That meant admitting to her two best friends that she'd lied in the first place.

How had everything spiraled so far out of control? It was a question she'd been asking herself all night long. Her feelings and the situation were like aa freight train that had jumped the tracks and was headed for a brick wall—and she was terrified of the impact.

She hadn't slept a wink since he'd dropped her off at her place last night, delivering a sweet kiss under the porch light. There wasn't anyone around and it wasn't for show. It was just for them. Like their time in his bedroom.

"This had better be good." Kat said, walking into the mudroom. She was still in her pajamas, her hair was standing on end, and she had sheet prints on her cheek. She also had the bloodshot eyes of someone who'd had too much wine and barely lived to tell the tale.

"Sorry I woke you up so early," Milly said.

"That's okay. It just meant that I got the best pick of the doughnuts." In comparison, Gemma looked as if she'd welcomed the sun with a rejuvenating round of yoga, and singing birds had picked out her clothes. Her choppy hair was effortlessly styled, her makeup flawless, and her outfit bohemian chic.

"Are those from Just Holes?" Milly asked, her mouth already watering.

"They're the only reason you're still alive," Kat grumbled.

Her friends walked into the family room and looked at the nearly empty floor and froze. "You've made some serious headway," Gemma said.

That's what happened when one needed a distraction. They went through their dead sister's things until the wee hours of the morning. But instead of feeling as if she were losing Zoe with every box she put in the Give Pile, she felt closer to her.

"It was time," she said simply. Just like it was time to let go of the heartache of the past and, instead, embrace the wonderful memories every item inspired.

"Then it's okay that you woke me up before Tiny Dancer nibbled my toes to go out."

"Don't mind her," Gemma said, leading the way into the kitchen. "She's just mad that Ranger Tight-ass offered to drive her home."

"He didn't offer, he dictated. Because that's how his kind are, they dictate as if they're the authority on all things."

"I thought it was sweet," Gemma said, setting the pastry box on the table and taking her seat.

Kat yanked out the chair and plopped down, pulling her knees to her chest so that her feet were resting on her chair. "It was high-handed, and had I not been drunk in thirty degree temps and the closest Uber was ten minutes out, I would have told him where to stick his tight ass."

"You did tell him that," Gemma said. "In fact, you told him in front of the entire party."

"Good. Then everyone will know the truth about him." Kat picked up a doughnut hole and popped it in her mouth. "Mmm. So good." She took another, quickly inhaling the whole thing. After moaning in ecstasy, she opened her eyes. "Why aren't you double fisting some jelly-filled holes?" When Milly didn't answer, Kat asked, "Is this about you disappearing into Jax's bedroom to have sex during his mom's party, because don't think your disappearance went unnoticed. When you guys never came back down, your mom and Peggy started talking baby names."

"This whole thing has spiraled out of control," she admitted out loud for the first time.

"You mean you shagging the town's bad boy?" Kat asked, going in for her forth doughnut hole.

"We weren't shagging last night." Not technically. Besides friction, nothing else was used. And she'd orgasmed. So hard she could still feel the aftershocks. "In fact, we aren't shagging at all."

"Wait, what?" Gemma asked.

Milly dropped her head to her chest, hiding behind the curtain of hair when she admitted, "We aren't even really dating." When no one said a word, Milly peeked a look. Both friends sat there open-mouthed. "We made the whole thing up."

Gemma lifted her hands up and let them fall to her sides. "I told you," she said to Kat. "I told you something was off."

"I don't believe you," Kat stated firmly. "There is so much chemistry the air crackles."

A bead of sweat dripped down Milly's back. "Chemistry isn't our problem."

"What is the problem then?" Gemma asked.

"It all started the morning after our one-night stand."

"Where you did shag?" Kat asked, and Gemma shot her a look. "What? Just clarifying."

"Where we did shag," she said. "My parents barged in on us. I was in nothing but his shirt and Jax was in his nothing but his jeans, unzipped low enough to show he hadn't bothered to put on any underwear. My dad freaked, my mom looked worried, and Jax looked like the perfect knight in shining armor. Then my dad gave me *the* look."

"I know that look," Kat said. "I only saw it once, freshman year, when he caught Zoe and me drunk, and that was enough to last a lifetime." She looked at Gemma. "Since you've never done anything remotely fun in your life, let me explain it to you. It's the 'You did something rash and irresponsible, and I am so disappointed in you' look."

"Then you get it," Milly said. "One Howard brow raise, and it just came tumbling out that we were dating. But the worst part is I introduced him as Lucas."

"Ho-ly shit," Kat said.

Gemma's response was a disappointed shake of the head. "How did Jax feel about that?"

"He was hurt and pissed, and I don't blame him. How could I sleep with the wrong twin?"

"We saw him at the bar, too, remember. I totally thought it was Lucas. We all did. I mean he was wearing loafers," Kat said.

"That's what I said!"

"So your crush on Lucas is—?"

"Completely gone." After talking to Lucas again last night, with his even demeanor and CEO energy, Milly didn't get a single zing. But when she kissed Jax she had all the feels. Too many feels. She looked at Gemma who had yet to say more than a few words. "What are you thinking?"

"That you lied to us," Gemma said, and the hurt in her voice made Milly's heart sink. Gemma had a long history of people lying to her. Her parents, her ex-husband, even her other friends who said they'd stick with her through the hard times after she lost her baby. Milly had become just another person in Gemma's life to bring her hurt.

"I know and I am so sorry," she whispered. "I never should have lied. I was going to tell you the whole story, but then Jax showed up on my doorstep and gave me a proposition. If I helped him with, well I don't want to break his confidence, but he needed help with his family, and I needed help with mine and it just seemed easier to keep the charade going than to tell everyone the truth."

"I'm not judging you," Kat said. "But Gemma is right, we're not everyone. You could have told us."

"I didn't know how without breaking my word to Jax. I made a promise to keep it a secret."

"Why are you breaking that promise now?" Gemma asked. "Unless the ... I don't even know what to call it."

"A relationship." No matter what was happening between her and Jax, it was a relationship. That she knew. "It might be only friendship on his side, but it's a relationship."

"And what is it on your side?" Kat asked quietly.

"I'm pretty sure it's a tiny crush," Milly said, and Gemma lifted a challenging brow. "Maybe more than a little crush." Milly rubbed her eyes under her glasses. "I am in so much trouble. He's here for another two weeks and how am I going to last that long without my clothes falling off again?"

"Then let them! Take the polar plunge into dating. Maybe it will jar you out of this funk and put a smile back on your face," Kat said around doughnut crumbs.

"Yeah, what's so wrong with enjoying every single second until he leaves?" Gemma added.

Milly closed her eyes with resignation. She'd already crossed the line and she didn't see a way back. "Because I think I'm falling for him."

She didn't think. She knew. And damn if that wasn't breaking another promise.

Chapter Eighteen

Take Life by the Balls
Fight for what matters.

Between training and helping with the Sierra Vista Cup, Jax had barely more than a few moments to himself. But he found himself wanting to spend those moments with Milly. Only she wasn't there.

She'd spent the first part of the week with her parents and worked from home yesterday to see them off. At least that's what she claimed. But Jax knew the truth.

The other night had spooked her.

Hell, it had spooked him too. Or so he thought. But the more days that passed without seeing her, the deeper this strange emptiness in his chest grew.

Thursday morning couldn't come fast enough. But when he got there, instead of seeing Milly at her desk, he found Peggy and Kent in the conference room, with the kids gathered around for the weekly board meeting.

Dropping his computer bag off in his office, he joined everyone. He glanced at the big pink box in the middle of the table and froze. When controversy was imminent, Kent used sugar to sweeten the blow.

"So it's a chocolate sprinkles kind of meeting?" Jax asked.

"There's a jelly-filled in there as well," Harris said with a smile.

"Will you two stop," Peggy said. "Your dad just thought it would be nice to bring along breakfast. Now, grab one and take a seat. We're just waiting on Brynn."

Jax took his designated chair, noting how tired Lucas looked. His shirt was wrinkled, his tie loose, his eyes bloodshot, his hair mussed. His starched and polished demeanor was seriously lacking today.

"You look like shit," Jax said in a *You okay* tone.

"Thanks for the commentary," Lucas said.

"Well, either you're wearing yesterday's clothes because you got laid or because you spent the night in your office. And since your screw-you factor is coming in at an impressive twelve, I'd go with the latter," he said in a tone low enough that only his brother could hear.

"I spent the night organizing some of the financials for the due diligence. Matrix Resorts wants it by May, which gives me a little more than three months to get my shit together."

Which gave Jax three months to figure out a plan that accommodated everyone. He knew there was a solution. It was right there, just out of reach. But the more invested he became in the Sierra Vista Cup, the more invested he became in the lodge and its future.

"How much work are we talking?" Jax asked.

"A deal this size? Four hundred pages of financials, ledgers—current and historic—operational contracts, supply contracts, property surveys, employment records … "

Four hundred pages of things Jax knew nothing about. His communication skills were best suited for social settings. If Jax believed in something, he could sell it to anyone. It was how he managed to land so many sponsors so early on in his career. He didn't do analytics and minute details, Jax did things big and loud.

Lucas, on the other hand, worked silent wonders with spreadsheets and presentations. He was a man who controlled his world with confidence and great authority. Right then, he looked like he'd gone to battle with Ares and lost.

Jax could feel Lucas's quiet defeat as if it were his own and that cut all the way to Jax's soul. He hated to see his brother struggle like this.

"How can I help?" Jax asked, and Lucas did a double take. "I know that most of what you're dealing with would be Greek to me and I type like shit, but I'm a great sounding board and a fast learner."

Before Lucas could answer, Brynn strode into the room. Dressed in her National Guard jumper, combat boots, and a slicked back bun, she looked like a bad-ass helicopter medic.

"Hey, fam." She gave a salute and then reached for a dough-nut. Right before she could grab one, Harris pulled the box to the center of the table, making it impossible for the pint-sized paramedic to get her sugar fix. "You remember I was the top of my class in hand-to-hand combat?"

Harris grabbed the last jelly-filled, Brynn's favorite, and took a giant bite, scarfing down a third of the pastry.

"Harris, stop teasing your sister," Peggy scolded.

With a smirk, Harris set the doughnut back in the box and slid it across the table. "It's all yours, sis."

Brynn defiantly picked up the doughnut and shoved the entire thing in her mouth, then gave a jelly-coated smile. Around bits of pastry, Brynn asked, "What did I miss?"

"Nothing," Kent said. "We were just getting started." Peggy and Kent shared a look that had unease winding through Jax's chest.

Peggy rested her hand over her heart and gave a watery smile. "We wanted to start off by saying all your help with the Cup hasn't gone unnoticed."

"Oh boy," Jax said. "This is sounding like a double-fister kind of talk."

"Is this because you still don't get the whole birds and bees talk?" Harris asked, looking right at Jax, and the rest of his siblings broke off into laughter. Even Lucas cracked a slight smile.

Peggy silenced them with a single clearing of her throat. "Now, where was I? Oh yes, I was talking about how sweet and considerate my children were. But really, watching all you kids work together has warmed our hearts. It brings me right back to when you were all still living in my nest, with family ski days, snow-castle contests, arguing over who gets to work the ski lift." She eyed them all. "And don't think I didn't know that was to talk to the girls."

Harris waggled a brow. "Being the oldest has its perks."

Jax might use his charm to get the women, but Harris's game was on a whole other level. Or it was, until he became a single dad and went from being the town's biggest playboy to the neighborhood's greatest playdate organizer.

"Your father and I have been reconsidering the sale of the lodge."

Brynn's face split into a smile. "You're not going to sell." She collapsed back into her chair and exhaled loudly. "Thank god! I knew that in the end you guys couldn't go through with it."

"We're still retiring," Kent said with finality.

Brynn threw up her hands in a fit. "But you just said you were reconsidering selling. I should have known when I saw the jelly-filled."

"I said we were talking *about* the lodge, not that we'd changed our minds about retiring. Your dad and I are ready to enjoy our golden years. We want to travel and explore and wake up in the morning to the sound of waves crashing on the shore-line. But we also want to respect your feelings on the possibility of a sale." Peggy and Kent shared a giddy smile that was full of secrets and excitement. "Which is why we've come up with an alternate option."

Shit.

Jax knew what was coming and he wasn't ready to take the hit. He hadn't had a chance to talk to Lucas about his conversation with Peggy.

"We've been thinking about what you all said when we told you about the offer, and it breaks my heart," Peggy said, her voice cracking. "We don't want to disappoint you kids, but one by one you left the nest until it was empty. Now you're all grown up and settled into your own lives." Kent rested a supportive hand on Peggy's shoulder. "It's time your dad and I left the nest too."

"Mom," Nolan said, her voice rough. "Don't cry. We get it. We don't like it, but we get it. You gave up so much to give us the best childhood, and now it's time to give yourself the best kind of retirement."

"Which we intend to do," Kent said. "But it was pointed out to me the other night that just because we're ready to fly the coop, doesn't mean that you all are ready. Your mom and I are excited for the next chapter, but that doesn't mean that you kids should be forced to turn the page."

Peggy pushed a button on the remote and a PowerPoint presentation flickered to life on the screen behind Kent. The title page read SIERRA VISTA FAMILY LODGE IS ABOUT FAMILY.

Maybe it was the look on Jax's face or the fact that they were twins but Lucas knew he was behind the change of direction. Lucas shot Jax a look so furious it nearly fried his nuts. "I was going to tell—*ow!*"

Lucas knocked Jax's knee with his own—hard. Jax knocked back.

"We have a proposition." The next slide resembled the opening credits for *The Brady Bunch* with a photo of each of the kids and Peggy and Kent, the final space taken by Emma. "Instead of selling to Matrix Resorts, what if you kids took over?"

Surprised and stunned looks flashed around the table. It was like a game of *Holy Shit* Simon Says. Except for Jax's face; his was feeling warm because Kent was looking right at him with those proud papa eyes and Jax could feel the disappointment and anger and betrayal rolling off his brother in waves.

"Mom," Nolan said. "None of us can afford to buy you guys out. Not even gold medalist over there."

"You wouldn't have to buy us out. It would be more of a passing of the baton, where our generation hands over the reins to the new generation. Just like how your grandparents handed Sierra Vista down to us," Kent said, and flipped to the next slide. It had the number of shares broken down equally between the seven of them.

"Are you happy?" Lucas snapped under his breath, but Jax was too stunned to speak.

He knew he had a board seat and maybe a few shares, but to own nearly one-seventh of the lodge was too much to take in. He didn't deserve one-seventh of anything. The Carmichaels had already given him the world.

"Peggy," Jax said. "When I mentioned letting us kids take over, I never meant to imply that I should receive an equal share. This isn't my heritage, it's theirs." Jax pointed to his siblings around the table, including Lucas. Lucas might not be blood, but all the work he'd done meant he deserved everything coming his way.

Peggy reached across the table and laid her hand on Jax's. "You are one of us, sweetie. And I'm going to keep reminding you until it sinks into that thick skull of yours."

Kent continued, "Now, this is a big decision—"

"Whatever it is, I'm in," Brynn said.

"Slow down, sweetie. This is a big decision and big thing for all of you to take on. Running this lodge will take all of you. And not just rallying when there's an event, but helping manage the lodge year-round," Peggy said.

"We don't expect you to give up your careers for this, but it will take a lot of sacrifice on your part," Kent added.

"I'm in," Brynn repeated. "I've got a year left in the National Guard and then I'm going into the reserves. I can help with ski patrol and search and rescue. Plus, I've always dreamed that I'd run a helicopter sightseeing company that works out of the lodge."

"My job isn't as flexible," Nolan said. "But I can moonlight at the lodge, overseeing security."

"I can hire a good crew and top-notch general contractor to handle all the maintenance on the lodge," Harris said.

Peggy clasped her hands, her eyes brimming with pride.

"I know I'm gone, a lot," Jax said. "But I also know I can bring in sponsors and donors, even find and train a new business development person to handle all the accounts. Work with legal, make sure everything gets buttoned up."

He knew that it was going to be hard juggling his life, but he'd have time in the off season. He just had to get through the next few months, then come spring he could really focus on growing the lodge's brand. Plus, he wasn't a spring chicken anymore; his knees told him that every morning when he climbed out of bed.

"I hate to admit it, but my competition seasons are numbered and when things come to an end—and they will—it would be great to have something like the lodge to come home to."

Something to grow with his siblings. Something to be a part of.

"Of course you do, sweetie," Peggy said.

All eyes turned to Lucas, waiting for him to say that he was going to captain this ship. And Jax saw the complacency in his eyes, knew he was going to agree to something he really didn't want to agree to.

Before Lucas could open his mouth, Jax jumped in. "And just like I'll need someone to help me, I think we should hire a new president, Kent," he said. "With you being in Santa Barbara, Lucas will need someone to manage the details so Lucas can steer the direction of the company. Or we can hire someone as CEO so Lucas can—"

Lucas abruptly stood and gripped Jax's arms, practically dragging him to his feet. "Can I see you for a moment outside?"

Once outside, Lucas slammed the conference room door and spun to face Jax.

"What the hell, man?" Lucas shouted, his jaw tight as he fisted his right hand. "You went behind my back?"

"I didn't go behind your back. Just because you didn't think it was a good solution doesn't mean that it isn't. In fact, everyone in there seems to think it's a pretty fucking great idea."

"An idea that only works if I stay on as CEO."

"I see you still have the whole-world-on-my-shoulders complex. Jesus, I should start calling you Atlas."

"And I see you're still a self-centered asshole, *bro*," he said as if he'd expected Jax to drop the idea just because Brother Knows Best didn't approve.

"You want out, okay, then here's your chance," Jax said. "You said your heart isn't in this anymore. I call bullshit, but you're too stubborn to recognize I'm right. But here's the thing, the hearts of everyone else in that room is in this, *bro*. We don't need you standing guard like Superman coming to our rescue. Lose the cape and just be Clark Kent. Sell some of your shares and give AvalancheEx another go."

Lucas narrowed his eyes. "Just like that. Just up and tell the man who took me under his wing, took me into his family, taught me everything I know, and told me I was as much his son as Harris and Nolan, that I'm out?"

"You were out when they wanted to sell. What's the difference?"

"The difference is that everyone is staying, and I'd be leaving."

And that was the crux of the problem. Lucas was so afraid of being like their parents that he'd rather stay in a shitty situation and make do than let someone down.

"Everyone has to run away from home at some point. Maybe it's your time."

"That's more your style," Lucas said.

Jax didn't question his anger. He loved their mom in the same perverse way Jax did. It was this twisted power struggle their parents held over them. Both abandoning their sons in their own unique way. But the pain was the same.

"You're pissed when I leave. Pissed when I come home. What the hell do you want?"

"You to be straight with me."

"You?" Jax shot back. "You want *me*? To be straight with *you*?"

"I screwed up, let it go," Lucas said, and Jax noticed he was missing the *sorry* part of the apology. "And why the hell didn't you tell me you talked with Peggy and Kent? Instead, I was blindsided in front of everyone. So much for having my back."

"Feels like shit, doesn't it?" The second the words left his mouth he regretted them. Lucas's entire demeanor changed. He went low, sinking into his stance like preparing for a row. His jaw was so clenched, one flick and it would shatter. "Are you serio—?"

That was all Jax got out before Lucas's fist plowed into his face, knocking the words back into his throat—and kicking Jax back several steps. It wasn't quite a stars-and-ringing-bells kind of punch but it hurt like hell.

"Shit." Jax probed his face for broken bones, then cracked his neck from side to side. He could taste blood, telling him he had a split lip which would likely swell to the size of a jawbreaker by nightfall.

Lucas looked damn proud of himself, shifting his weight side to side, stupid-ass grin on his smug face.

"How does being blindsided feel, prick?" Lucas spat.

Jax took a step forward and let his fist fly, catching Lucas right in the nose that he always held so high in the air. The nose he used to root around in Jax's private life and complicate shit. The nose that thought his shit didn't stink.

On contact there was a loud crunch, followed by a sharp pain in Jax's knuckles. Jesus, his brother had a hard head.

"I think you broke it." Lucas wiped his nose with the back of his hand, staining his shirt sleeve in the process.

"It's not broken. It's a little owie. Do you need a Band-Aid?"

Lucas lowered his shoulder and rammed Jax backward until he hit the wall with a thud. Lucas was going for a jab to the ribs when someone demanded to know, "What is going on?"

Jax shoved Lucas off him and both men stared each other down for a brief moment. So much was being said in those few seconds before they broke eye contact.

Jax looked behind Lucas to find Milly looking exactly like his life preserver in a tumultuous sea crashing against the cliffs of rage and regret. What the hell had happened? He and Lucas didn't fight. Ever. Oh, they'd been in fights, but it was always them against the world. Even when one or the other wasn't necessarily down for the cause. But that was how they worked—in tandem. Well, they used to.

Now, they were both circling around each other, waiting for the other to pounce.

"Oh my god, are you okay?" she asked, looking at Lucas and, well, shit that hurt. He watched her walk up to his brother—and right past him—coming to stand in front of Jax.

She was dressed in fitted jeans that were distressed around each one of her curves, a bright-blue, soft-looking sweater that fell off one shoulder, exposing a tiny black strap that made him wonder what lacy thing she had on beneath. Her eyes were wide with concern.

She reached out and gently ran a finger over his split lip and he barely resisted the urge to groan. Damn, Lucas knew how to throw a sucker punch. He had three choices:

1. Play it up and maybe get some loving out of it—*total dick move.*
2. Brush it off—*his normal MO.*
3. Hit Lucas again—*his fists were on board.*

Jax went for the first and Lucas knew what he was going to do before he even made a move, because his brother rolled his eyes.

Jax cupped Milly's hand and held her finger against his lips and then kissed it. And, damn, if it had zero to do with proving their relationship was legit.

"I'll be okay," Jax said, kissing another finger. Then another.

She turned to Lucas, but not before taking Jax's hand in solidarity. "Are you okay?" she asked his brother.

"Never been better," Lucas said, then shot Jax a *To be continued* glare. "Next time you ask to come onto my island, remind me to shoot a hole in your boat."

Chapter Nineteen

Take Life by the Balls
Dream under the stars.

"What are we doing?" Milly asked Jax, feeling as if she were on unsure footing.

"We are having another adventure," he said. "Now stop fidgeting."

"If I could just see where you're taking me." She reached up to her eyes and he took her hand, dropping it back down to her side.

"The blindfold stays on."

"Is that really necessary?"

"All great nights start with a blindfold. Wouldn't you say?"

The night had started out great indeed. Jax had called her out of the blue and told her he had a surprise in mind and to dress warm. There was a blizzard moving in from the east, white-out conditions were expected. Mother Nature was flexing her muscles, cracking one knuckle at a time.

Milly had taken more care than she'd like to admit in picking out her outfit. After a few costume changes she'd settled on her favorite pair of jeans—the ones that made her butt look like J.Lo's—a light gray sweater that had a deep scoop neckline, and knee-high leather boots that were definitely more fashion that

function. She topped it off with a bright green and white scarf
and just enough makeup to make it look like she hadn't spent a
half hour on it—which she had.

She'd chosen to wear her hair down and natural, light waves
spilling over one shoulder. Her neck on display.

Since people were encouraged to stay indoors and ride out
the storm, she hadn't a clue as to what he had planned. But when
he'd walked her through the lobby of the lodge a few of the
employees gave them a curious glance. Then they'd arrived, at
what she assumed was his room, and he'd tied on the blindfold.

"I'd say a blindfold in public makes a different statement
than one in front of a hotel room door."

"A suite," he amended.

"Are the events of the evening on the approved list?"

"Why?" he whispered, his breath grazing her neck. Her
insides turned over in response. "You worried you won't be able
to keep your tongue off me?"

Yes. Yes, she was. Not that she'd let him know that. Milly
was already in serious danger of getting too involved with a man
whose life was spent chasing the next storm. And her life had
been uprooted by enough storms. But when she was with him,
like this, it felt as if they were in the eye together, with the world
clashing around them.

And that was a scary place to be.

"I think I can resist," she lied.

This time when he spoke, his lips grazed the outer shell of
her ear. "Then why are you scratching your wrist?"

Damn him! She *was* scratching. Irritated, she stuffed her
hands into her front pockets. She could almost hear his amused
smile.

"Shall we get on with the show?" she asked primly.

His hands settled on her hips and the very air around them
seemed electrified. "I have a ladies first rule." Steadying her

against his front, he walked them through the doorway and inside. She barely heard the lock engage over the pounding of her heart.

He guided her deeper into the room. She could smell the scent of pine, feel the warm glow of a lit fireplace, and taste the hunger that was stirring in the depths of her being.

"Ready?" he asked, and before she could ask "Ready for what?" he was removing the blindfold.

There was no bright light blurring her vision, no crowd of people waiting to surprise her. In fact, the only thing that lit the room was a roaring fire in the hearth and, what seemed like, a million fairy lights twinkling overhead.

On the floor were two sleeping bags, side by side, and in front of the fireplace was a flannel blanket set out like a picnic with all the ingredients for hot dogs and s'mores. In the middle sat a cooler filled with beer and soda.

"What is this?" she asked.

"This is you and I camping beneath the stars."

She turned in his arms. "You did this for me?"

He looked at her strangely. "I promised you I'd help you complete as many adventures as possible and this was one of the things you and Zoe talked about." It was said as if it were a foregone conclusion that he'd go so far out of his way to create this special moment for her. "I know it isn't in the great outdoors, but camping in single-digit temps isn't all that it's cracked up to be. No matter what those sub-zero sleeping bags would have you think."

"It's perfect." She went up on her toes and gave him a gentle kiss to the side of his lip that was still a bit swollen. "And sweet."

"Sweet?" He made a face. "Don't let the guys overhear you or they'll start calling me Princess."

He was trying to play off the whole thing as nothing more than rolling out a couple of sleeping bags, but she knew better. He'd put thought and imagination behind this.

"So what's the itinerary?"

He chuckled. "That's the point of camping. No schedules, no plans, just an itinerary-free night that we play by ear. We'll roast some hot dogs, make s'mores, drink a few beers, and play a game or two of Jenga Roulette."

"What's Jenga Roulette?"

"It's like regular Jenga, only on the bottom of certain blocks there are questions that you must answer honestly. If not, you lose a piece of clothing."

"I'm guessing you don't play this with your family."

"Actually, we do. I just added the piece about losing your clothes."

"You have me held captive, under the stars, with chocolate and beer. The clothes stay on, Prince Charming."

"My favorite sex position?" Milly asked, and Jax schooled his features. "Somehow I doubt that Peggy and Kent would approve."

"I may have added a few new questions." He leaned in until she could smell the scent of smoky pine on his clothes. "Creative license and all."

Oh, she remembered just how creative he could be, which was not helping her resolve this ridiculous crush. Because that's all it was, she'd decided, a simple crush that happened when two people had earth-scorching sex. But his thoughtful surprise was making it hard to keep things in check.

They'd had a fun campout fondue, using only their hands and long metal skewers. They'd talked about work for a little and he'd adopted this shy boyishness when he told her about the two new sponsors he'd brought on board. When she'd mentioned the fight between him and Lucas, he'd deflected and pulled out the Jenga game.

She'd volunteered to go first, selecting a block from the middle, rolling her eyes when she read the Sharpied words on the bottom.

"I think you already know my favorite sex position," she said.

"I do, but I want to hear you say it. That's the rules of the game. And we both know how much you like rules."

"I think you're making up the rules as we go along," she said, and his charming-as-hell grin told her he was. "Okay, fine, my favorite position is doggy style." She placed the block back on top. "Your turn."

He pulled one out from the bottom and flipped it over. It was blank.

"Wait, where's the question?" she asked.

"Not all the blocks have them."

She narrowed her eyes. "Does that mean I get to make one up?"

"Just remember, this is a tit-for-tat kind of agreement."

"So I can ask you anything?"

"Anything. But it goes both ways."

Where did she even start? She had so many questions she wanted answers to. Including why he was so afraid of commitment. He had all the qualities that would make the perfect partner, but he was always holding something back, and that scared her as much as it drew her to him.

"What are you best at in bed?" she asked, and he tilted a knowing brow. "I want to hear you say it."

"It involves my tongue and my head between your thighs," he said, and a quiver ran the entire course of her body.

As if they were discussing the weather, he set the block on top. "Your turn."

Milly took a block out of the bottom of the stack, which was harder than anticipated because her hands were slightly shaking.

She flipped it over and let out a breath. Blank. She wasn't sure what was more nerve-racking, a predetermined question or a spontaneous one.

"Regretting your addendum to the rules?"

"No." Her hand was halfway to her wrist when she pulled it back. He chuckled. "Fire away."

He took a swig of his beer, then rested back on his palms, his upper body facing Milly. "What turns you on?"

He wanted honesty, so she went with honest. "Your tongue and your head between my thighs."

All of his easygoing, nothing-gets-to-me façade crumbled beneath the heat building between them. His gaze dipped to the V of her legs and held, so long she felt her thong go damp.

She picked a random block from the top and didn't bother to turn it over. She knew what she was going to ask.

"What's your favorite place to be massaged?" she asked, her breath coming in short puffs. And, *would you look at that*, she had shifted so close their knees were touching.

He laughed softly and the sound flickered down her belly on a direct course for the Southernmost Parts of Milly. He had this ease about him, a superpower. He could make her feel completely aroused and little off-balance.

"I could show you, but it requires the use of your tongue," he said, drawing a shudder from her.

Unable to sort through the onslaught of emotions—yearning, desire, the need to make this a full-on under-the-stars experience, she rose up on her knees and said, "I bet I can just use my mouth. No tongue required."

"Angel," he groaned, and she knew his reserve was crumbling, which should have had her running scared, but it turned her on.

Assuming the whole *Dirty Dancing* crawling-across-the-room position, she made her way across the blanket, not stopping until her hands were on either side of his thighs. She brought her mouth a hair from his, "Is it a bet?"

He hadn't budged from his position, still leaning back on his palms, legs crossed, shoulders bulging under his weight. So while they were chasing each other's breath they weren't touching at all—and it was erotic as hell.

"If I win the bet," he said, skating his mouth down her throat, "I get five minutes of my tongue on your body."

"Fair is fair."

She'd barely gotten the words out of her mouth when Jax's descended on hers. He sucked her lower lip, careful not to use his tongue, she noticed. She gasped and would have fallen into his strong body had he not lifted her onto his lap. A hand gripping each thigh, he scooted her snuggly against him, running his palms down her legs, then locking her ankles behind his back.

"How am I supposed to massage your favorite part from this position?"

"I thought we'd work up to it." He wrapped his fist around her hair and gave a sharp tug, groaning when her neck was visible. He didn't waste any time, burying his face and teeth into the gentle slope where the neck meets the shoulder. He stayed there for a long moment, nuzzling and breathing her in. "Your scent alone makes me hard."

"No verbal foreplay, remember?"

"So then I won't mention that I am so hard for you I'm afraid the second you take me into your mouth I'll blow."

Milly had never been all that into dirty talk, but Jax was a masterclass dirty talker—and she liked.

"I think I'm the one who's going to be doing the blowing." She reached between them and found the button of his jeans. She could feel the strain on the zipper, his erection pushing to be released. And she was going to release it—in more ways than one.

Fusing their mouths together, he delivered a kiss that blew her socks off. Slow and sensual, taking his sweet time to drive her out of her mind. It was so easy to get lost in what he was offering—easy, casual, temporary, no strings, and no stress. With her body wrapped around him the way it was, she felt feminine, powerful, desirable.

A single *pop* of the button later and his jeans were unzipped. She tugged at the hem of his shirt and yanked it over his head. She let out a throaty moan. Memory hadn't done his chest justice. The man was chiseled, his athletically honed body was one for the records book.

"Mmm." She started at his shoulders, sculpting around them before sliding slowly down his pecs to his abs, taking in each and every one of his six pack. When she reached his waistband, she slid her hand beneath the soft cotton and down his smooth length.

"Angel," he whispered, his head dropping all the way back. And, *man*, did she love it when he called her that, all throaty and rough, like sandblasted concrete.

She gave a stroke from base to tip, tightening her grip on the ascent and getting a little creative at the bottom. Quickly, she found a rhythm that had him pushing into her hand.

But then he held her hand still.

"Are we stopping?' she asked.

"We're taking a moment to think this through," he said quietly. "Once these pants come off, we both know what's going to follow. And I made you a promise that there would be no sex between us. And I take my promises, especially to you, very seriously."

Jax might be giving off more boyfriend vibes that her ex. But his bachelor status was, to her knowledge, still firmly in place.

"I know, which is why I'm rescinding the no-sex rule." She reached for him again, and again he stopped her.

He tipped his head so that he was looking her in the eyes and cupped her cheek. "This wasn't why I brought you here tonight."

"I know. It makes me want you even more," she said. "I want you, Jax. I want *you.*"

"Then I promise to break every rule," he said, as if she'd freed a stallion from its pen. Jax kissed her with a heat comparable to the surface of the sun.

Chapter Twenty

Take Life by the Balls
Never shy away from a challenge.

*J*ax was going to make up rules just so he could break them. Now, it was about deciding where to start. Well, she was straddling him with her hand down his pants, and her tits were right there for the taking. And he couldn't wait to hold them, lick them, suck them into his mouth until she was rubbing up against him.

"Lose the sweater," he said gruffly.

Her answer was to lift her hands in invitation, which was sexy as hell. Always one to pull his weight, Jax slid his palms under her shirt and up her sides, his thumbs spanning around her front so that he grazed her nipples on the way.

He tossed her shirt on the floor and, *holy mother of God,* they were even more magnificent than he remembered. A perfect handful of wet dreams hiding behind black lace that was so sheer, her nipples were playing a game of hide-and-seek and his dick wanted in.

Not wasting any time, he went right for the goal, sucking her through the fabric of her bra until she was hard and tight, then bit down gently.

"That feels good," she said.

"I was aiming for mind-blowing." This time he bit down a little harder and she arched her back, pushing into his mouth.

"Speaking of blowing...I know exactly where to start."

She tiptoed her fingers from his navel to her neck, then placed two hands on his chest and shoved him backward onto the sleeping bag. She slid her way down his thighs, taking his jeans and boxer briefs with her. She stopped at his knees, using his clothes as restraints so he couldn't move his legs.

He was about to protest when she leaned forward and took him in her mouth. No warning, no buildup, just covered him from tip to base and that sweet mouth was so hot he nearly came then and there.

"Hell, angel," he gasped, his lids closing.

"You might want to open your eyes, or you'll miss how I get you off without using my tongue." His eyes flew open and he found her looking up at him and she covered him again. And again. Her mouth doing some kind of magical pass that had his balls tightening.

If he were able to think straight, he'd notice that while she was using her mouth, her tongue hadn't come into play.

She looked up at him through her lashes, and he could tell she was very proud of herself. His little hall monitor loved that she was breaking the rules without actually breaking the rules. He loved her creativity. Hell, if she got any more creative, he might not get out of the room alive.

He let her do one more pass, he couldn't help himself, then he cradled her face. "One more and I'm out of commission for at least ten minutes and when I come, I want to do it with you screaming my name."

"I can scream your name now, if you want?" She tilted her head to, well, take his head in her smart little mouth, when he stopped her.

"I want to be inside of you." Even as he said it, his erection jumped as if reaching for her. "With my hands all over you, caressing every single inch of skin, while my mouth takes yours. And there *will* be tongue involved."

"That's a big order."

"I'm a big man," he said, and she laughed.

It was the most beautiful thing he'd ever heard. It was spontaneous and real and erased every ounce of sadness he'd witnessed in her eyes over the past few weeks. She looked happy and free—and he'd done that. A strange tightness tugged at his chest, but he ignored it.

"So I've seen." She licked her lips, then stood. In a flash her bra was on the floor and she was peeling her jeans—which put her ass on glorious display—down her legs. His breath caught. She looked beautiful. The fire cast a warm glow around her body, almost creating a tempting silhouette as her hair hung in light waves down her swollen breasts. The twinkle lights above reflected in her eyes, making them sparkle.

She combed her fingers through her hair and, producing a hairband from nowhere, she tied her waves into a high ponytail that was begging to be pulled. Jax's lungs refused to take in oxygen.

Whereas that first night she'd been somewhat shy about him watching her, tonight she stood there letting him look his fill. He inventoried every curve and dip, then crooked his finger at her.

With a smile that scrambled his mind, she strode toward him. And when he said strode, he meant strutted, those full hips moving from side to side, her shoulders back so her breasts jutted out, not an ounce of that shy girl he'd met on the slopes.

Nope, Milly Smartt had come to life and it was magnificent.

Just when Jax thought it couldn't get any hotter, Milly turned around. Looking over her shoulder, with eyes locked on him, she went down on her knees. She placed her palms flat on the floor and pushed that glorious ass backward.

Damn.

"I figured we'd try my favorite position, then yours." She scooped her ponytail to one side so it fell like a rope, exposing her neck. "Unless you want to go first?"

Before she could move, Jax had grabbed a condom out of his back pocket, finished shedding his pants and was behind her, curving his body around hers. And while all he wanted to do was bury himself inside of her, he took his time.

"First things first." Leaving her on her knees, he guided her up until she was kneeling in front of him. Wrapping one hand around her hair, he tugged her head to the side and placed open-mouthed kisses all the way down the column of her neck. His other hand slid down the middle of her torso, between her tits, down her smooth stomach, and between her legs.

"You're already wet for me," he growled.

"It seems to be a constant state of being when I'm around you."

With a grunt of approval, he sunk his finger in, first one, then two. Her head fell back against his shoulder, and he tugged her hair to maintain access, which she willingly gave. Then he was surrounded by her floral scent, her silky curves, and the softness that could only be described as feminine.

He moved his fingers in and out, loving how her hips pressed into his hand, her ass pressed back against his erection. The image she created was so sexy he could get off just like this.

Moving his thumb, he found her pleasure button and pressed down hard, then made soothing circular motions. She let out this sexy little sound, so he did it again.

He could feel her tighten around his fingers, coiling and soaking him. His thumb pushed harder, then feather soft, bringing her right to the edge and then backing off. He paid attention to her as she moved, when she moaned, cataloging every little thing she liked, and what she loved.

And she was loving on his hand as if it were hers to conquer. Her head rolled languorously toward him, and she tilted her chin up. "Kiss me," she said, and he wasted no time taking her mouth with his. And there was nothing languorous about it. It was raw and hungry and when she parted her lips, he moaned a sigh of rightness.

He took a moment to breathe her in. She tasted like s'mores and sex and felt like heaven.

She was there, desperate for release, so he picked up the pace, going deeper until he hit the right spot and just like that, she flew apart around him. Her body trembled with her release and her hips jerked back against him, and he was lost.

Before she could catch a breath, he grabbed the condom and was wrapped and sliding home. She let out a gasp of surprise and the pressure pushed her forward. She caught herself with her hands, using the floor for support.

Jax wrapped fingers around her hips, pressing forward and into her. In that position he was able to go even deeper than before. When he hit full hilt, she cried out his name.

He pulled out and slid back in, repeating the motion until they found a slick, unhurried rhythm that set his body on fire. Slow withdrawal and even harder penetrations, with her pushing back every time he jutted forward.

"Harder," she said. "I want... it... harder." Her voice escalated with every word, the last damn near rattling the windows. Which only drove him higher.

And so he did. She had to drop to her elbows to support herself, and he could hear her tits moving with their rhythm. The sound and the traction was so right, so perfect, he felt himself getting closer and closer.

"Jax, I'm going to—"

She didn't even get the last word out before she detonated. He could feel every one of her shudders around him. The pressure built until it needed to release, and he popped, screaming her name and pumping into her until he could barely move.

Before he collapsed, he rolled to his side, taking Milly with him so that they were spooning. After some long gasps of breath she turned to face him.

"What now?' she asked quietly. He knew she wasn't talking about the night, she was talking about them. And he wasn't willing to go there.

"Now," he rolled her onto her back, "I'm going to put my tongue and head between your thighs."

Jax woke up curled around beautiful.

Hell, that word didn't even begin to describe Milly. She was on her side, snuggled into his chest, one bare leg slung over his. After a night where they'd put the Kama Sutra to the test, they'd crawled into a sleeping bag and melded together like a single being.

But now, in the light of the morning he was having serious questions. Not regrets. He could never regret a second with Milly. But he was afraid they'd broken more rules than intended.

While he wanted to spend as much time in Sierra Vista as possible to help with the family lodge, he still had a career, which was demanding and ate up every free moment of his life. He'd sacrificed a lot to get to where he was; he didn't want to walk away from it now.

But he also didn't want to walk away from Sierra Vista. And his family wasn't the only pull.

Chapter Twenty-One

Take Life by the Balls
Go all in.

It took two solid days for them to set up for the Sierra Vista Cup, which was to start tomorrow at seven a.m. It had been an all-hands-on-deck kind of situation, with Milly at the helm. They couldn't have managed without her, and everyone on the team knew it. Including his family.

They'd set up a staging area for the athletes with snacks and beverages, a designated spot for competitors to register and receive their numbers, and a viewing area for the spectators, surrounded by a mesh barrier that had banners from all the sponsors—all twelve sponsors, who pledged five figures each.

Over the past few days, Jax and his siblings had had several strategy meetings, each filling the rest in on how their respective teams were operating. But it had been Milly, with her spreadsheets and velvet touch, who smoothed out every detail so that it all came together to create a cohesive event.

His eyes automatically scanned Bigfoot's Brews and, as if she were a homing beacon, he found her in a split second. She was at the far end of the bar talking with the owner of a local brewery who was delivering the extra kegs.

She was dressed in knee-high boots, dark jeans, and a blouse that had all these tiny buttons, which he wanted to undo—with his teeth. And those boots were the kind he would ask her to leave on in the bedroom. She'd worn her hair in a high pony-tail—and he'd bet his life savings that it had been a conscious decision on her part to drive him crazy.

He wasn't the only one to notice. When she walked into the room the entire male population stopped to appreciate a beautiful woman. And she was beautiful. And smart. And tenacious.

She had this dynamic energy that was inspiring and infectious. She led with an understated assurance that made people want to be around her. Then there was that quite poise about her that turned him inside out. He'd once mistook it for shyness, but now he knew better.

"I haven't seen you smile that like that since you won your first competition," Peggy said, approaching him.

Jax was behind the bar wiping down the counter. He had come in early to help set up for tonight's opening. With only one restaurant at the lodge, and not a single vacancy, he knew tonight would be a madhouse. Normally, he'd be hanging with the other athletes, but tonight he wasn't a participant, he was Sierra Vista's head of sponsor and business development, working the event just like the rest of his family. He had a meeting at seven with a buddy who was a VP for the Xtreme Games, but until then he was free, so he'd offered to fill whatever slot needed filling and he'd been stuck with barback duty.

"I'm just practicing my bartender face."

Peggy did not look convinced. "Either way, I'm just glad to see you smile."

Peggy's eyes locked on his in a way that made him feel like she could see right through to his soul.

Man, when did it get so hot in here?

"The other night we were talking about next chapters. What is your next chapter?" she asked. "I know you love what you do, but have you considered what comes next?"

He'd been considering it more and more as of late. Jax hadn't felt this kind of comfort and rightness since that first night he'd slept at the Carmichaels nearly twenty years ago. Sierra Vista was home and somewhere along the way he'd forgotten that.

Snowboarding was a young man's sport and, while Jax wasn't old by society's standards, he was quickly reaching retirement age. And he'd always told himself that when he went out, he'd go out on top.

He never considered any kind of sales position—he wasn't a suit kind of guy and he never would be—but he'd managed to create partnerships with several companies in a matter of weeks while still being true to himself. And he was damn good at it. Almost as good at it as he was at snowboarding. Even more, he'd helped his family hold on to something that was a huge part of their history and, he hoped, a huge part of their future.

"Some of my best memories were made right here. I spent the first part of my life working alongside my family and I think, when it's time, I'd like to spend the next part of my life doing just that," he said, even as he felt his lip ache from running into Lucas's fist.

Peggy rapped one finger on the bar top as if genuinely amused by his answer. "While I love to hear that, I was asking more about Milly and where she fits."

Jax's palms began to sweat. He'd managed to avoid conversations about Milly with his family. Actually went out of his way to avoid "the" talk. At first it had been because he didn't like deceiving them, but lately it had been for another reason altogether. Because talking about Milly led to thinking about Milly and thinking about Milly led to him showing up on her doorstep at midnight. He told himself that it was just because he wanted her, but that want was turning into something much more powerful.

Man, he'd complicated the hell out of what was supposed to be a simple arrangement. And he'd known it was only a matter of time before Peggy wanted answers. And it appeared his time was up.

"We just started dating," he said. "We're not even thinking beyond the next few days." Because then Jax would have to go back to his regularly scheduled life. And while his body was craving the rush of a win, his heart was craving something else.

Something he couldn't have.

Milly was the kind of woman who deserved to be the center of a man's world and Jax's world didn't allow for that right now. She deserved adventure and he wasn't about to hold her back. She also deserved someone who knew how to love—and that wasn't him.

"With Kent, all it took was a single look."

He glanced across the room to see Milly, catching her mid-laugh, and his heart did this odd little jump. If he were the right guy, he could see how one look could do it.

"Don't get too excited," he warned. "My life is complicated and she's still trying to figure out her next chapter. The last few have all been about her sacrificing everything for others. She has enough people pulling her in different directions. She doesn't need another string to worry about."

"I'm sure you'll figure it out." And with that Peggy walked off leaving him with alone with these unsettling feelings.

He was leaving. That was the plan. It had always been the plan. Their arrangement began with a clear understanding that they had an expiration date. So then why was this sense of urgency pressing in on his chest?

As if sensing his swirling emotions, Milly's gaze roamed to his. Tilting her head in concern, she studied him. Instead of falling back into his usual *life's great* attitude, he let her see his truth. They stood like that for several beats, walls down, staring at each other from across a busy bar and it felt like a page started to turn.

Jax had just thrown back a beer with an old friend, Jeremy Gibbins, who helped organize the Xtreme Games, when Lucas slid onto the barstool beside him.

"Tim, we'll take two more," Lucas said to the bartender, pointing to Jax's beer and indicating two bottles of a local ale.

"You here to deliver another cheap shot, then go crying to Peggy that I beat you up?" Jax asked.

"Haven't decided. And I didn't tell Peggy shit. Everyone in the conference room heard us yelling. Hell, everyone in the office heard." Tim delivered the beer and the two sat in silence for a moment.

"I saw you with Jeremy Gibbins," Lucas finally said. "I didn't know he was coming."

"I invited him under the guise of a free vacay, but really I wanted to pick his brain about how the Xtreme Games operate."

Lucas lifted his beer and took a long pull. "Any good pointers?"

"Yeah, including that he might be interested in moving west if the right opportunity presented itself." Jeremy had all but handed over his résumé. "He loves his job, but he's reached the ceiling and unless the founder steps aside, he's not moving up anytime soon."

"So what? You're already looking for my replacement?"

Jax fiddled with his bottle, rolling the rim between his thumb and finger. "If that's what you want?" When Lucas didn't speak, Jax pulled Jeremy's business card from his pocket and slid it toward his brother. "I was thinking more of a president to your CEO. But that decision's up to you."

Lucas grunted. He was sitting forward, elbows folded on the bar, apparently riveted by the condensation on his bottle because he didn't even spare Jax a glance.

"So, is this us now?" Jax asked. "Surface questions and the occasional grunt?"

Lucas slid him a sidelong look. "It's a step up from throwing fists."

Jax wasn't so sure about that. At least when they'd been fighting there was some kind of emotion behind it. This? This was uncomfortable and stale as hell.

"Why did you come over?"

"I wanted a beer."

Jax coughed "*Bullshit*" into his hand. "There are a handful of open stools, but you chose this one, why?"

"I was going over the numbers and we've generated a quarter more revenue than our best year. Which is pretty impressive since two months ago we had the lowest enrollment in the history of the event. Including the inaugural year."

Jax let out a low whistle. "What happened?"

"You." Lucas turned to face him. "You happened. Between the new participants you attracted and the sponsors you brought in, I think we'll be able to swing that house in Santa Barbara without selling the lodge. At least the down payment."

"Is this where you tell me I ruined your life?"

He shook his head. "Nah, this is where I tell you that you were right."

Jax cupped his hand around his ear. "Say that again?"

Lucas shoulder checked Jax so hard he nearly fell off the stool. "Kent dropped by my place this morning to have one of his *chats*." Jax grimaced. Kent's chats were kind of like marathons, they could last anywhere from an hour to the end of time and you always ended up sweaty and exhausted. "He was so excited about how the event was coming together that he admitted he never wanted to sell. He just thought it was his only option. And I had practically signed away the family legacy."

"You can still be a part of the legacy from a distance," Jax said quietly. "Just because they changed their minds doesn't mean you have to."

Lucas lifted a single shoulder and let it fall. "I thought about that, but I guess I'm more like Kent than I'd like to admit. The thought of someone else running this place while it's still in the family doesn't sit right."

"Does that mean you're staying on?"

"Honestly, I don't know what it means. I told Kent I'd stay on until the end of the year and then we can revisit."

"What about AvalancheEx?"

"It's been back-burnered for five years, what's another year?" Lucas tipped his bottle up and drained it. "Anyway, I just wanted to say thanks for all of the time and energy you put into the event."

"You don't have to thank me. I'm your brother," Jax said. "This is my family too and this place means a lot to me."

A small smile broke through the tension. "I'm glad you remembered. Because even though you're a dick, you mean a lot to this place too."

Chapter Twenty-Two

Take Life by the Balls
*Say yes even when
it scares you.*

Milly was at the finish line.

"This event has never run so smoothly," Brynn said.

She and Milly stood along the fence line with the other few hundred spectators, waiting for the next run to begin. Besides a snafu with the porta-potties—half the amount ordered had arrived—everything had gone as planned. The deliveries came in correctly and on time, the swag bags had been stuffed and passed out, and Peggy had pointed out that this was the smoothest the event had ever gone. She'd also pointed out how handsome Jax looked that day.

Unlike the rest of the employees, who were in Sierra Vista team polos, Jax wore a dark gray button-down, untucked from his pants and with the sleeves rolled to the forearm. His shoes were business casual and his face was clean-shaven. He looked like one of those models from a cologne ad.

The last time she'd seen him he'd been talking with one of the event's sponsors. That had been seven hours ago. Milly barely had time to breathe, yet she couldn't help scanning the crowd for a peek at the man who made her smile. And as tired as she was—she'd been going since five a.m.—her cheeks hurt from smiling so much.

"I have a great team working with me." In fact, her team had been amazing. They'd gelled immediately and functioned like they'd been working together for years. Surprisingly, she worked better with them than she did with the crew she'd spent four years working with in New York. And the work was fun and challenging. Being a part of an event that meant so much to so many people fulfilled something inside her that her old job never had. "Plus, your family makes it easy to do my job."

Brynn laughed. "My family has been acting like we're three-year-olds in a presidential debate. Whining, shouting, and a lot of tantrums, with the occasional punch being thrown."

Remembering Jax's split lip had been enough to stop her heart. "Do they do that a lot? Jax and Lucas?"

Milly's expression must have been intense, because Brynn said, "My, my. You look like you want to throw a few punches yourself. Any of my family members in particular?"

"I plead the fifth."

"Welcome to the world of having brothers. They're more of an *act first, have a beer after* kind of creature. In fact, they use the least amount of words possible when communicating. Personally, I think it has to do with the missing leg in the chromosome." Brynn's smile vanished. "But I will say that Jax and Lucas have had a rough go of it the past year. Now that they've acted like idiots, I'm sure they'll be hugging it out sometime soon."

"I hope they do before Jax leaves."

Brynn studied Milly with curious interest. "You know, Jax only needs a reason to stay."

"Jax lives for the slopes," Milly said quickly. Too quickly to allow herself to think of possibly being one of his reasons to stay. Because their relationship wasn't real, she reminded herself.

Even though the last few nights had felt more real than any relationship she'd ever been in.

Jax hadn't said anything to let her know that he felt it too, but she knew he did. It was in the way he held her and the way he cared for her—and about her.

"That doesn't mean he can't make Sierra Vista his homebase. His first couple of years on the circuit he still lived at home. He'd come back all the time. Then Cindy happened and, as always, came between them," Brynn said, hands on hips. "That woman drives me nuts."

"Wait. That wasn't the first time?" Milly had been under the impression that this had been the first blowout between the brothers.

"Oh, nothing as big as avoiding each other for a year, but even as kids they always had different opinions of what Cindy's involvement in their lives should be. Lucas took to my family like a kid starved for love. Jax took a long time to open himself up to the idea that he was one of us."

"I think he still struggles with that," Milly said.

"Lucas treated our family like his, only spending time with his mom when he had to. Jax split time between houses. I think he was too afraid to sever ties like Lucas did, in case our family turned our backs on him. So when Lucas met with Cindy secretly I think it was Jax's biggest fear coming true. But just like when he was a kid, he's slowly opening back up." Brynn's expression went soft. "I think you have something to do with it."

"Me?" Milly croaked. "No. I don't think so."

"We've all seen the way he looks at you."

"How's that?" She wanted to know. Because she saw a wealth of emotion every time their gazes met, but for all Milly knew, she was fabricating it because that's what she wanted to see.

Gah!

Milly had begun to think of Brynn and her family as more than employers. More than Jax's siblings. She'd come to think of them as friends. And that friendship was all based on a big fat lie.

"Like he's happy," Brynn said. "And I haven't seen him happy in a long time. So thank you."

Milly didn't know what to say. Scratch that, she was afraid to say anything for fear that her voice would betray her.

"And I think you're happy too," Brynn continued.

She was more than happy. Milly felt alive and excited about what came next. She hadn't had this much freedom in her world, freedom to choose where she wanted to live, what she wanted to do, and who she wanted to do it with, since college. But that freedom also came with hard decisions.

"I'm not sure where I'll end up. My old boss offered me my job back, but upgraded."

"Have you accepted?"

"No," Milly said. She'd been meaning to get back to Leah but kept putting it off. Every time she picked up her phone to call, she found something else important to do—such as painting her toenails or deep-cleaning the kitchen.

"Well, you might want to put off answering."

"Why?"

"I wasn't going to say anything until later, but I don't want to miss the chance."

"The chance for what?"

"This event was so successful that we're considering hosting more events throughout the year, which means we'll be looking for a full-time logistics coordinator, who would run the entire division. Do you know of anyone who might be interested?"

"Are you serious?" Milly said before she could curb her enthusiasm, and Brynn laughed.

"Is that a yes?"

"Maybe you should take some time to consider your options," Gemma said.

Milly closed her tablet and sighed. She was in the middle of solving the problem of a missing crate of champagne when Gemma and Kat came in hot.

"Brynn told you." She sent Brynn an imaginary, through-the-ether high five to the forehead for having such a big mouth.

"Nope. Nolan told me when he was ticketing my car to ruin my day," Kat said.

"You *did* park in a loading zone," Gemma pointed out.

"I was unloading my sister and a dozen of her friends. So I may have left the car for a bit to watch the last few runs of the day. So what?"

"You were parked there for over three hours," Gemma said.

"Whose side are you on?"

Gemma put her hands out, palms up, claiming Switzerland status. "Just stating facts."

"Fact," she said with a sharp flick of the finger. "He's annoying. Fact." Another finger shot up. "He's insufferable. Fact. He's arrogant."

"Um, Kat," Milly said, making a slicing motion over her neck, but Kat was too busy fact-ing herself into a tizzy to notice that her annoying, insufferable, arrogant neighbor had joined the conversation.

"Fact. He's full of himself," Kat went on.

Legs in a wide stance, smile in full effect, Nolan crossed his arms over his chest, which was waging war with a black Sierra Vista Security shirt. Nolan's pecs were winning.

"Fact." Kat spun around to face him, as if the entire past few minutes were for his benefit, and held up a single finger. Her middle one. "Ranger Tight-ass is a pain in *my* ass."

Nolan glanced at Kat's middle finger, then scanned her from head to toe, the corners of his mouth lifting into a smile as they made their way back up. "Fact," he said. "If you turn around, I can massage the pain right out of that ass."

"In your dreams, Ranger Carmichael," Kat said, knowing that he wasn't a ranger but a federal agent, and knowing that it irritated him.

"You're always in my dreams." He winked.

"Uh! Like I said, *full of himself.*"

Nolan's gaze went over Kat's head to meet Milly's. "Congrats on the job and welcome aboard."

Milly rolled her eyes. "Is there anyone Brynn didn't tell?" Even as she said it, she froze. Her mom. Her dad.

Jax.

God, she didn't want them to hear about this through the grapevine. "I haven't accepted yet," she clarified. "I said I would think about it. So could you all please add that to the story when you pass it along?"

"Gotcha," Nolan said and lifted his ball cap in a gentlemanly gesture. "Ladies." He turned to Kat and said, "Trouble," then he left.

"Back to the secret at hand," Gemma said. "Are you really considering it?"

"Why don't you sound happy?" Milly asked confused. "You two have been harassing me to stay in Sierra Vista since I graduated college. If I take the job, I'd be staying." Milly had a sister, so she knew what Gemma and Kat's shared looks meant. They were silently talking about her behind her back, while she was standing right there. "This is what you wanted."

"But what do you want?" Gemma asked.

To be happy.

And, just like that, her mind was made up. Milly couldn't think of any place she'd like to settle down more than Sierra

Vista. She'd pushed through the grief and felt closer to her sister's memory than ever. In fact, she felt as if she'd never really lost her sister. Her sister was in her heart. Memories were forever and memories were meant to be made.

And she wanted to make them here, in a town that offered so many adventures she had yet to tackle. And she wasn't just talking about fun, she was talking about having a full and exciting life that included more than just a career and family. One that included happiness and fulfillment and love.

She was in a town she loved. A house she cherished. With friends around her and parents whose love was so large they wouldn't give her a moment's peace. Yet, until recently, she'd never felt so alone. She'd thought about nothing other than going back in time, before cancer and death and the consuming grief. She'd felt like she was going under. Except when she was with Jax. He made her feel connected to something larger, more powerful than loss.

Milly's chest constricted and her head went a bit dizzy.

Love?

Oh god. Love—question mark unnecessary.

Milly closed her eyes. Somewhere between their one-night stand and camping under the "stars," this faux-mance had become real. So real she felt like laughing and crying all at the same time.

Milly had fallen in love. Fully, hopelessly, and stupidly in love with a man who wasn't even hers. But could he be hers? Milly had overcome so many obstacles these past few months— many of them with Jax by her side. Yet, come next week he wouldn't be by her side. He wouldn't even be in the same country. He'd be in Germany and then it was Switzerland and then, well, she didn't know where, except it wouldn't be here.

Any desire she had to ask him to stay, to make Sierra Vista his homebase, would be flat-out selfish.

She'd tried the long-distance thing with Dillon, and it had blown up in her face. How was she supposed to make it work with a globe-trotter when she couldn't make it work with a guy who was just a commuter plane ride away?

You've overcome harder obstacles, she reminded herself. She'd uprooted her life for Zoe, relocating, figuring out work and life and everything that comes with a cross-country move.

She was a logistics coordinator for goodness' sake. Her job was to figure out how to get something from point A to point B—and sometimes that meant going through the entire alphabet until point B came up again. It also meant knowing when to zag when others expected you to zig.

She was ready for a little zagging in her life.

"What do I want? To say yes."

"And why do you want to say yes?" Gemma asked.

Milly glared halfheartedly. "Not because of why you think." When they didn't look convinced, she added, "Or because of *who* you think."

"Ah huh," Kat said.

Clearly, she wasn't winning over this jury.

"I know it seems rushed, but my *what's next* has been on my mind since Zoe's funeral and staying here, building a life here, is what makes the most sense," she said, and it was the truth. Looking back, she'd been making this decision slowly—one step at a time. One adventure at a time.

Gemma's expression stated that she thought Milly's next step was in the wrong direction. "So you're going to burrow here in Zoe's things."

"No. I'm not staying because of what I've lost. I'm staying because of what I've found. This is where I want to be. This is where I belong."

Kat raised a brow. "And?"

"And yes, maybe it has something to do with Jax."

"I thought that was all pretend," Gemma said.

"Geez, Debbie Downer," Kat said to Gemma. "Let the girl have some fun."

"I'm okay with fun." Gemma took Milly's hand. "More than anything I want you to have some fun. If anyone deserves it, it's you. I just don't want you to make a huge decision based on something that started out as a ruse." Gemma's expression was filled with so much concern Milly began to waffle a little. "Is this still a ruse?"

"No," Milly whispered. "Not to me it isn't."

"What about Jax?" Kat asked.

Milly shrugged. "I guess I'll find out when I tell him I'm staying in Sierra Vista."

Chapter Twenty-Three

Take Life by the Balls
Put it all on the line.

Jax wasn't all that familiar with strings, but over the past month he'd created enough strings to tear him in four different directions.

It was as if he were being emotionally drawn and quartered.

He had his career, his family, the lodge, and now Milly—a rope noosed at every limb—and he was about to snap.

Christ, how had things gotten so out of hand so quickly?

He stood at the bar, with a beer in hand, watching the Carmichael and Smartt families mingle as images from Peggy's birthday rewound in his head like a dream in reverse. The way Milly had so seamlessly slid into the family fold had a done a number on him.

He took a long pull of IPA and tried his best to reconcile this happy-family moment with the regret knotting in his gut. Every time he breathed it felt like he had a chest full of crushed glass. In a month, Milly was able to find her spot in a way it had taken Jax decades to accomplish—and he still struggled with his role in the Carmichael clan.

He was a bit of a triangle in a square hole—he fit, but half the space was vacant. With Milly that vacancy had been filled with her laughter and support and understanding. And the thought of losing that was already too much to bear. He couldn't imagine what it would feel like a year from now when things ended. Because they would end—as soon as she figured out that the guy she thought she knew wasn't him.

Jax wasn't some suit wearing, recovered bachelor, who knew how to stick. He was more like Cindy than he'd like to admit. Where she'd disappeared into a bottle, Jax vanished into his career. It was the downside of the job. But a necessity to win. And Jax liked to win.

Shit, was that what this was about? Winning Milly over to prove he was better than his brother? Even as he thought it, he rejected the idea. But that had sure as hell been a part of the motivation in the beginning. And what kind of guy sets out to prove he's the better twin? A guy who doesn't deserve a woman like Milly.

He had no idea she had been seriously considering moving to Sierra Vista. Why would she give up that big life waiting for her back in New York?

His eyes immediately tracked to her. She was talking with Peggy, Gennie, and Brynn in this family moment straight out of a Norman Rockwell painting, as if this was something that happened every weekend.

It did happen every weekend, you idiot. He just wasn't around enough to take part. Give it another season or two and things would be different. But until then?

Until then he'd be busting his balls to finish what he started when he decided to pro, while pulling as much weight as he could with the family business. That didn't leave the kind of time for a relationship. Just like that Norman Rockwell painting, this wasn't the real deal, and it was time Jax started to remember that.

He knew what he had to do and, damn if that wasn't a sucker punch to the gut.

Setting his beer on the bar, Jax wove through the crowd, his feet getting heavier with each step. By the time he reached Milly it felt like he was wearing brick shoes.

"Hey," she said with a giant smile when he approached. Then, as if they were the couple of the hour, she rose on her toes and kissed him. He should have pulled back, but he couldn't. He wanted to taste her one last time.

Needed to taste her one last time, so he pulled her into a quiet corner.

She must have sensed the urgency behind his response because, with one of those little moans he loved, she ran her hands up his chest until she was clutching his collar and opened her mouth to him.

He deepened the kiss, inhaling her as if it were his last breath. And maybe it was. His lungs sure as hell knew something he didn't.

He wasn't sure how long they held each other, but slowly distant whistles started to break through the haze. By the time he pulled back the entire bar was cheering them on. Glasses tinkling, hands clapping, even a few cat-calls. And behind them were Peggy and Gennie, looking on as if that summer wedding was a reality.

"Just like the first time," she said, not knowing that this would be their last. It was the universe's way of hammering it home that they'd come full circle. "Only I didn't have the blindfold."

When he didn't laugh, she tilted her head with curiosity. "Is everything alright?"

He didn't want to acknowledge the emotion he saw swirling in her eyes. Because if he did, he wouldn't do what he needed to, which was the right thing. "Can we go somewhere and talk?"

"Sure," she said brightly and took his hand. "Where to?"

"Somewhere where we won't be overheard."

Her laugh ricocheted off each wall of his chest. "The last time you said that we ended up breaking a few rules."

The reminder of the rules caused a painful ache to form behind his ribs. If he'd just followed through on his promise, just stuck to the plan, the next few minutes wouldn't have to happen.

"Is that what we're doing? Breaking some rules?" she asked, taking his other hand and leaning into him, her body pressing all the way against his, her mouth grazing his neck until it was next to his ear. "Because if so, I need to let you know that I might have forgotten my panties tonight."

His mind flashed back to waking up with Milly's naked body wrapped around him. The feel of her silky warmth beneath his hand as he ran it down her spine. The way his heart beat in rhythm with hers.

Shaking it off, Jax guided her further down the hallway that led to the manager's office. When they were out of range of others, he turned her to face him.

"You look so handsome in your fancy shirt," she said, coyly plucking at the bottom button. "And this?" She nuzzled his fresh-shaven cheek with her nose.

"I'm not really a starched kind of guy. Never will be," he reminded her. The collar of his shirt was suddenly suffocating. He pulled at it, but it didn't help. Not only wasn't he a starched guy, but he also wasn't a good enough reason for her to stay.

Wrong twin.

That's how this whole thing started, right? Milly thinking she was with Lucas. Maybe somewhere along the way Jax had started wanting to be the right twin. And maybe in trying to be somebody he wasn't, he'd given off signals that he shouldn't.

"I'm betting you'd look even better out of it," she said.

To stop her from unbuttoning his shirt, he trapped her hand over his chest. He was certain she could feel his heart thrashing. "I heard Brynn offered you the logistics coordinator job."

She sighed and his gut twisted. He had no idea why the thought of her choosing Sierra Vista over New York unsettled him. But it did.

"My hope was to get to you before the gossip line, but it moves faster than wildfire around here," she said.

"So, you're staying?"

"I was thinking about it." Again was that flirty coyness. She was breaking his heart.

"I looked into it and there is no way we can match the salary you'd get in New York," he said. "You'd be taking a demotion." Sierra Vista was a family-run company that did smaller events. They couldn't offer the kind of projects she'd be working on in the publishing world. There just wasn't that kind of career ladder available in Sierra Vista. Not to mention she'd be walking away from a city that she told him she loved.

Lucas had passed on his dream in order to help the Carmichaels, then kept everything a secret to make sure Jax went after his own dream. Jax couldn't let that happen to someone else he cared about. "You said that your freedom was in New York."

"I thought it was, but maybe not. I mean, freedom can be lonely and money isn't everything. I've loved working on this kind of project. It's exciting and challenging. Plus, my family is nearby. My friends are here. You're here." His inner turmoil must have shown on his face because her smile wilted with confusion. "Is that a problem?"

"I'm not here. In a few days I'm gone. I made that clear."

"I know you're leaving, but you're going to be back to work with your family. And we'd be working together on the events that are sponsored."

And *this*, right here, was what he was afraid of.

"You said long distance wasn't something you were interested in pretending. And this is pretend, remember?"

She dropped his hand and her face crumbled in on itself. "Is it? It that what you think? That this is all still pretend?"

He gripped the back of his neck and squeezed. "It doesn't matter."

"But it does." Her eyes were pleading. "Yeah, long distance isn't optimal, but I'm willing to try. I'm willing to see what happens and continue this."

"Continue what? What are we doing here, Milly?"

"What do you mean?"

"I mean, how is this supposed to work?" he asked. "Our relationship started with a dare and a misunderstanding that led to a lie. A lie that has grown to encompass every aspect of our lives. Our family, our friends, our careers. Everything we have is based on a lie."

"So our meet-cute wasn't the norm."

"I'm not a meet-cute kind of guy." And wasn't that the problem. Milly was the meet-cute kind of woman, who deserved to have the prince riding in on his white horse offering the happily ever after. But Jax was packing up to ride out of town. "I think somewhere between pretending to be together and working together, we've gotten caught up in this make-believe world where you and I are a match. I'm not your match, angel."

"Yes," she said quietly. "You are and you know you are."

"This," he said, pointing to his shirt, his slacks, his dress shoes. Even rubbed a hand over his beardless jaw. "This isn't me. Being a nine-to-fiver isn't me. Nightly family dinners and barbeques on the weekends isn't me." He listed off everything he knew a woman like her wanted in a partner. "What you're looking for isn't me."

Too bad what he was looking for was standing in front of him, her eyes brimming over with heart-wrenching emotions he was responsible for.

"Am I not allowed to change my mind?" she argued, angrily wiping at her tears.

"I haven't even taken you on a proper date."

"Every time I was with you felt like a date. Fun and exciting and I treasured each and every one."

"Fun and exciting gets old. The rush that comes from seeing me off and welcoming me home gets old. The weeks apart get old. You want stable and commitment minded."

"And you think you aren't those things? You're wrong." She shook her head sharply. "I don't want a Lucas. I want you. And I know you want me too, but you're just too scared to ask for more."

He went utterly still. "We've never talked about a *more*. Not one time."

"It was written in every kiss, every single touch, every time we were in bed together. It's already more and you know it." Her eyes were now burning with anger and something else that was hard to swallow.

"All I know is that if we continue like this, someone will get hurt." He reached out for her hands, but she wrapped them around her stomach. "I don't want to hurt you."

"It's too late for that," she whispered, and the acceptance he heard there, as if she had anticipated the pain and disappointment, shredded his chest. He'd take anger any day over the anguish that now filled her eyes.

"You don't do long distance. Your words," he said. "My life is crazy and hectic and—"

"Your life is more scheduled than mine. You know exactly where you'll be every day. When you're competing, where you're competing, when you'll be back in Sierra Vista. So that isn't an excuse. I mean, you'll be back in town after the season."

"And then I'm gone again. That's what I do. I leave. I think it's best that we just end with a clean break."

"So what are you suggesting? That when you're back in town we act like we don't love each other?"

Jax emptied his lungs, creating the space he needed to process the information. Those four letters rocked his foundation in a way that sent him reeling. If he didn't do *more*, he sure as hell didn't do *love*.

"I know I just scared you," she said, her tone that of one who was talking to a terrified child. "But it's true. I love you and I'm pretty sure you love me back." She took a gentle step forward and in a barely-there voice said, "I know you haven't had the best experience with love and trust. But you can trust me, Jax. You can trust what I'm saying." He was unable to speak through the sheer amount of fear coiling in his throat. "You don't have to say anything. I just need you to give us a chance."

He didn't know what would shatter him more, her admission or knowing that he was going to have to reject it.

"I care for you." He took a step closer, reaching for her hands. She let him take them this time. "More than I've ever cared for a woman." His heart was pounding, and his palms were sweating worse than at the beginning of a race. He was dreading the next few words, but they had to be said. "I don't love you, Milly." Even as the words came out, his heart rejected the statement. "I never meant to mislead you," he said. "This all just became too much."

She jerked her hands back as if she'd been branded and all the emotions drained from her face. "You mean, *I'm* too much."

"That's not that I said."

"No, but it's what you mean." She couldn't even look him in the eyes. "I know you care about me, Jax. You're hiding behind your career and your fear of commitment and real emotions and love. The same thing you've been doing to your family all this time."

She waited a beat for him to speak, but he had nothing. She was right of course, there was nothing he could say that would make this any less painful.

"I get that our relationship is complicated and unorthodox, and I imagine we'll make mistakes along the way, but I am willing to try, willing to put my heart out there and see if you're man enough to pick it up. And I hope to God you are because I might not know how to do the whole faux-mance thing, but I know how to love. I have been doing it my whole life, and it is terrifying and intense, and I know it can seem like a lot at first, but it can also be safe and freeing if you allow it to be." She looked up at him and all the fear and nerves and love shone through. "I have fought too hard for too many people in my life. This time I want someone to fight for me. Fight for me, Jax."

He wanted to fight, more than anything. But he knew that sometimes fighting wasn't enough. Sometimes love wasn't even enough. His silence was his answer.

"Understood." Milly turned to leave, then paused. "For the record, I didn't decide to stay because of you. I decided to stay because my happy is here in Sierra Vista. I hoped you'd want to be a part of it, but with or without you I'm going to find it. And Jax, I hope that whoever that next person is, you allow yourself to find your own happy."

With that she walked away, but not before he saw the tears spilling down her cheeks.

He tried to call out to her, but her name got stuck on the tip of his tongue, too afraid to break free. Pain lanced through him, nearly bringing him to his knees. Not only had he done the same thing as the men in her past, he'd also been no better than his parents—walking away when love became too much.

Chapter Twenty-Four

Take Life by the Balls
Never be afraid to make a mistake.
At least you took the risk.

Milly knew her life was a lot. But hearing Jax explain away her love so easily hurt. Even worse, she still had another few hours of work. Usually at an event like this, she was the last to leave. Which meant she spent the next three hours keeping track and signing off on each and every rental: from chairs to porta-potties, firepits to sound equipment—if it was set to go back to the vendor, then it was Milly's job to oversee. And she was going to do her job like her heart wasn't in a million pieces.

Unable to stomach seeing him again, she'd also kept track of Jax. It was the only way she could successfully avoid him. So when the bonfire started, she released her team to enjoy the festivities while she stayed back in one of the empty offices. Not her cubicle or anywhere obvious, but one that was reserved for smaller team meetings.

She knew Jax was looking for her, at least a dozen people had told her. Then there were the texts.

Jax: Are you okay?

Milly: Okay isn't how I would describe my current emotional state.

Jax: I shouldn't have dropped that on you tonight.

Milly: And the Bastard of the Year prize goes to...

Jax: I know your parents don't leave for another few days. We can keep up the pretense. Just the rules would have to go back into play.

To which Milly had responded:

Milly: I don't need you to pretend to like me. Thanks for the offer but kindly fuck off.

Then her phone had gone achingly silent. So silent that she couldn't breathe through the space of it.

If she thought the pain of losing Zoe was crippling, it was nothing compared to the icy ache filling her chest now. It burned so cold, one sob and she would splinter into a million shards.

Milly knew all about loss. Had learned how to embrace it, how to put the pieces back together. But nothing in the all the books she'd read about loss had prepared her for this kind of devastation.

She spent her entire life sacrificing what she wanted to make others happy, but she was ready for her own happy. She was ready for someone who would take all the love she had to offer and match it beat for beat.

But Jax wasn't willing to even meet her halfway. In a humiliating and crushing moment, he'd shoved her love back in her face.

The last of the guests trickled back to their hotel rooms around eleven, but Milly found some extra things to keep her busy to ensure her parents would be asleep by the time she arrived home. She needed a good old-fashioned cry session, and she didn't want to do that in front of an audience who would have questions. She especially didn't want to cause her father any stress. She knew she'd have to come clean, but that could wait until tomorrow.

After stealing a box of day-old doughnuts from the staff room, Milly drove home. The pressure building in her chest made her body too small to contain the loss. She quietly unlocked the door and tiptoed into the family room.

She didn't need a light to see that someone was waiting for her. *Zoe.*

As if by magic, her urn had been moved from the mantel to the kitchen counter. How many times had she caught Zoe sitting on the counter in the middle of the night eating the last of the ice cream or Halloween candy? Needing to be close to her sister, Milly hopped up on the counter, facing Zoe, and tore off a hunk of doughnut. It tasted like cardboard. She took another bite and another bite, each one becoming more frantic. It felt like if she didn't fill her mouth, all the emotions would come spilling out and she'd never get them back.

She'd never get back the feel of his hands in her hair, the way he made her laugh, how safe she felt wrapped in his arms, the spark of happiness that lit whenever he called her angel.

"It was a lie," she whispered to Zoe. "All of it was a lie but to me it was more real than anything I've ever felt. But now it's over and I don't even know what story I'm supposed to tell people. Did he dump me? Because he did. Or do I get to say I dumped him, because he deserves it."

"Or maybe you just tell the truth."

Milly turned to find her dad standing in the kitchen looking at her with his round belly and a shirt that read I JUST WANT TO DRINK BEER, EMBARRASS MY KIDS, AND SLEEP.

"Dad?" she choked out, rushing into his arms.

He picked her up into his safe embrace and cradled the back of her head to his chest. He'd held her like this so many times over the years.

"What's wrong, Milly Moo?"

The sound of her childhood nickname broke the floodgates and the first sob rolled through her chest and broke free. Unable to control them, a second one ruptured, followed closely by a third. And by the time Milly's eyes were too full of tears to see, she was pouring herself into her dad's arms until they were both sitting on the cold kitchen tile.

"I need Zoe," she whispered, and Howard held her closer. "I need her advice and her laugh and the way she'd interrupt me every two seconds to let me know what a badass I am. I need her so much right now and she's not here."

"I need her every second of every day," her dad admitted.

"It was getting easier. Going through her things, going on adventures. It was like she was right by my side. And then tonight, tonight was awful and for a moment I forgot she was gone. I forgot that I couldn't come home and crawl into her bed and cry. I forgot until I saw her ashes."

Milly felt her dad's chest deflate on a shaky, emotional breath. "I heard you sneaking in and for a moment I thought it was her. I had my dad voice ready to catch her in the act."

Milly looked up and gave a watery smile. "She was too old for your famous dad voice a decade ago."

Howard tugged her closer. "You girls will never be too old for my famous dad voice." They sat up against the fridge doors as he tucked her hair back. Strands stuck to her tear-streaked face. "But right now, I think you need one of my famous dad hugs."

She did. So badly she clung to him and buried her face into his strong I've-always-got-you arms. And that made the tears flow even harder.

Her dad was her rock, always had been. No matter what was going on in Milly's life, her dad had been her hero. He'd saved the day so many times and rather than tell him the truth that she wasn't ready to let Zoe go, she'd lied to him. And that lie turned into another and another until—

Oh my God. Jax was right. Their entire foundation was based on a lie. How were they supposed to make something meaningful out of that?

"I blew it, Dad," she admitted. "I had something really special, and I blew it because I was too busy trying to make everyone else happy that I destroyed what made me happy." She met his gaze through her blurry one. "Jax and I were pretending."

"I know."

"I didn't mean for it to get so far out of hand. It's just that I picked him up at the bar and brought him home and then you and mom showed up and—" She broke off when his words registered. "You knew?"

"You picked him up at a bar?" he said, Dad Tone in full effect.

"Back to you knowing. When did you know?"

"When you called him by the wrong name." This was from Gennie who walked over and sat next to Milly, making her the center of a Smartt family sandwich.

Milly looked up. "I can't believe how awful that must have been for him. I really hurt him thinking that I'd slept with his brother."

"But everyone got over it," Gennie pointed out.

"I didn't get over it," Howard said. "In fact, I still want to kick the guy's ass."

"It was my fault," Milly defended.

Howard brought Milly's hand to his lips and kissed her palm. "Just like no means no, it's always the man's fault. Always. Now, you remember that."

"Why didn't you guys say something?" Milly asked, wiping some tears—and a little snot—on the back of her hand. "You just let me keep lying."

"First, we wanted to see how far the lie would go," Gennie said with a mischievous grin.

"First, I wanted to knock his teeth in," he said.

"But good sense prevailed," Gennie said to her husband. "It was just too exciting to resist, which was why I kept talking about babies and weddings, just to see how far you two would go with it. I must say, you were both extremely committed."

"That was you spreading the rumors? To, what, ferret me out?"

"Couldn't let you have all the fun with such a juicy lie," Gennie said. "But then ... " She clasped her hands to the non-existent pearls around her neck. "Then we saw that kiss on the porch and, *yowzah*, the sparks there went far past pretend. So, Peggy and I decided to play along, knowing you two would figure it out."

Milly choked on air. "Peggy knew?"

"You and Jax are both terrible liars. You practically had hives covering you from head to toe." Gennie reached over and lifted Milly's sleeve. "Isn't that interesting. No hives now. Why do you think that is?"

"Because now you know the truth."

"A minute ago, you said you loved him, and yet not a single hive."

Milly yanked up her sleeve, then groaned. It was even worse that she thought. She hadn't just talked herself into a fake love, she'd really fallen hook, line, and sinker for a guy who wasn't willing to fight for her. "I'm such an idiot."

"No, sweetie," her mom said. "This is a textbook case of how men are stupid. Sometimes they need a little space to come to terms with the fact that they're already sunk."

"He doesn't love me," she whispered through the humiliation.

"Sweetie, you know better than that," Gennie said. "So does your heart."

"My heart is as flat as a pancake rolled by a steamroller. And even if he does love me, it's not enough for him to give this a try."

"Then he's an idiot," Howard said.

"No, honey, he's a man."

Chapter Twenty-Five

Take Life by the Balls
Accept no refunds on love.

Jax plunked his room key down on Lucas's desk.

"What's this?" his brother asked.

"I'm heading out," Jax said as if that had been the plan all along. His once-in-a-lifetime angel was gone, and that was all on him. "With the Cup being over, I figured I could use a few days to familiarize myself with the next mountain."

"So this has nothing to do with you and the logistics coordinator?"

It had everything to do with her. He couldn't stop thinking about the look on Milly's face when she'd walked away. Or the feeling in his gut to watch another person he loved disappear on him. Then again, this was what he'd asked for, wasn't it? A clean break.

And what kind of man implies a woman would give up her life for him? Another thing she was right about was that he ran from confrontation—just like her ex, which made Jax a grade-A coward. And he couldn't stand one more minute to pass with him and his brother at odds. A new leaf he could attribute to Milly.

Milly would be proud—if she were talking to him.

"This has to do with us." Jax yanked the chair out and took a seat. "This stupid fight has gone on long enough. I'm leaving and I can't go unless we fix this. I refuse to go unless we fix this."

Lucas sat back in his chair, body language pushing a solid ten in the pissed-off category. "So, you help out with one event, then you bail early? And here I thought you'd changed."

That made two of them.

"Fine. Where do you want me to start?" Lucas asked.

"At the beginning."

Lucas eyeballed him for a good long beat, his brow lowering until he was practically squinting.

"I didn't include you in that breakfast with Cindy because I didn't want to give you false hope. The last time she'd gone off the wagon, you went to a dark place and I didn't want you to go back there. I wasn't going to tell you until I saw her walk through the facility's door. And I was right, she didn't go."

Jax's body went rigid. "Why didn't she call me?"

"She didn't call me either. Her 'boyfriend' did when she backed into a parked car, drunk. I bribed her with money and she actually showed."

With every word he said Jax's shoulders lowered slightly. "Why didn't you just tell me that?"

"Are you kidding? I've been trying to tell you for a year. And the last time I brought it up you punched me in the face, then walked off like a tantrum-throwing toddler."

Jax hadn't walked, he'd ran—hard and fast.

"I know that face," Lucas said. "I had that face. What aren't *you* telling me?"

"I punched you because Mom called me a week later asking for money. She told me that you gave her money again and that she'd used it on the down payment on the lease."

"The only money I gave was to the rehab center and she bailed after one week."

"Well, shit, I actually gave her money, scot-free," Jax said.

"Well, who's the dumb brother now."

Lucas sat back and laughed; Jax joined in. It felt good. To laugh about their mom instead of arguing.

The tension and anger dissipated and what was left were two brothers who had been played against each other by the one person who was supposed to keep them safe. But none of that mattered, when they were each other's ride or die.

"I think you still take the trophy because you walked away from the best thing in your life."

"You take the trophy. At least I gave a relationship an attempt. When was the last time you gave it a try?"

Their eyes locked together for an interminable amount of time. "Did you really give it a try?" Lucas asked. "No, no you did not."

Brynn popped her head in. "You guys roshambo for the title of Biggest Idiot?"

"What the hell, Brynn?" Lucas asked. "Did you have your ear to the door?"

"Do you even have to ask?" she said, then walked over to sit on the corner of the desk. "So, roshambo or ax throwing? A good old fashion wood-chopping competition? Oh, I know. Why don't you guys pitch yourselves off Vista Peak and whichever idiot makes it to the bottom first is the winner."

"No point. I'm the bigger idiot," Jax said.

Brynn's face went sad. "You really are. You broke her heart, Jax."

A fact that he already knew and didn't need reminding. "Is she okay?"

"What do you think?" Brynn asked.

If she was half as bad off as he was, then he was even a bigger asshole than he thought. He hadn't slept in three days. His eyes were scratchy, his mind scrambled, and his heart in pieces. And he deserved it. "Have you seen her?"

Brynn kicked the side of Jax's boots with the toe of her shoe. "The question is why haven't you?"

Lucas looked at him, long and hard. Then a knowing smile curled at his lips. "He knows why. He's just too chicken to own it."

Brynn threw her hands up in exasperation. "Men are such idiots."

He was an idiot. He'd been fighting in his head about what was happening in his heart and what was happening he could no longer deny because no matter how far he ran, it wouldn't change the facts. He loved her. Hard stop.

Jax stood. "Holy shit." He turned around aimlessly. "You're right!"

"That you're an idiot or that you love her?" Brynn asked. "I just need to get the details right, before I tell Mom."

Chapter Twenty-Six

Take Life by the Balls
*Hold on to love like it is
a box of doughnuts.*

Milly meant what she'd said—she was going to find her happy. But that would have to wait until tomorrow.

Today was the first annual Zoe Smartt's *Classy Crap This Way* garage sale to raise money for breast cancer research. Milly had decided the best thing to do with Zoe's things was to pass them on to others who would love and cherish them.

The response from the community had been overwhelming. Donations came in from all around town, people showed up to work the event, and the Carmichaels even offered their ballroom.

"How much is this, honey?" Ms. Tilden, Milly's neighbor, asked, holding up Zoe's autographed poster of Justin Bieber, wearing nothing but his Calvin Kleins. "I always had a thing for blonds."

"It's a pay what you feel kind of event. So whatever you think that's worth, it's yours." Milly had decided to leave it up to the customers how much they felt comfortable paying. She'd discovered people pay more when it's for a good cause. And putting a price on Zoe's things was impossible since she would have marked everything *priceless*.

"Will forty do?" Ms. Tilden asked.

"That's very generous. And my sister would love it to know that Justin is going home to a fellow fan."

Ms. Tilden pulled out her reading glasses and slid them up her nose. "Here, I thought this was Leif Garrett," she said, but handed over two bills.

"I was going to buy that for Ranger Tight-ass and superglue it to the hood of his car," Kat said. "I guess you saved me going to jail for vandalizing an officer's vehicle." Kat slung an arm over Milly's shoulder. "How are you holding up?"

"My heart feels like roadkill, and I haven't slept in over a week," Milly said honestly. She was done with lies. "But I'm wearing a pair of Zoe's bitchin' boots."

"The offer still stands. I have the perfect place to hide his body. Plus, murder goes well with those boots."

A little bubble of laughter escaped. It might have been a small sob. "My boots and I would like to remain murder-free."

Plus, she could never hurt Jax. Even though he'd crushed her, she still loved him. She was afraid she always would.

"There you are," her mom said, rushing over to Milly. "Here, let's give your hair a little brush." Gennie finger-combed Milly's hair. "And slightly tousled."

Milly batted her mom's hands away. "What are you doing?"

"Oh, I wish I'd brought my new lip gloss, Sexcapade. It's a shade between red and mauve. Very modern and sultry. Kind of like Julia Roberts in *Pretty Woman*." Gennie turned to Kat. "Dear, do you happen to have any lip gloss or mascara?"

Kat pulled the neckline of her shirt out and dug around in her bra. She came up with a phone, car keys, a business card with someone's number scribbled on the back, and sixty-three dollars and seventeen cents. "Sorry, no lip gloss. But I can—"

Kat grabbed Milly by the cheeks and pressed her lips to Milly's—hard—then smudged them around. She pulled back and smiled. "There, you are now wearing Stiletto Red. You're welcome."

"About your shirt, Milly. Does the neckline go any lower?" Gennie asked, then started tugging at the hem of Milly's sweater. "It will have to do."

"Mom, what's going on?"

Milly realized that the entire ballroom had gone so still she could hear her own heartbeat. With an encouraging smile, her mom stepped aside, and Milly's breath caught in her throat. Because there standing ten feet away, wearing snow-covered boots and a winter sweater was Jax.

Their eyes met and her body immediately started to melt— stupid body.

We're mad at him, remember? He broke our heart, remember? He let us walk away, remember?

But no matter how many times she reminded herself of these facts, she couldn't help how her heart yearned for things to be different. Yearned for a different outcome where they went in search of their happy together.

With an unreadable expression, Jax started forward in a direction that looked like he was on a direct course with her. The crowd parted for him, people's phones coming out to video the entire thing. Milly's palms began to sweat.

"Go on, sweetie," her mom fake whispered.

"We don't even know why he's here," Milly whispered back.

"All you have to do is look at his eyes and you'll know everything you need to."

But Milly couldn't move. It was as if her feet were crazy-glued to the ground. But her heart was keeping double time, going faster and faster with every step Jax made. Then he was there, standing in front of her, and a nervous smile touched his lips.

"You're back," she whispered.

"I'm home," he corrected, and that one word sparked a small glimmer of hope in her stomach.

"For how long?"

"As long as it takes."

"Can you speak up," Peggy called out from the back of the room. "I've got the TikTok going and my followers can't hear you. And if you can turn a little to the right, the light will really catch your hair, sweetie. You want your hair to look glossy in the video compilation at the wedding."

Milly looked around to see that the entire room was watching them as if this were some rom-com where the boy asks the girl to be his forever. Only, she'd offered him forever and he'd passed. But he was here and that had to mean something. Right?

"Ignore them," he said, cupping her hip and tugging her closer. "For once, this is about us."

"Us?" she repeated. "There is no us, remember?"

"Milly—"

She shook her head. "You wanted a clean cut, now you need to stay away."

"I can't," he told her. The crowd moved in closer, making a circle around them.

"You can't have it both ways, Jax. I get it, you're scared but so was I. Only, I was willing to take the leap and you decided to let me fall alone."

His hand slid up her arm to cup her jaw. "That's not true. I fell with you. I fell so hard I got scared."

"What are you saying?"

"It was never fake for me. From that first kiss I think I knew."

She tilted her head because she couldn't be sure she'd heard him right. "Then why did you let me think otherwise?"

"Testosterone syndrome," Gennie said, and murmurs of agreement went up around room.

Jax ignored everyone. "Lucas said it's because I'm an idiot."

"You and Lucas made up?"

"Yes. And now I'm attempting to make up with you."

She shook her head. "But you're leaving."

"But what if I want to come home."

"Do you?"

"Of course I do. I love you, Milly," he said and at those three words a smile went full bloom on her face and she couldn't hide the tears welling in her eyes. "I'm sorry that it took me so long to realize it, and I'm sorry that I hurt you. You were right, I ran away before you could remember I was the wrong twin, but I'm done running. There I was standing at the top of the mountain looking down and I realized that if I didn't take a chance, there'd never be anyone waiting for me at the bottom." He ran the pad of his thumb down her cheeks. "Don't cry."

She nuzzled her cheek into his hand. "They're happy tears. And you were never the wrong twin."

"Yeah?"

"I love you back. But you already know that."

Jax's mouth came crashing down on hers in the sweetest kiss in the history books. "God, I love you," he murmured against her lips. "So much, I couldn't breathe without you."

When they pulled back, the crowd was whooping it up and cheering them on. Jax smiled one of his breathtaking smiles "You told me you were chasing your happy and I decided I wanted my happy too. You're my happy, angel. You're my happy and my home."

Jax gifted her a tender and sweeping kiss that had her heart somersaulting in her chest. It was the kind of kiss that spoke of adoration and felt like a cherishing caress. The kind of kiss that could only come from love.

Jax pulled back and she looked up into those warm green eyes and felt herself fall all over again. She'd come to Sierra

Vista for love, and she was staying for love. And she couldn't be happier.

Jax tipped her chin up. "One more?" he whispered against her lips.

"You can have all the mores."

Thank you for reading FAUX BEAU. To read more about Millie and Jax in an EXCLUSIVE epilogue go online and enter this link:

www.marinaadair.com/fb-epilogue/

Want more Marina Adair?

Read on to Kat and Nolan's story, book #2 in my Sierra Vista series, *Second First Kiss*, a witty and tender enemies-to-lovers romantic comedy!

Chapter One

Kat Rhodes's sister had disappeared off the planet. One minute she was there and the next she was gone. A never ending theme in Kat's life, it seemed.

She refreshed her Find My Friends app, but Tessa's dot had mysteriously disappeared an hour ago, which meant she was not at the library prepping for her STAS and likely up to trouble. The kind of trouble Kat had once invented.

Boy trouble.

Those days were long behind her, or so she thought, until she became the keeper of a teenager. She wasn't Tessa's legal guardian, but she was working on it. Which was why she was at Sunrise Falls—the stomping grounds for underaged partiers in Sierra Vista—instead of at work, spying on her sister's extracurricular activities. Activities that she likely included keg stands and hooking up.

"I'm so going to get fired," she mumbled to herself.

This was the third time she'd had to leave work in the middle of a shift to adult. Karma was definitely paying her back for all the grey hairs she gave her dad when she'd been Tessa's age. Unfortunately, Karma wasn't paying her a salary—a problem since Kat desperately needed money. Between college loans and paying off the back property taxes on her dad's house, she was so in the red, her life was always in emergency mode, like the constant flashing of the exit sign during a plane crash.

Grab the parachute and escape while you can.

Only she couldn't escape. She and Tessa were working on building trust. Another theme in Kat's life.

Trust was harder for Kat than love. And she wanted to trust her sister, she really did, but recent history hadn't afforded Tessa that privilege. Five years ago, when Kat had walked away from her dream college to home from college to help care for her sister, Tessa had been a sweet, rule-following, people-pleaser who was more into boy bands than bad boys. Then she'd grown boobs and attracted the interest of town bad boy, TJ Locke, and things rapidly changed. All those people-pleasing tendencies had transferred from her family to her crush.

Checking to make sure there were no bears or coyotes in the near vicinity—Kat hated bears—she hopped out of Betty Davis, her grandpa's 1967 yellow dodge dart, which looked like a banana on wheels. Grabbing the bolt cutters from the backseat, she approached the metal gate which was blocking her entrance to the park's grounds and had a chain wrapped around it, securing it shut. Screwed to the center of the imposing gate was a big, official looking sign stating:

FEDERAL FOREST PARK RULES:

1. OPEN FROM DUSK TO DAWN
   Um, that won't work. It was nearly ten at night and Kat was going into that parking lot.
2. NO ALCOHOL
   Based on the thumping base in the distance that rule was broken by about a hundred underaged teens.
3. NO PETS

Kat looked at Tiny Dancer, her miniature pony who had attachment issues and thought she was a lawn mower. "One bleat out of you and your name will be glue."

Neigh!

"Rebel!"

Kat studied the rest of the rules and nearly rolled her eyes when she realized there were twelve. Including but not limited to: No fires, hunting, camping, littering, or unauthorizes groups over twenty.

Geeze, they might have well listed: No fun.

12. No unauthorized motor vehicles during off hours.

That was going to be a problem since she wasn't about to hike it a quarter of a mile through the woods in the pitch black. Even the moon was working against her—a thin slice about as bright as a single Christmas tree light. Then again, just like she knew how to handle herself—a necessity when you grow up the poor kid in town, with a bipolar mom—she also knew the importance of self-reliance.

She gave one last look at the sign, and the bolded: All violators will be prosecuted to the full extent of the law, and shrugged off the warning. Sometimes bending a little rule, or twelve, was the right thing to do. And catching her sister in the act was the right thing to do. Too much was at stake for Tessa to be out partying on a school night.

"Buckle up," she told Tiny Dancer, "Things are about to get interesting." Gripping the bolt cutters, she was ready to slice through the metal when she realized someone else had broken rule one, since the chain was in fact already cut.

"I guess we're only violating the Entry part in this impromptu B&E."

Neigh.

Kat unwound the chain, letting the heavy metal clank against the steel gate and pushed it open. Hopping in Betty, she drove over the storm grate and pulled around the bend, where she found a parking lot full of cars. Enough to account for Sierra Vista High's entire football, basketball, and cheerleading teams.

She was going to kill Tessa.

With an exhausted breath, she drove off the pavement and onto the gravel shoulder, inching up as far as she could get to the base of the trail, blocking any and all exits. She wasn't about to miss her sister's escape.

Turning off the engine she pulled out her phone.

Kat: How's studying going? You figure out the answer to $E=MC^2$

Tessa: …

Then the dots disappeared while her sister was likely concocting yet another lie.

Tessa: No, but I'm learning how to conjugate "My sister's annoying" in French.

Kat: You'll have to teach me that one. I imagine it will come in handy. What time will you be home?

Tessa: Don't worry MOM. I'll be home by curfew.

Kat: Good. I got off early so we should get home around the same time.

Which was in twenty minutes. More than enough time to get home from the library but booking it all the way from Sunrise Falls? Never going to happen. It would take her ten minutes alone to hike through the dense forest after dark sober.

Kat hoped to God her sister was sober.

Tessa: You don't have to do that. I have my key.

Kat: And I have a headache. See you in twenty.

Kat waited a whole three minutes for a response—not even a single blinking dot—before sliding her phone in her pocket with a sigh. This was going to be a fun night. Not. She didn't like playing the heavy or pulling on the Hall Monitor hat, but if she was going to prove to the court that she could provide a safe and loving environment for Tessa, then she'd wear however many hats as it took.

Kat rolled down the window and let the fresh spring air wash over her. She smelled of curly fried and malt beer. She felt like she'd been run over by a snowplow. This second job as a bartender was going to kill her. After pulling her nine-to-five at the county as an IT specialist—which was more of a glorified DMV clerk—she worked the closing shift at Bigfoot's Brews three nights a week. Man, would her peers at MIT laugh their asses off if they could see her now.

Bigfoot's was a bar and grill located inside the largest ski lodge in the area and a hot gathering spot for tourists and locals alike. It was this stunning combo of rustic-luxe and cabin chic with vaulted wood ceilings, pounded copper tabletops, and floor to ceiling windows that soak in the mountainess views—which was currently showcasing the evergreen ridges with white capped peaks dusted in residual snow from the long winter.

Kat felt like she'd had a long winter as well—one that started when her dad lost his job as a lumberjack and had to reinvent himself as a cross-country truck driver. That had been five years and a few abandoned dreams ago. But family meant everything to Kat, so she'd do whatever it took to keep her small family together—even if that meant getting custody of Tessa over her father.

Not that Abe was a bad father, he was just unavailable. Literally. As in gone for months on end while on long-hauls.

He wasn't a bad dad; he just didn't excel in the parenting department. Never had. He was more interested in being the "cool" dad rather than being a "solid" dad, who his daughters could count on. When Kat was Tessa's age, she'd had no curfew, no boundaries, no guiding hand, and absolutely no rules. She'd run wild and made mistakes—big mistakes that almost cost her MIT.

Big mistakes that had big consequences. Painful consequences.

But she was done with mistakes. For Tessa, she was going to turn in her Bad Girl crown for PTA tiara. On the outside, working at a bar might not look like a responsible job, but she made more money in three nights of tips than she did forty hours a week at the county.

A rational person would quit the day-grind for a few more nights a week at the bar, but the bar didn't provide benefits—like health insurance. And if Kat were going to gain custody of Tessa she needed to at least appear as if she had this whole adulting thing down. Adulting wasn't really her thing, but she was trying. For her sister she'd always try.

Good thing she was a master of deception.

Kat had been pretending since she was a kid. Pretending to be happy, pretending her home life wasn't unstable, pretending people's judgements didn't hurt. Especially pretending that she had her shit together. Truth was, she didn't know how things would play out from day to day—let alone how to raise a brooding, trouble-seeking teen. And that scared her.

"Let's see how she talks her way out of this one," Kat said.

Neigh.

Kat rested her head back on the seat and closed her eyes. She wasn't lying about the headache. It was the equivalent of the thumping bass in a Snoop Dog song.

Boom. Boom. Boom, it went. Right behind her eyes.

As if sensing her discomfort, Tiny Dancer wiggled himself out from his seatbelt and stuck his head between the front seats, giving her ear a little nibble.

"If you want a nibble, you'd better buy me dinner first."

"I get off at eleven."

Kat didn't bother opening her eyes. She'd recognize that voice anywhere.

Nolan Carmichael. Her neighbor, nemesis, and everyone's favorite federal agent. Everyone, that was, except Kat. He might be the sexiest man in Sierra Vista, but he was inflexible, closed off and straitlaced. He was so ridged he made the mountains look smooth. Plus, guys like him never messed with chaos and Kat's life was chaos personified. And people like Nolan never changed their stripes.

Not that she wanted him to. Unlike the rest of the female population in their small mountain town, she had zero interest in Ranger Tightass.

Then why did you kiss him? her inner bad girl asked.

Because it was a dare and I never turn down a dare.

Her inner bad girl called bullshit. And it was a bullshit excuse. The dare had been a fun game of *Buckle Up,* where the dare-ee had to take off the belt of the man who walked through the door next—with her teeth. To her dismay, Nolan happened to walk through that door. Wanting to see him squirm she'd challenged him, and just like her, Nolan couldn't pass up a challenged. Kat had whipped that belt off in under fifteen seconds, then—in a moment of sheer insanity—she planted one on him.

They'd been circling each other ever since. For months she given herself permission to admire from afar, but she'd never allowed herself to act on it. Until she did and one awkward kiss—well, she couldn't really call it a kiss, it was more of an impromptu brush of the lips with zero warning and zero time to rally. But he'd still managed to create a spark brighter than fireworks on the Fourth of July. Which was why Kat had been avoiding him.

She didn't have the time or the bandwidth to do anything more than casual. In fact, ever since she'd come home from Boston to help take care of Tessa she'd sworn off relationships.

Not that she'd ever really had one. Kat wasn't really the "bring home to mom type"—something she'd accepted over the years—so she'd become a one-night-stand champion. A discrete one-night champion.

With their mom suffering from a chronic case of Dead-Beat syndrome, and their dad being a cross-country truck driver, he'd missed birthdays, Christmas, and showing up for Tessa's aren't-teacher conference.Tessa was falling through the cracks, and Kat was determined to catch her—only Abe wasn't into signing over custody. He thought it made him look like a bad father.

And that mean Tessa really only had Kat as a role model. The irony wasn't lost on er—or the rest of the town.

Things got really bad when Abe got injured on the job and fell behind on, well, everything. It took him two years of physical therapy to heal, but he had to find another career. To this day, Kat never understood how, out of all the possible career choices, a father of an eleven-year-old could pick a job that put thousands of miles between him and his family. Maybe if he had a partner who stayed at home.

Then again, he did. Kat. He asked Kat to walk away from the future possibilities Boston represented to come home to help out with Tessa when he got injured that help became eventually became a fulltime job, until Kat found her dream of finishing college was no longer an option.

"You'll have to get off on your own. I don't accept nibbles from men who kiss like corpses," she said referring to that kiss three months ago.

"Is that your way of asking for a second round? Because I promise you, one kiss and you'll be begging me to use my tongue—and not just on your mouth."

A tiny trill of anticipation flickered in her belly. A demoralizing feeling. And something that would never happen again.

She finally turned her head to acknowledge Nolan's presence and her tongue turned to dust. Instead of his department issued uniform, he was in faded jeans that were soft in all the right places, a red and black flannel that was waging war with his biceps—and losing—and a black ballcap turned backward. He looked like Thor and Paul Bunyan had a lovechild.

He was bending over slightly, his hands resting on the hood of her car, his face so close she could make out every dark hair of his scruff.

"What are you even doing here?" she asked, working hard to keep her gaze from landing on his lips. Either he was a mind reader or she had a very bad poker face, because he smiled this annoying, *You're totally thinking about round two* smile.

"I should ask you the same."

She closed her eyes again and rested her head on the seatback, feigning boredom. "I plead the fifth."

"That only works in a court of law."

"Well, you always walk around flashing your big badge and pistol like you're the judge, jury, and executioner, so forgive me if I got confused." She waved a dismissive hand.

"You've been checking out my big badge and pistol, Trouble?"

"Don't let it go to your head, Ranger Tightass. You prance around like a peacock with cuffs. It's impossible to miss."

She felt him move closer, now resting his forearms on the sill of her window. "First my pistol, and now my cuffs. Is that your way of asking what I'm doing when my shift ends?"

She straightened and leveled him with a look. "While you're clearly finding this amusing, I've got a job to do, so if you'll kindly screw off."

"I have a job to do, too. Like writing you up for trespassing after dark."

She shrugged as if unconcerned, when inside she was nervous. She couldn't afford a ticket. She could barely afford her streaming channels. "I'd just throw it back in your face."

He smiled. "Then, I'd have to write you up for littering."

Tiny Dancer took that moment to let his presence be known with a loud neigh. Nolan lifted a brow. He and Tiny Dancer went way back. All the way back to the day that Tiny Dancer decided to sharpen his teeth on Nolan's new truck, then drop doodie on Nolan's boot.

"Before you bring up the fact that he isn't leashed, know he hasn't stepped foot out of this car."

"Have you?"

"That's none of your business."

"It is when you're sitting in a secluded area in the middle of the night, alone." He said it as if he were genuinely concerned for her safety.

"Are you worried about me, Ranger?"

"Yes," he said and there was a quality to his voice that caused a warm bubble to start in her belly and slowly rise into her chest. When was the last time someone had been worried about her? She couldn't remember. "Camping out here isn't just illegal it's a stupid idea."

And the moment had passed.

"Sorry, Mr. Fun Police, you aren't even in uniform, so I don't have to listen to you drone on about rules and bylaws."

"I'm always in uniform." A truer statement had never been said. He was uptight no matter what he wore. He was also sexy as hell. "And when I found the gate open, I thought I'd investigate.'

"It was already open when I got here." He looked at the bolt cutters on the passenger seat and lifted a brow. "Hand to God, someone got here before me." She did a sweeping pass with her hand to highlight the dozens of cars in the parking lot. "It could have been any of them."

"Yet, you ignored the no trespassing sign anyway and drove off road."

"I was just checking to make sure people weren't up to shady business. You should be thanking me, not harassing me."

At that precise moment a belt of loud laughter ricocheted off the mountains surrounding them and filtered through the pines. He straightened and turned toward the trail leading to, what Kat knew, was a raging party.

Just great. Here she was trying to catch Tessa in the act, and a lawman was there to pay witness. Tessa better be sober or there would be words. Lots and lots of words.

She opened the door and stepped outside. A little shiver chased the hairs on the back of her neck—that had nothing to do with how good he filled out a pair of jeans. Even though spring had come, winter was still holding on, bringing low temperatures and cutting winds.

She leaned back against the car. "What are you even doing here?"

"I can't talk about an ongoing investigation," he said and she gave a dramatic eye roll for his benefit. "So why don't you head on out before I call the tow truck?"

"No can do, Ranger," she said knowing full well that he was a special agent for the US Forest Service special agent who was usually armed to the teeth and took down bad guys who did bad things on federal land. "I'm in the middle of a stakeout and I can't turn back now."

"Boyfriend?" he asked.

"My sister."

His eyes softened with understanding and something too close to empathy for her liking. It wasn't a secret that Tessa was staging a rebellion against the world. And Kat couldn't blame her.

Abe drove big rigs to help pay the bills, and took on as many hauls as he could get to chip in, but Kat wondered what would hurt Tessa more, losing the family home or losing the last few precious years with her dad before she heads off to college and, according to her sister, never steps foot back in Sierra Vista.

"If she's at the party I will get her home safely," Nolan said. "I promise. But you staying here isn't an option."

There was a strange urgency to his voice that she didn't understand. "And I promised to kick my sister's ass if she snuck out again, so my promise trumps yours." She held her head high. "I'm not leaving here without Tessa."

Nolan studied her for a long moment, and she wasn't sure what he was thinking but she didn't like it. "Well, I hope she gets here before the tow truck."

She pushed off the car and walked right into his space, craning her neck so she could meet his gaze—which was dialed to amused.

"Seriously? I'm parked in a sea of cars and you're harassing *me*?" She poked him in the chest and her finger bounced back. The man was built like a Viking—imposing, indestructible and so sexy one might call him irresistible.

"They're next." A chant of *"Chug. Chug. Chug."* filled the night sky and Kat let out a defeated breath. "Is your sister at the party?"

Kat's shoulders drooped with exhaustion. "She's supposed to be at the library, but her Find My Friends dot mysteriously vanished. Which means she's up to no good."

"How did you know to come here?"

"This is exactly where I'd be if I were trouble."

He chuckled. "IF?"

She crossed her arms defiantly. "I've actually grown up." *Some.* And not by choice.

He looked her up and down, pausing in specific places— places that began to tingle. Treacherous tingles.

"Trust me, I know," he said quietly and those tingles went from treacherous to straight out traitors. "Every time you take out the garbage in those itty bitty pajama bottoms I'm reminded of just how much you've grown up."

She gasped and looked him in the eye. "We hate each other."

"Hate is a strong word."

"Loath. Dislike. Detest. Irritate. Annoy. Abhor." His smile hitched higher with every word. "I give Tiny Dancer a treat when she poops in your yard. I steal your tomatoes in the summer. I reported you to the Community Board last month because your sequoia dropped pine needles on my property. I blow my leaves onto your lawn in the fall and shovel snow on your side of the easement in the winter."

"That's an awful lot of effort for someone you loath, dislike, detest, irritate and annoy."

"Don't forget, abhor," he said, lowering his voice to intimate levels "I'm surprised you haven't started pulling my pigtails."

"We're at war. I'm not wooing you," she said but he didn't look convinced. "Is there tension between us? Sure. We're both attractive people so there might be a tiny bit of chemistry." That was the understatement of the year. When they were together the air crackled. Then he'd open his mouth and say something that brought out his uptightness and she'd be reminded that he saw the world in black and white and she'd learned to survive in the gray. "But we aren't going *there*."

"I know," he stated with so much certainty she wanted to knee him in the nuts. She was the one to shut things down, but for some reason hearing him agree made her stomach pinch.

"Then why are you watching me take out the trash?"

He stepped closer and lowered his voice. "Hard not to when you do it every time I leave for a shift. Like clockwork," he said. "Almost as if you want me to watch." He reached out and ran the pad of his thumb down her jawline. "Do you want me to watch, Trouble?"

Did she? She never used to wear her silky pjs until Nolan moved next door. But that was just a coincidence, right? It had to be.

Oh right, she remembered now. When her best friend passed last year, Kat inherited Zoe's entire wardrobe, including an impressive collection of itty-bitty pajamas. Silk wasn't really Kat's jam, she preferred steel-toed, but wearing Zoe's clothes was like getting a little piece of her friend back. It just so happened that Zoe's passing coincided with Nolan becoming her newly single, and apparently nosy, neighbor.

"What a total guy thing to say. I know this will probably blow your mind, but it's not all about you, Nolan. Did you ever think that maybe I wear them for me? Or maybe I had an overnight guest, and I wore them for him."

Nolan's nostrils flared and his mouth went into a tight, unhappy line. Perhaps *he's* the one who wants to pull *her* pigtail.

"Maybe." He casually lifted one massive shoulder and let it fall. "Maybe not."

She threw her hands in the air. "Oh my god. Next are you going to mansplain the nonverbal signals around wearing pajamas in the morning?"

"I could. How about tomorrow morning over coffee?" he said.

Kat would rather drink from a gas station toilet than share her morning coffee with Nolan. She opened her mouth to tell him exactly that, but nothing came out. She cleared her throat and tried again and only a strangled breath escaped, turning to mist in the chilled air. Not that Kat was chilly. Oh no, her body was reacting as if she were a nuclear plant in the middle of a meltdown.

He stuffed his hands into his pockets and rocked back on his heels. "Cat got your tongue, Kat?"

"Clever. Did you come up with that all on your own?"

"I have others I can share with you while I make you my famous frittata."

She couldn't tell if she was being serious or just yanking her chain. The bigger mystery was, did she want him to be serious?

Kat loved men. The breadth of their shoulders, the smell of testosterone, their rough and capable hands. Nolan had all of those in spades, but they drove each other crazy—and not in a good way. He was also an officer of the law and her grumpy neighbor. Not to mention, her best friend's soon to be brother-in-law. So when her joke of a kiss a few months back sparked something deeper she'd turned tail. And he knew it.

"What happened to *"I know."*"

Before he could answer a shrill ring cut through the night, but neither of them moved. It was as if she were stuck in some kind of hormone-charged standoff with her sexy and insufferable neighbor. Without breaking eye contact, she pulled her phone out and answered.

"Hello?" she said

"Kat?" a guilt-filled voice came through the phone.

It was Tessa. Who would rather die than actually talk on the phone. Who was supposed to be home in ten minutes and hadn't appeared from the woods. Who Kat was supposed to be focusing on instead of sparing with her sexy and insufferable neighbor.

"If you're calling to extend your curfew, the answer is a big, fat, hells-to-the-no."

She could hear Tessa take in a big gulp of air. "I know you're going to be mad at me. So mad. But you promised that if I ever needed you that you'd pick me up, no questions asked. Are you going to keep your promise?"

Kat's smile vanished and as if sensing that something was off, Nolan's posture went from competitive to protective. "Always," she said.

"Can you come get me? I'm at Sunrise Falls."

"I'm already here. At the base of the trail."

There was a long pause where she was certain Tessa was doing some quick math that equated to *Caught Red Handed*.

"Okay, I'll be there in a few—"

A loud *pop* blasted simultaneously through the phone and the blackness of night. A sound so violent it felt as if the ground beneath Kat's feet vibrated. So terrifying her heart stopped mid-beat.

"Was that a gunshot?" she asked, but Nolan was already on the move. Weapon drawn, protect and serve in full effect, he disappeared into the night.

Read on to check out Teagan and Colin's story, <u>Situationship</u>, a hilariously smart and reunion romantic comedy!

Chapter One

*If life gives you lemons, it's only fair that a
guy with vodka isn't far behind.*
—Unknown

Teagan Bianchi was at the crossroads of Forgiveness and Letting Go when her GPS crapped out—a problem of living life on autopilot for too long. In the past she would have relied on her intuition. But intuition was one finicky prick.

"Are we there yet?" a tiny voice asked from the back seat. It was the fifth time since their last potty stop. One of thousands on their trip from Seattle to California.

Teagan always encouraged curiosity in her daughters, so it wasn't the question that bothered her. It was the feelings it evoked. It made her feel like a fraud. Even worse, a failure.

"What does your tablet say?" she asked Poppy, her elder daughter by seven minutes. After thirty-three weeks of sharing thirty-six centimeters, the twins had come out of the womb inseparable.

"Da blue dot is by da red dot," Poppy said, her Ts sounding more like Ds.

"What number does it show?" She glanced over her shoulder at her daughter, and all four years of her smiled back, filling Teagan with a sense of purpose. With the disillusionment of her marriage in the rearview mirror, she was moving away from her immediate past and toward a happier and simpler time.

"Five," she said, holding up the coordinating number of fingers. "One, two fwee. Four. Five."

"That's right. Good job," she said, and a bark of agreement came from the back seat as a wet nose nudged her shoulder.

Their horse-sized puppy, who'd broken free from his crate—with help from his two partners in crime—wedged his head between the two front seats.

"GD, back seat only."

Garbage Disposal barked excitedly at the mention of his name, then took a flying leap, and 120 pounds of dog landed on the passenger seat with a thud. Teagan leaned right, pressing herself against the window to avoid being smacked in the face by a wagging tire iron.

"You want me to pull over and put you in the cage?" she threatened but he panted happily and stuck his head out the open window so he could drool on the cars behind them. Part Portuguese water dog and part Great Dane, Garbage Disposal looked like a buffalo with two left feet fathered by Mr. Snuffleupagus. While he more than lived up to his name, he had a heart the size of his stomach.

Teagan pulled through the quaint downtown, noticing gas-lamped streets, brick sidewalks, and awninged storefronts, then turned down Lighthouse Way, where the landscape opened, revealing the crystal blue waters of the Pacific Ocean. Coiling with intensity, the waves gathered speed before crashing against the cliffs ahead. On her left sat rolling hills dotted with cypress trees and rows of bright-colored Victorians. To her right was the road to fresh starts, childhood memories...and heartache.

It was the last part that had panic knotting in her chest and activating her internal countdown. She was *one, two, fwee, four minutes* away from the place she'd called home for most of her childhood—well, the happy parts anyway.

Pacific Cove was a sleepy beach town nestled between Monterey and Carmel. Settled by Episcopalians, it was a sea of steeples on a stunning horizon. It was later home to many military families during World War Two, thanks to its location close to three military bases: Army, Navy, and Coast Guard. Teagan's grandmother had been one of those Navy wives whose last missive from her husband had been a *Just in Case* letter with his wedding ring enclosed.

Grandma Rose had reinvented herself in this very town, and Teagan could too. Or at least that was the hope.

"Are we there yet?"

At a stop sign, Teagan turned back around to look at Poppy. "You just asked that question."

"Lily wants to know. You said we'd be there at *fwee-oh-oh*. And it's *four-oh-oh*." Hushed negotiations ensued. "Lily say that four comes after fwee."

Teagan's ETA hadn't accounted for the wind drag of towing a twelve-foot trailer or the volume of potty breaks. "We're about four minutes out from Nonna's." Even though Nonna had passed and willed the beach cottage to Teagan, she always thought of it as Nonna Rose's house.

"We're about four minutes out from Nonna's." Word for word, Poppy repeated their ETA to Lily and then, doing their twin thing, her too-big-to-be-toddlers and too-small-to-be-schoolkids had a complete conversation without saying a word. "She's gotta go number one."

Better than number two. "Sweetie, can you hold it for just another few minutes?"

Lily, who was having a silent conversation with the tops of her shoes, shook her head, then gave a thumbs-down to her sister.

"She said no," Poppy translated, and Garbage Disposal barked in solidarity.

Teagan had known that last juice box was a bad idea. Almost as bad as adopting a rescue puppy three months before moving two states away. A clumsy, untrained, former outside dog who loved to be inside and eat Teagan's shoes, handbag, tampons—the list went on.

"Five minutes, that's all I'm asking for."

After an intense exchange of looks, Poppy said, "Fwee works but not four."

Teagan gunned it. She knew better than to tempt fate. Especially when Lily's Go Time was about as accurate as a nuclear countdown clock. T-minus fwee was Go Time—toilet optional.

She blew through the stop sign and took a hard right onto Seashell Circle. An ocean-soaked breeze filled the car—reducing the stench from Lily's bout of car sickness, which had kicked in her twin's sympathetic reflex.

Winding her way down the hill, she made the final turn into her old neighborhood and a sense of rightness, a sense of home, swept through her body. Because there it was, the purple and white Victorian where she'd spent the first half of her life making memories.

They'd arrived, intact, if not a little wrinkled around the edges, to begin their fresh start, leaving behind a history of pain and disappointment.

Complete with clapboard siding, massive stained-glass windows, and widow's walk, Nonna Rose's house—now Teagan's house—butted up to pristine beach, which was shared by the neighbors on Seashell Circle. At one time, this house had meant everything to her but as she pulled up to the empty drive, she was reminded that Nonna was gone, and Teagan's earlier excitement was painted with a coat of sorrow.

Another thing she intended to change.

With nine seconds to spare, Teagan pulled into the drive and pushed the button to open the side door. Her daughters freed themselves from their boosters and a flurry of arms and legs exploded out of the car. Garbage Disposal sailed through the window as if it was a fence and he was a thoroughbred at the Royal Cup.

Lily ran behind the big magnolia tree in the front yard, lifted her sundress, and squatted—a recently acquired skill. Adhering to the *where one goes, the other follows* philosophy, Poppy did the potty-squat even though she didn't have to go. Garbage Disposal barked and ran circles around them.

Teagan dropped her head against the steering wheel, accidently honking the horn and dislodging a cheesy poof from her hair. Yup, that pretty much summed up the past year.

She looked at the dog hair stuck to every surface, including but not limited to the passenger seat, the dash, and interior roof of the car. Then there were the grape juice stains on her armrest and clothes.

"Why couldn't you have packed lemonade?" That was the one chore she'd left for the morning: packing the kid's snack bags. Somehow in her exhaustion, she'd packed cheesy poofs and grape juice. It was almost as if karma was doing it on purpose.

She thunked her head to the wheel again, wondering about her next move.

"Careful, you might knock something loose." The voice startled her—in more ways than one.

She must be hearing things. Her sleep-free, peace-free, caffeine-free state was to blame. Surely when she looked up, no one would be standing outside the window smiling. The voice definitely had a smile to it. And brought a feeling of nostalgia that had her heart racing.

Don't stroke out.

Teagan closed her eyes for a moment to compose herself. Hard to do when she smelled like vomit and looked like roadkill.

With the bright smile of someone in control of their world, she looked up and—*yup.* She was definitely hallucinating. Because standing outside her window was a blast from her past, who did *not* look like roadkill. No, her unexpected visitor looked cool, calm, and incredibly handsome.

How was it she'd forgotten his family owned the vacation house next door to Nonna Rose? And how was it that the first time she'd seen him since her divorce she looked as if a convenience store bomb had gone off around her?

Colin West, in nothing but bare feet, wet jeans, and bare chest, still damp from washing his truck, looked like the sexy-dad-next-door.

He twirled his hand in the universal gesture for *roll down the window* and, even though her heart wasn't in it—it was lodged in her throat—she complied.

"Excuse that." Teagan looked at her daughters racing around the yard with their sundresses repurposed into superhero capes, leaving them naked. "I'm sorry, they're … it's been a day."

"Been there."

At the foreign voice, Garbage Disposal's head poked out from beneath a shrub. Covered in leaves, with one ear flopping topsy-turvy, he chewed on a garden hose—the neighbor's garden hose.

"Um, I think my dog … " *Oh boy.*

Garbage Disposal lurched. Hard and fast, galloping across the lawn in record time with all the grace of a flamingo in a snow-bank. He was infamous for licking toes, knocking spillable things off tabletops with his tail, and knowing the precise latitude and longitude to give the ultimate doggie-high-fives to the crotch.

"Watch out, he's bigger than he looks. … "

With a single hand motion, Colin said, "Down," and Garbage Disposal lay down, resting his head on his big paws, looking up at Colin as if he were his new master.

"Good boy." He crouched down and gave the dog a good rub, which ended with Garbage Disposal rolling over on his back, proudly showing off his doggie bits.

"How did you do that?"

"Magic," he said, sitting back on his heels. That was it. No "Hello" or "Good to see you" or even "Why the hell are you here?" Just a single evocative word.

"Magic."

"He's still got some puppy left. How old is he?" he asked, his attention still on the dog.

"Oh, I have no idea. He isn't mine," she lied.

"Funny, he thinks you're his pack."

"Pack, smack. He looks all cute and innocent and, okay, he's kind of mine. The girls and I went to the shelter and he followed us home."

Colin chuckled.

"And before you tell me what a good dog he is, he's a dog training school flunk-out." Not that anyone could tell, since Garbage Disposal was giving a good-boy wagging of the tail as if he'd earned a gold star in obedience school, when in reality he'd flunked out three times. "Probably why he kept following us when we told him to stay."

"There aren't bad animals, only bad teachers." Colin looked up, his gaze tinged by amusement.

"Are you saying I'm the problem?"

At that exact moment, Poppy jumped up on the porch step. Hands raised to the heavens as if she were some Amazon warrior ready to wreak havoc on the mere mortals, she tied her dress around her neck and pumped a single hand in the air. Lily followed suit until there were two nearly naked tots chasing a dog around the magnolia tree.

"It *is* me," she admitted.

In a very Colin-like move, he rested his arms on the car door frame above her head, leaning in and getting up close and personal. It took everything she had not to stare at his chest, which—with his forearms on top of the door—was at direct gawking level. Looking at his face wasn't any better. He was near enough that she could ascertain he hadn't shaved recently and that his eyes were glimmering with amusement.

"Are you laughing at me?"

"Wouldn't think of it." He didn't bother to hide his grin. "First rule in long trips, superheroes aren't just for boys. Pack dress-up capes, coordinating flags, and plenty of tiaras or they'll get creative." He chuckled. "Just wait until they're teens."

"Is it worse than the terrible twos?" she asked.

"I thought they were older than that."

"They're four, but still going through the terrible twos. I'm afraid it's a permanent condition. You're a doctor. Tell me it gets easier."

"Vet," he clarified. "And I wish I could. Maddie hasn't been easy in seventeen years."

Right about now, Teagan would give anything to go back and be a bright-eyed, naive, and trusting teenager again.

When had everything become so difficult?

"Maddison's a teenager?"

"Unfortunately," he said. "In fact, you just missed her stomping off and slamming the door because I looked at her wrong."

"How did we get so old?"

His eyes slowly slid down her body. "You don't look a day older than you did that summer before sophomore year, when I first saw you."

She smiled with the same mischievous smile she'd worn when she snuck out her bedroom window and met him at the cove. It had been her first time sneaking out, her first time skinny-dipping—oh, she'd had a lot of firsts that night. She could tell by the smile on his face, his thoughts weren't far from hers.

"Just be grateful yours don't talk back yet."

"Only one talks." It hadn't always been that way. Lily had always been the quieter of the two, more cerebral, but after her dad moved out, Lily stopped talking. To anyone who wasn't her twin.

"Even better."

"Oh, Poppy talks enough for everyone in the family. In fact, there wasn't a silent moment on the entire trip from Seattle."

He looked at the small trailer behind her. "Movers coming tomorrow?"

"Nope. This is it." She swallowed because *this was it.* This was the moment every recent divorcée dreaded. The *where's your other half* question.

Surprisingly, he didn't say a word about Frank's absence, but his gaze did shift to the empty passenger seat, and she thought she'd be sick.

Her ex. Her lying, selfish, bonehead of an ex, who'd cost her family nearly everything. The writing was still wet on the dotted line of the divorce papers, but they'd separated a year ago, when things took a turn for the worse.

She knew all too well how confusing it could be for kids when their parents reenacted *The War of the Roses* on a regular basis. By the time Teagan's parents divorced, things had become so bitter, she'd promised herself if she ever had kids, she would never put them through that, so she'd stayed in her marriage as long as she could.

She'd tried so hard to make it work. Frank wasn't a bad man; in fact he was an incredibly sweet man and a good father. But he lived with his head in the clouds and his money on a poker table.

For a long time, she'd obsessed over what she could have changed. Done differently.

"You okay, Bianchi?" His voice was quiet, and she knew he'd figured it out. He only used her nickname when he was razzing her or concerned for her. This time it was a little of both.

She waved a dismissive hand. "Oh, just tired from the drive." Her pants were going to burst into flames for that lie. But the last thing she wanted to do was talk about her last ex with her first ex.

He studied her and then thankfully let it go without any further questions. "If you need help unloading the trailer, I'm right next door." She was tempted to take him up on the offer. She was exhausted, her back was killing her from the long drive, and she still had to empty the boxes in the U-Haul trailer, which was due back tomorrow before ten. But his voice held a cool distant tone.

Maybe the past wasn't buried in the past. Not that she blamed him.

"I've got it," she said, even though she totally didn't have it.

"If you change your mind." He jabbed a thumb over his shoulder.

"Noted."

His face went carefully blank, and he stepped back from the car. "I forgot. You're good at notes."

Well played but *ouch*.

"If you change your mind, let me know. Oh, and for the record, lemonade is overrated, unless it has something stronger in it."

Continue *Situationship*

Read on for Adair's hilarious and tender romcom, *RomEantically Challenged*, which is a modern take on *Crazy Rich Asians* meets *Three Men and a Baby*.

Chapter One

The moment Anh Nhi Walsh stepped into her wedding dress and shimmied the eighty-year-old silk over her hips, she knew there had been a mistake.

A mistake so terrible, all the chocolate in the world couldn't fix it.

Annie had pulled a thirty-six-hour shift, so her brain was a little slow on the uptake, but the longer she stood in her silver Louis Vuitton heels and yesterday's makeup, the more certain she became that even the world's best push-up bra couldn't compensate for the obvious.

This was not her dress.

"Oh, my god," she whispered through her fingers.

Sure, the gown had arrived on her doorstep in the trade-marked cream blush-colored striped box, special delivery from *Bliss*, Hartford's premiere bridal design boutique. And, yes, that was the silk gown Grandma Hannah had hand-carried from Ireland, now billowing around Annie's waist. But *this* was *not* Annie's dress.

Annie's dress was elegant and sophisticated, a heartfelt tribute to her grandmother, the one person Annie had wanted by her side when she finally walked down the aisle. Grandma Hannah wouldn't let something as insignificant as death keep her from her only granddaughter's wedding. But Annie had wanted to feel her in more than just spirit.

Which was why she'd commissioned a modern-day restoration of the 1941 Grecian gown with cap sleeves and embellished mermaid train, cut from the same cloth that the most important woman in Annie's life had worn on her special day.

Annie pulled the bodice of the gown to her chest and wanted to cry. The too-big, too-long, and most definitely D-cup rendition was that extra-special kick in the gut she needed to find closure.

Six years as an ER physician's assistant had instilled in her a rational calm that allowed for quick and efficient assessment of any situation. Taught her how to differentiate between the life threatening and painfully uncomfortable. With that in mind, she pulled up the planner app on her phone.

"Add, *Murder fiancé,* to my To Do list," she instructed.

"*Murder fiancé* added," the digitized female voice said. "Is there anything else I can help you with?"

"Yes." Because Annie understood murder wasn't a rational response, and besides, Dr. Clark Atwood was no longer her fiancé. Or her problem.

According to the elegant handwriting on the linen thank you card that *Bliss* had included with the gown, that responsibility now fell to Molly-Leigh—with a hyphen—May of the pin-up curves and double-Ds.

Anh Nhi—always mispronounced—Walsh of the boyish build and perky but barely-a-handful B's had moved on to bigger and better things. And that didn't include cleaning up her ex's messes.

Not any more.

"Call, Dr. Dickless," she said.

"Calling Dr. Dickless," the female voice chimed. Annie had de-programmed her sexy 007 British narrator the day she'd heard of Clark's upcoming nuptials. She was taking her new man-free existence seriously.

Clark picked up on the first ring. "Jesus, Annie. I've been calling you for weeks," he said, as if she were the one inconveniencing his life.

"I've been busy with my new job, decorating my new place, apologizing to my relatives because it seems that "The groom's marrying another woman" isn't an acceptable reason for airlines to grant a refund."

Four months ago, Annie had awoken to an empty bed, an emptier closet, and an awaiting text on her cell:

Sorry, Anh-Bon, I can't do this. U R the best thing in my life, and if I could have made it work w/ anyone, pls know that it would have been you. IDK if I'm cut out to be husband material. Forgive me.

It had taken an entire week for her to realize that the wedding, the romantic Roman honeymoon with walks along the River Tiber, the future they'd spent three years building toward was gone.

It had only taken a single Instagram post of her ex of just one month and a perky blonde with the caption "I finally found my one ★true love★" for Annie to give her two weeks' notice—which was more courtesy than Clark had spared her—and apply for a temporary ER position in Rome.

Once the offer came in, she packed her suitcase, sent in a change of address, left the rest of the gifts behind for Clark to return, and promised herself a future full of exciting opportunities and exotic destinations. She had become a traveling PA because she'd wanted to see the world, and her six-year layover in Hartford was over.

Now, it was her time.

"You do have a lot going on—how did you find the time to add "Murder fiancé" to the top of your To Do list?" he asked, and Annie flipped her phone over to check for a listening device.

She was about ready to rip out the battery when Clark added, "You still have me as a recipient on your calendar."

"Just because I forgot to delete you, doesn't give you the right to read my personal stuff," she accused.

"Hard to ignore a death threat or my personal favorite, "Alone time with B.O.B." Clark let out a low whistle. "Five times a week. How many batteries are you burning through?"

"Not as many as when I was with you." Annie cringed, thinking back to all the reminders she'd put on her To Do list over the past three months. God, she was going to be sick. "And if you saw that, then you had to have seen that I contacted *Bliss* to cancel the alterations and return my grandmother's dress. Untouched." She looked at her reflection in the mirror. "This isn't her dress, Clark."

"Yeah, about that." She could hear the familiar squeak of leather as Clark reclined in his office chair. "I guess there was a mix-up between orders, and your grandmother's dress was used to make, uh, Molly-Leigh-Leigh's gown."

Annie eased onto the couch and rested her head on her knees.

"How did Molly-Leigh-Leigh end up at Bliss?" she asked. The question exposed an ache so deep, it was as if she were reliving the breakup all over again. Because *Bliss* wasn't the kind of off-the-rack-shop most brides visited. It was a custom gown boutique that specialized in vintage restoration and had a wait list six months long.

Bliss didn't work with just any bride and Annie hadn't wanted any old dressmaker to handle her most precious family heirloom. Which was now retrofitted to support Dolly Parton, the New Year's Eve ball in time square, and the scales of justice—that never seemed to tip in her favor.

"She saw a sketch of your dress in the wedding journal and fell in love with it."

Annie jerked her head up and glanced out the window to the back deck, breathing out a sigh of relief when she spotted her wedding journal. The evening's marine layer had come in fast, leaving a light dusting of dew, but it was right where she'd tossed it, beside the pool, under the patio table, in a box labeled Dirty Laundry, Dry Oatmeal, and Broken Dreams. "How did she see my wedding journal?"

"*Our* wedding journal," he corrected, and a bad feeling began to swirl in her belly. "I had one of the nurses make a copy of it for me."

"That's an inappropriate use of hospital staff and supplies. And why? You barely went to any of the appointments."

"I went to the ones that mattered."

"You mean, the one. The *one* that mattered to you," she corrected. "You showed up twenty-minutes late to the cake tasting. And only because you were determined that it *had* to be carrot cake. Nobody likes carrot cake, Clark. Nobody."

"My mom does. And so does Molly-Leigh."

Ouch.

"I guess you found your perfect partner," she whispered, raising her hand, her ring finger looking heartbreakingly bare.

Other people's choices are not a reflection on me, she whispered.

They were the words her therapist had given her when she was younger and suffered panic attacks whenever confronted with a situation that left her feeling inadequate. Throughout her teens she wore it like armor. As an adult, she liked to think it was more of a coping device when insecurities paid her an unwelcomed visit.

"You still owe me half of the deposit," she reminded him.

"That's my Anh-Bon," he said softly, and once upon a time, the nickname would have given her heart a flutter. Today it made her want to throw up. "Always calling me on my shit. Without you I never would have gotten through my selfish stage."

Annie laughed at the irony.

Growing up the adopted child of two renowned therapists, and the only rice cracker in a community of Saltines, Annie had acquired the unique ability to identify and soothe away people's fears. She could find a solution before most people realized they had a problem. It was what made her so good at her job. And so easy to open up to.

The nurses at the hospital had taken to calling her Dr. Phil.

Annie was a good girl with a good job who managed to attract good guys with the potential for greatness when it came to love. Her life had been a non-stop revolving door of serial monogamists, each with a fatal flaw that kept him from finding *the one*. For most of their time with Annie, the men were convinced *she* was the one. Then, ultimately, she'd fix what was broken and make some other woman enormously happy.

Annie had wife-in-training written all over her DNA. In fact, she was so good at helping her boyfriends overcome their issues, four of her last five had met their wives within months of breaking it off with her. The fifth had married his high school crush, Robert.

Then came Clark. Her practical knight in blue surgical scrubs, with an amazing family, a solid life plan, and an unshakeable foundation. He was the first guy to get down on one knee, tell Annie that, for him, she was it.

Foolishly, she'd believed him.

And when he'd recanted, confessed he wasn't husband material, that it was him not her, she'd believed that too. Until four weeks after ending their engagement, when he and Molly-Leigh had "put a ring on it."

"Well, you have a lot to be called on. Let's start with the money for the dress you now owe me."

He sighed, long and loud. "How much?"

"Four million dollars."

"Oh, for the love of God."

"No, Clark, for the love of my grandmother's dress. *My* grandmother's dress." Her voice cracked, and so did her heart.

"Anh-Bon..." The sympathy in his voice was real. Sadly, so was the pity, damn him.

"Five million dollars. Price just went up! And before you Anh-Bon me one more time, don't forget you also owe me half of the cost of the cake, the three-hundred-and-fifty invitations," of only which fifty were hers, "and the deposit I put down to hold the venue." Being the mature bride-to-be, she had insisted on covering. God forbid she appear incapable of being a full partner in their union. "Since I haven't received anything from The Hartford Club, I'm guessing the check was mailed to you?"

It was the only reason she could come up with for why her bank account was still short ten grand. Ten grand she desperately needed.

"You can forward me the check," she continued. "I assume you know how to break into my contacts and find my new address?"

"It's not breaking in if the owner grants you access," Clark teased. Annie didn't laugh. "Come on, Annie, don't be like that. I'll Venmo your half of the cake cost now, and I'll pay you back the deposit for the venue after the wedding."

"Pay me back?" Annie's hold on the dress slipped, the silk sliding nearly past her waist before she caught it. "What is there to pay back? The planner specifically told me that if the venue was rebooked by another party, she'd send a refund. The venue was rebooked over a month ago. Where's the refund, Clark?"

"Molls and I met my parents there for lunch and I remembered what a great location it was." His tone was wistful. "Historical but with modern conveniences. Intimate but large enough to hold everyone. Classy but not too expensive."

Perfect but not for me. "Get to the refund."

"It checked off all our wedding wants and more, Annie. When Mom asked about availability, we were told they still had us booked for that weekend."

"Impossible. My mom told me she canceled it."

Clark's answer was a long exhale through his mouth that made Annie sick. "She never canceled it, did she?" Annie tilted her head back and closed her eyes. "That's why my grandma's dress was still at Bliss."

"She said she was hoping we'd work it out. I thought." His words were followed by a long—that's not happening—pause that caused her insides to heat with embarrassment. A reaction that often accompanied her mother's match-making attempts. "Under the circumstances, it would be a shame to let such a beautiful venue go to waste."

That bad feeling had moved through her chest, working its way up to twist around her throat. "What's a shame is that I spent two years waiting for that perfect venue. Half my wedding budget to reserve that venue." Her hand fisted in the silk at her waist, the pressure wrinkling the silk. "Clark, please tell me that you didn't promise Molly-Leigh my venue."

"I didn't know what to do. She took one look at the giant windows and said the light from the afternoon sun illuminated the hall as if it were lit by a thousand candles. What was I supposed to say?"

"That you've been there, done that, dumped the bride, so that venue is off limits."

"I tried, but she said after experiencing the magic of The Hartford Club, she couldn't think of a better place to get married."

At his comment, Annie's chest gave a painful little squeeze. Afraid it would grow, she held her breath so long she thought she might pass out. Reaching behind her, she popped the top two eyehooks of her corset to let her lungs expand far enough to take in air.

It didn't help.

"Grab a pen and paper because I can think of a thousand other places to get married. Ready? Great. Now jot this down, "Anyplace that isn't where you were going to walk down the aisle with another woman". Or how about, "Find a place that won't hold my ex's money hostage". That's my rainy-day money, Clark." She stressed. "I need it back."

"It's supposed to be a dry summer, but I promise I'll pay you back after the wedding. It will just be easier and less confusing that way."

"For who?" she asked. Clark remained silent but Annie could hear the devastating disregard for her situation. Annie pressed two fingers to the center of her forehead and massaged the creases. "It's my grandparents' wedding date."

"I know," he said softly. "Which is the other reason I've been trying to get ahold of you. I wanted to get your thoughts before we committed to anything."

"The dress isn't up for discussion. Period." Realtering it again would be daunting, maybe even impossible, but there was no way in hell her grandmother's dress was going to be worn by any woman other than a Walsh.

"Of course not," he said, doing a piss poor job of hiding his disappointment. "I was referring more to the day of the wedding."

Annie had worked with Clark for six years, lived with him for three of those, so she knew his moods and quirks. Knew by the long, soft pauses between words that renowned surgeon Dr. Clark Atwood wasn't providing options. He was delivering a prognosis.

Whatever hopes Annie had about the possible outcome of this conversation was beside the point. Clark had weighed the possible scenarios, come to his decision, and nothing was going to get in the way of his wedding. It was going forward regardless.

Any rational person would shout a resounding, "Fuck off" to the universe, Clark, the inventor of carrot cake, and—she popped another eyehook—all of Victoria's rib-crushing secrets. But anger wasn't a luxury Annie had ever afforded herself.

"Clark, it doesn't matter what I think or even what I say. It's your wedding, you've made up your mind, and I'm no longer the bride."

Her heart gave an unexpected and painful bump, followed by enough erratic beats to cause concern. Not with resentment. Not even anger. She'd learned long ago that resenting other people's happiness didn't lead to her own. It also wasn't jealousy hollowing out her stomach.

No, the familiar ache she felt coiling its way around her bones and cinching was resignation. Resignation over losing someone who had never really been hers to lose.

Too tired to hold on any longer, Annie released her grip on the silk and the dress slid to her hips, leaving her with only a matching corset set, heels and an overwhelming sense of acceptance, followed by acute loneliness.

"I know," he said gently. "But you're still my friend. When we broke up, we both promised to do whatever it took to keep our friendship. I don't want to lose that."

"You convinced me you weren't ready for marriage, and four weeks later you were Instagraming love sonnets about another woman."

"That was shitty timing on my part. I should have handled it better." He released a breath and she could almost picture him resting his forehead on the heel of his hand. "I don't even know how to explain what happened. Meeting Molly-Leigh was unexpected and exciting, and I know it seems completely insane but . . . suddenly everything made sense, the pieces all fell into place, and I couldn't wait another second to finally start my life."

Annie expelled a breath of disbelief, which sent Clark back pedaling.

"God, Annie, I didn't mean that how it came out. I just, well, when it's right one, when it's your person, you know it. And there's this urgency to grab on and hold tight. No matter what."

That's exactly how Grandma Hannah had described meeting Cleve. A single spin around the dance hall and—*bam*—they were in love.

"And when you said you loved me? Was that a lie?"

"No. I meant every word I said, and I still do. But over time it was clear that we were better as friends. You and I both know that."

Yeah, she did. But the rejection was still raw. Her best friend now belonged to someone else. And that hurt most of all.

"Good to know," she said. "Because I expect all my money to be Venmoed to me by tomorrow."

"I'll see what I can do," he said then did the whole *hand over the mouthpiece while talking to a make believe secretary.* "What? Yeah, I'll be there in one second. Prep OR—"

"—Seven," Annie said in harmony with him and he went silent. "Yeah, remember I was there when you made up OR seven to get off the phone with your mom?"

"Which is why I'd never be stupid enough to use it on you. I really am needed in the OR," he lied. "Gotta go."

"Don't you dare hang…up on me," she said the last few words to herself because he'd already hung up.

Annie dropped the phone on the couch and wondered, not for the first time, when it would finally be her time to belong. She wasn't greedy. One person would be enough.

Her grandparents had belonged to each other. Her parents, to their patients. Which was why she'd been so understanding of Clark's late hours, his dedication to his career. Because in that world, she knew where she fit. Now she felt like she was in a freefall, spinning out of control, unsure where she was going to land.

Continue RomEantically Challenged

Read on to check out Darcy and Gage's story, *Chasing I Do* **a reluctantly funny, feel-good enemies-to-lovers romantic comedy!**

•

Chapter One

Darcy Kincaid had dreamed about this day since she was six and uncovered her mother's stash of Southern Wedding magazines in the basement. After a lifetime of planning, handpicking two thousand of the palest of pink peonies, and her entire life savings, she was about to pull off, what she believed to be, the most romantic I Do in history. The sun was high, the sky was crystal blue, and a gentle June breeze carried the scent of the nearby primrose blooms and ever after.

Today was the perfect day to be married, and the rose garden at Belle Mont House was the ideal backdrop. And Darcy wasn't about to let a tail-chasing wedding crasher ruin her moment. No matter how charming.

Not this time.

"Nuzzling the bride's pillows before the wedding will only get you escorted out," Darcy said to the four-legged powderpuff in matching pink booties and hair bow.

The dog, who was more runway than runaway, dropped down low in the grass, eyes big black circles of excitement, tail wagging with delight—her jewel-encrusted collar winking in the sunlight.

Darcy squinted, but could only make out the first word. "Fancy." The little dog's ears perked up and her tail went wild.

"Such a pretty name," Darcy cooed, taking a cautious step forward. "I'm Darcy; it's nice to meet you. I'm going to come a little closer so I can get a better look at your collar and find your mamma's number. Is that okay?"

With a playful snort, the animal's entire body was wiggling as if so excited by the idea of making a friend she couldn't hold in the glee. Darcy reached out to ruffle her ears, and Fancy, confusing Darcy's movement for time to play, snatched up the pillow and gave it a good shake.

"No!" Darcy cried, halting in her tracks while little bits of stuffing leached into the air, causing perspiration to bead on her forehead.

Fancy, on the other hand, wasn't worried in the slightest. Nope, she gave another rambunctious whip of the head before jumping up and down with the pillow as if this were all fun and games.

Sadly, this situation was about as close to fun and games as natural child birthing. Not only was the vintage silk pillow, a family heirloom passed down from the bride's great-grandmother, in danger of becoming a chew-toy, but the bride's ring was swinging dangerously from the aged ribbon.

And this wasn't just any bride. Candice Covington was the former Miss Oregon, a Portland mover and shaker, and the first bride to be wed at the newly renovated Belle Mont House. Candice was already in the bridal suite, her beloved in the tower room, and two hundred of their closest friends and family were set to start arriving in just over an hour—and the dog looked content to nuzzle the pillow all afternoon.

With its teeth.

"Stop!" she said in her most authoritative tone, putting her hand out.

To Darcy's surprise, the dog stopped. Her snout going into hypersniffer mode, she dropped the pillow to the grass and rose up to smell the air. Seemed Fancy had caught the scent of the prosciutto-wrapped figs sitting on a chair that Darcy had been tasting, and she stood up on her hind legs, then walked around in three perfect circles.

"Someone's got moves," she said. "Not bad, but mine are better."

A decade of planning events for Portland's pickiest clients and four years in the trenches as a single mother had taught Darcy the art of positive redirection. She'd lasted through potty training, teething, and chickenpox. This stubborn ball of fluff didn't stand a chance.

Eying the flower arrangement on the closest table, Darcy grabbed a decorative stick and gave it a little shake. "Want to play with the stick for a while?" The dog sat, eyes wide, head cocked to the side in an explosion of cuteness. "We can switch toys before you destroy the pillow, okay?"

"Yip!"

Tail up like a heat-seeking radar, the dog hit the fetch-and-retrieve position, pointing her nose toward one of the open fields.

"Ready?" Darcy wiggled the stick again for show. "Go get 'em!"

The stick flew through the air, going as far in the opposite direction as it could. Darcy released a sigh of relief when it cleared the fountain and landed in the middle of the field.

A low growl sounded, followed by a blur of white fur that bolted past.

Those little legs working for the prize. A position Darcy could relate to.

Located in the prestigious West Hills, Belle Mont House was three stories of Portland history with extensive manicured gardens, six bedrooms, a grand salon, and captivating views of the city and Mount Hood—all of which needed to be meticulously cared for. And Darcy was the sole caretaker.

She had driven by the old property a thousand times over the years. But she hadn't really recognized its potential until after her world had fallen apart and a heartbreaking betrayal had left her life in tatters—much like the foundation of this forgotten house. Unable to watch something so beautiful and full of history crumble, she'd saved it from demolition, then spent every penny and waking moment renovating it back to its original grandeur. In return, Belle Mont had given her something even more precious—a future for her and her daughter.

Today marked Belle Mont's first day in operation as the year's "Most Romantic" wedding destination in the Pacific Northwest and Darcy as its planner extraordinaire—according to the editor at Wedding Magazine, who'd left a message earlier about sending a high-profile couple to check out the location.

A couple so hush-hush, the editor refused to give the name for fear that the press would show. But if they decided that Belle Mont was their dream wedding venue, and Darcy could accommodate them with the last Sunday in July, the only date that worked around the couple's hectic schedule, then Belle Mont would land a huge spread in the August issue.

The endorsement alone was enough to make her say yes on the spot. Not to mention the profit for hosting such a lavish event would go a long way toward helping pay back all the money she'd invested into the renovation—and secure her future in Portland.

A future that now resided in the jaws of a dog that could fit in her pocket. Fancy snatched the stick and darted across the lawn toward the twinkle-lit and peony-covered gazebo in record time—all with the pillow still in its jowls.

"Hey," she called out, "we had a deal!"

The dog's tail went up as if flipping the bird at their deal before she ran beneath a row of chairs and struck a different kind of pose altogether. A move that showed enough doggie bits to prove that under that pink bling, Fancy was all male. And about to shit all over Candice's perfect day.

A situation Darcy knew all too well.

"Had I known you had a stupid stick down there, I wouldn't have bothered trying to reason with you."

In Darcy's experience, men loved the forbidden almost as much as they loved their stick. So she fumbled with her skirt, pulling it above her thighs, and gave chase. Fancy took off, and man, those toothpick legs could fly. Ears flapping behind him, butt moving like lightning bugs in a jar, the pooch headed straight for the rose garden, which lay directly across from the aisle runner that had Candice and Carter spelled out in the palest of pink peony petals.

"Not the runner!" she cried, only to watch in horror as Fancy raced up the center of the white pillowed Egyptian cotton, his legs pumping with the speed and grace of a cheetah in the wild, leaving a few dozen miniature muddy paw prints and a tornado of petals in his wake.

"No, no, no!" she called out. "Not the rose garden."

Terrified of the damage he could do to the roses and the pillow, she picked up the pace and rounded the white iron fencing, gravel sliding under her heels as she burst through the gate and snatched the pillow right before the Fancy dove his fancy-ass—and Candice's ring—into the fountain.

"Got it!" she yelled, but the celebration quickly faded as her momentum carried her forward—and right into the stone cherub boy's watering hole.

"Oh god, no!" Darcy yelped as water exploded around her.

Having landed ass first, she felt the cold wetness seep through her silk skirt and slosh into her shoes. Her brand-new designer shoes she'd found at a consignment store and purchased especially for today. "Please, no."

She clawed the edge of the fountain and pulled, mentally willing herself out of the fountain—but she couldn't gain any positive momentum.

No matter how hard she tried, she just couldn't pull herself out.

Refusing to give up, she looked around for Fancy, hoping to either send him to find help or pull him in with her. But he'd vanished, right before the wedding, leaving her waist-deep in his mess.

The situation was so painfully familiar, Darcy wanted to cry. Then devour the entire wedding cake in one sitting.

"Are you okay?" a husky voice asked from above.

"Thank god you're here," she said, pushing her hair out of her face and looking up, expecting to find one of her kitchen staff.

But instead of a clip-on tie with a comb-over, Darcy's unexpected hero looked like an underwear model in a dark blue button-up and a pair of slacks that fit him to perfection. And his arms—oh my, those arms—were impressive, perfect for helping a lady in need.

Although Darcy had worked hard to not be reliant on others—a lifetime of letdowns could do that to a girl—she knew that sometimes it was okay to take an offered hand. And those hands were big and solid and— whoa—reaching forward to wrap around her hips and easily lift her out.

Her feet hit the ground, and she did her best to wring out her shirt. "I'm sorry if I'm getting you all wet."

"You never have to apologize to a man for getting him wet." He chuckled, and Darcy, realizing how that had come out, went to move, but his arms tightened, stilling her. "Make sure you're okay first. You were moving pretty fast when you dove in."

Not as fast as her heart was racing.

Closing her eyes, Darcy took stock. Her chest tingled, her head was light, and a wave of delicious thrill jumpstarted parts she'd long believed dead. In fact, she was as far from fine as a woman who had sworn off men could get.

"I'm good. Thank you," she lied, trying to gain some distance without falling back into the fountain, which was not an easy task. He was so big, he filled the space, leaving nowhere for her to go. She brushed off her elbows, which were scraped up, but she'd live, then started to straighten when a big hand appeared, Candice's ring resting in its palm.

"I believe you lost this."

"Thank you," she whispered, a wave of relief washing over her. "You have no idea how—"

Darcy looked up, and the words died on her lips and dropped to the pit of her stomach, where they expanded and churned until—oh god, she couldn't breathe.

Her unexpected hero wore slacks and tie fit for Wall Street, a leather jacket that added a touch of bad boy to the businessman, and a pair of electric blue eyes that she'd recognize anywhere. They'd always reminded her of a calm, crystal clear lake. Today they were tempestuous, like an angry spring storm.

The change wasn't a surprise, given the last time they'd seen each other. But the deep ache of longing it brought on was.

"Gage," she said, her heart pounding so loudly she was certain he could hear it thumping in her chest.

It was the first time she'd seen him since the funeral, a thought that brought back a dozen memories—some sad, some of the best moments of her life, but all of them a painful reminder of what had been lost.

"Hey, Pink," he said in a tone that implied that had he known it was her he would have let her drowned.

She swallowed back the disappointment, hoping he didn't notice that she was shaking. "What are you doing here?"

"It looks like I'm helping you find your wedding ring." He took her hand in his and slid the ring on her finger. The sensation was so overwhelming she jerked back.

Gage Easton was over six feet of solid muscle and swagger. He was also sweet and kind and, at one time, one of the few people she thought she'd always be able to count on. If things had gone how Darcy had dreamed, he would have made for one heck of a brother-in-law.

An even better uncle.

A swift shot of guilt mixed with the swelling panic in her throat, her reckless secret pressing down until she was choking. But Darcy swallowed it back and refused to shoulder all of the blame.

Life was filled with hard choices. While Gage's twin had chosen to be unfaithful, Darcy had chosen their daughter's happiness.

She would always choose Kylie.

Gage looked at her bare feet, then aimed that intense gaze her way. "I would have thought that after jilting Kyle like you did, you'd have started wearing running shoes to these kinds of events."

Although Gage had a big heart, he was still an Easton. And when someone messed with one brother, they messed with the whole clan. The only way to survive was to hide your fear and never stand down.

Shoulders back, chest slightly puffed, Darcy made her body appear bigger, the way she had when she'd been a young girl and encountered a stranger at her breakfast table. She'd walk into the kitchen and pretend she was big and strong—someone not to be messed with.

Her mother had a thing for rot-gut whiskey and bottom-shelf men—and made a habit of bringing both home. Sometimes they stayed the night, sometimes they stayed the year, but Darcy never knew who—or what—she'd encounter in the one place that should have felt safe.

But this was her home now, and she'd do whatever was necessary to protect it.

"After five years, I would have hoped you'd realize your family wasn't the only ones who were hurting," she said. "I may have walked out on your brother, but I wasn't the one who let him drive that night."

Gage Easton felt the truth of that statement hit hard, the power of it nearly taking him out at the knees. Darcy wasn't a confrontational person by nature, but she knew how to stand her ground. No doubt a trait she'd picked up from dealing with his family.

He hadn't seen her since the funeral. Nobody had. Not that he'd blamed her. His family had still been reeling from the aftermath of the wedding that never happened, when tragedy struck again, tearing a chasm between Darcy and the Eastons that could never be fixed. His brother, Kyle, was gone, and with the overwhelming and sudden grief that had been thrust upon his family, most especially his mom, a lot of the blame had been unfairly placed upon Darcy. There were so many times he wanted to reach out, make sure she was okay, but he'd spent the majority of their relationship keeping his distance, certain that no good could come from letting himself get too close. And he wasn't looking to test his theory.

Not today.

"Are you okay?" he asked, waving a hand to her elbows, which were scrapped and he was certain smarting.

"Nothing that won't heal," she said, and he knew she wasn't talking about the gravel burn. "I just have to change my skirt and shoes."

"You might want to change the top while you're at it." He grinned. "Not that I mind the view, but it might cause some heart problems with the older guests."

Darcy's gaze dropped to her shirt and the two beautiful buds peeking through the translucent fabric, and she gasped. Hell, Gage was in his prime and her top was causing some serious gasping and heart palpitations on his end.

"Don't worry, I didn't peek. Much." He leaned in and whispered, "Although, if you know you're going to take a swim, you might just consider skinny dipping. You'd get the same effect, only you wouldn't have to hang-dry your lace bra and panties."

"You can't see my panties."

No, he couldn't, but she didn't need to know that. The narrowed eyes and pursed lips were enough to tell him that she was ticked just thinking about him seeing her panties. And that was a far better state than the tears that had been threatening a moment ago.

"Look," she said pointedly, crossing her arms over her chest, which did nothing except pull the fabric tighter. "I'm grateful that you found the ring and helped me out of the fountain, and I have no clue as to why you're here"—her tone said she didn't care to find out either—"but I need you to leave."

"Don't worry," he said. "I didn't come to ruin your big day. I'll get out of your way as soon as my meeting is over." And he found the abomination in bows he was stuck dog sitting.

"Oh, it's not my big day," she clarified. "I'm the planner for the wedding that is supposed to start in less than an hour."

He looked at her outfit and, while cream in color, it wasn't bridal attire. The skirt, the buttoned silk top, even her hair said professionally elegant. Not bride-to-be.

A heaviness that he didn't even notice he'd taken on lifted at her admission, and he wanted to kick himself. She wasn't getting married? So what? It didn't matter. Kyle was gone, Gage was still struggling to make peace with things, and Darcy would always be off-limits. No matter how great she still looked. Even scratched up and sweaty, she was as gorgeous as ever.

"Well, if you'll just direct me to the manager's office," he asked. "I'm late, and don't want to keep him waiting."

She looked at her watch and froze, an expression of resignation washing over her.

"Actually, you're early," she said, so full of dread she felt sweat bead on her forehead. She stuck out her hand. "Darcy Kincaid, owner and exclusive planner for Belle Mont House. I believe the editor from Wedding Magazine said you'd be dropping by tomorrow."

Continue *Chasing I Do*

About the Author

Marina Adair is a *New York Times* and #1 Amazon best-selling, whose fun, flirty contemporary romcoms have sold over a million copies. In addition to the Sierra Vista series, she is the author of the St. Helena Vineyard series, which was turned into the original Hallmark Channel Vineyard movies: *Autumn in the Vineyard, Summer in the Vineyard*, and *Valentines in the Vineyard*. Raised in the San Francisco Bay Area, she holds an MFA from San Jose University and currently lives in Northern California with her husband, daughter, and two neurotic cats. Please visit her online at MarinaAdair.com and sign up for her newsletter at www.MarinaAdair.com/newsletter.

Sign Me Up!

Printed in Great Britain
by Amazon

17099476R00182